Also by Jane Ashford

The Duke's Sons

Heir to the Duke
What the Duke Doesn't Know
Lord Sebastian's Secret
Nothing Like a Duke
The Duke Knows Best
A Favor for the Prince (prequel)

The Way to a Lord's Heart

Brave New Earl
A Lord Apart
How to Cross a Marquess
A Duke Too Far

Once Again a Bride
Man of Honour
The Three Graces
The Marriage Wager
The Bride Insists
The Bargain
The Marchington Scandal
The Headstrong Ward
Married to a Perfect Stranger
Charmed and Dangerous
A Radical Arrangement
First Season / Bride to Be
Rivals of Fortune / The Impetuous Heiress
Last Gentleman Standing
Earl to the Rescue
The Reluctant Rake

Earl's WELL THAT ENDS Well

JANE ASHFORD

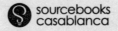
sourcebooks
casablanca

Published by Sourcebooks Casablanca, an imprint of Sourcebooks
P.O. Box 4410, Naperville, Illinois 60567-4410
(630) 961-3900
sourcebooks.com

Printed and bound in the United States of America.
OPM 10 9 8 7 6 5 4 3 2 1

One

As Arthur Shelton, seventh Earl of Macklin, walked through his home on his way to bed, he could hear the sharp scratch of sleet on the window glass, driven by a bitter late-January wind. A draft fluttered the flame on the candlestick he carried. The new year was beginning with a long, hard freeze. He was glad his children and their families had gotten away well before this storm hit, even though their departure had left the house feeling empty. The sound of his grandchildren's feet pounding down the corridors and their high, childish voices calling to one another had been such a pleasure.

On impulse, he turned and went into the gallery. The long room stretched out before him, scarcely lit by his one candle. It was frigid, too, with no fires lit. He passed the portraits of his ancestors, their ranks a panoply of English history, and stopped near the far end, raising the candlestick to better illuminate the painting that hung there. It had been done nearly twenty years ago and showed his wife, Celia, in the early years of their marriage, a lovely young woman in a gown of sapphire silk and lace.

He gazed into her serene blue eyes. The artist had caught the little half smile that so often graced her features. That smile had drawn him across a ballroom to wangle an introduction and a dance. When they'd talked, its promise had been fulfilled. Celia had possessed warmth and humor and an eager gusto for life. How she would have enjoyed the holiday visit just past! How unfair that she'd missed it, along with so much else.

Arthur caught his own reflection in a dark windowpane. It was almost as if they stood side by side again. Except that Celia was still young, and he was nearly fifty. It was true that his dark hair had no gray. His tall figure remained muscular and upright. His square-jawed, broad-browed face showed few lines. But he was not the young man who had wooed and won her and brought her here to Macklin Abbey.

More than ten years Celia had been gone now, struck down by a raging fever before she reached forty. It had been a hard death. She'd fought it with all her strength, and he'd sat beside her and tried to lend his own. There was nothing worse than seeing the one you loved suffering and being able to do nothing, Arthur thought. Even now, a decade later, that pain lingered.

He gazed into Celia's painted eyes. While his friends were sowing their wild oats in London society, he'd been getting to know her. He hadn't envied them, hadn't regretted even when they joked about his stuffiness. He'd had no doubts when he stood up beside Celia and made a vow for life. He'd expected to fulfill it, with all the joys and sorrows, complications and difficulties the years might bring, right down into old age. But fate had stepped in and changed the rules, and he'd been left alone. That, he had never planned.

Arthur allowed himself a brief pang, thinking of all the duties and familial pleasures he'd experienced without Celia. He'd carried on. When he looked at his children, he thought he'd done well. But it had been a long time since he was Celia's husband. Arthur met the eyes of his reflection once again. He thought of the four young men he'd helped this last year with the grief that oppressed them. He'd had some small part in establishing pockets of happiness scattered around the country, with their three wives and an upcoming wedding. They had each found a new life.

Perhaps this was a lesson he should learn for himself as well? A shock went through him at the idea, and at the realization that it had not occurred to him before. Odd that it had taken near strangers to plant the notion of change. But now that it had appeared, the idea began to take root and unfold.

He would go down to London early this year, Arthur decided, perhaps as soon as next month. He could see how young Tom was getting on in his theatrical adventures. That lad always had some interesting tale to tell. And who knew what else might turn up?

As he continued to his bedchamber, the earl's step was lighter.

⁓

"Now then, Yer Honor, have ye taken a wrong turning?" called a mocking voice.

Arthur turned to see a group of young men

lingering near a shop front on the shabby London street. They all grinned at him. He judged they were apprentices having a rare day out on this first clement spring afternoon.

"Naught to worry about," said another of them. "This is a respectable neighborhood. No footpads lurking in the alleyways to cosh you and lift your purse 'round here."

"Naw, just mouthy coves making a nuisance of theirselves," said Tom, who sauntered up just then and joined Arthur.

A volley of good-natured insults followed. Arthur gathered that the parties, near in age, knew one another and rather enjoyed a verbal tussle. And Tom exhibited a flair and volubility that Arthur hadn't seen in him before. "Yer naught but a beslubbering dog-hearted flapdragon," he told one of the group. "And Alf there is a weedy, toad-spotted puttock." He rolled out the final word with obvious relish, as if it had a savory taste.

"Well, you're a gudgeon," replied one of the apprentices.

Tom shook his head in mock disappointment. "That's the best you can do, Jem Dowling? Where's your imagination, ye pribbling jolthead?"

"Jolthead," repeated the one Tom had called Alf. "Jolthead." He grinned as if the sound alone was hilarious. And indeed the whole group seemed to admire Tom's eloquence. Arthur began to suspect that they goaded him just to hear the result.

"Shall we go, my lord?" asked Tom, with a gesture fully worthy of the stage.

"Milord, is it?" called one of the apprentices. "Well, ain't we grand?" The group began to mince about the cobbles and bow to each other, drawing a laugh from their target.

Arthur fell in beside Tom, and they walked on. "That was extremely...colorful," he said.

"It's that fellow Shakespeare," replied Tom. "Reckon you'd know already that his plays are chock-full of first-rate words."

"Ah, yes. So you've been reading Shakespeare?"

"Puzzling it out, all I can get my hands on," answered Tom cheerfully. Tom was nearly always cheerful, which still surprised Arthur sometimes, considering the lad's history.

Tom had spent his earliest years scrounging through the rubbish on the streets of Bristol, with no knowledge of his family or even his last name. After a series of odd jobs, he'd taken to wandering the countryside on his own, where he'd encountered Arthur and then joined him on his travels for a while. Exposed to the inner workings of the London theater in the course of their adventures, Tom had discovered a desire to join that colorful world.

Nearing sixteen, the lad was beginning to grow into his features, as well as the large bones that showed in his hands and wrists. He seemed to have sprouted several inches in the last few months, Arthur thought. Tom's homely, round face was gaining definition. He'd taken to wearing his brown hair longer, tied with a bit of cord at the back. His blue eyes continued to look out on the world with amiable curiosity.

"I'm thinking of Jesperson," said Tom.

Arthur realized that he'd missed a remark or two. "What?"

"For my name," said Tom. "Mrs. Thorpe calls it a stage name, but I reckon it'll be more than that for me since I ai…haven't got any name of my own."

"Ah. Jesperson?"

"Because I'm just-a-person," replied Tom with a broad smile.

Arthur laughed. "Mrs. Thorpe would know best about that choice." Arthur had introduced the two. His unusual friendship with the acclaimed London actress had come through her banker husband.

"She's been right kind to me," Tom acknowledged. "Found me a job building scenery pieces. They call 'em flats, did you know? Because they're flat, I reckon. Can't be because they're boring, since they ain't." He offered this information with gusto. Tom had a passion for learning, if not for schools.

"And you're enjoying it as much as you expected?" Arthur asked, though he was fairly sure he knew the answer.

His young companion nodded. "It's like I said before. I feel at home at the theater."

It was true that many actors were as rootless as Tom, Arthur thought. They formed a class of their own outside the bounds of conventional society. Tom's lack of antecedents didn't brand him there, as it would almost anywhere else. "I'm glad," he said.

They turned into the street where Tom was living. Arthur and Mrs. Thorpe had helped find him a room that was near the theaters but outside the raucous passageways that tended to surround them. His landlady looked after him like a ferocious mother hen.

"No, you will not look inside it!" declared an accented female voice just ahead. "You will go away and let me be!"

Arthur looked over the head of a passerby in time to see a woman confronting a burly fellow who was reaching for a cloth bag she held, as if to tug it from her grasp. She stepped back, swung the sack in a wide arc, and struck him square on the nose with it. The man roared and raised a fist. Tom surged forward, but Arthur moved more quickly, stepping ahead of the lad to stand behind the woman. Arthur met the attacker's angry eyes, showing his readiness to intervene by gripping his walking stick.

The fellow glared at him for a long moment. Then, with a growled oath, he whirled and strode away.

The woman turned. But when she saw Arthur and Tom, the satisfaction in her face faded to a frown. "Oh, he went because you were standing there," she said. She stamped her foot. "I thought I'd bested him."

"You bloodied Dilch's nose," said Tom. He offered her a jaunty bow. "Only thing wrong with that is—it weren't me as done it."

"He made me angry," she replied.

"As he does," Tom acknowledged. "You got in a good hit. What's in the bag?"

"Vegetables," she replied, with an ironic smile and a shrug. The word had three syllables in her smoky voice with its slight foreign lilt.

"You faced off with Dilch over vegetables?" Tom grinned.

"It is the principle of the thing."

Again the words had more sounds than a native English speaker would have employed. This woman's speech was like warm honey pouring over one's ears, Arthur noted.

"We must do something about that man," she added.

Tom agreed. Arthur said nothing, because in plain fact he couldn't. Her presence had struck him like a coup de foudre, and his famous aplomb had temporarily deserted him. It wasn't simply the chiseled beauty of her face or the grace of her figure, clad in a gown with a unique air of fashion. He was ravished by the crackle of vitality in her eyes, so dark as to seem black; the glint of auburn in her raven hair; the aristocratic arch of her nose; the unconscious nobility in her stance. What was this magnificent woman doing in a seedy street, fighting off ruffians with a bag of vegetables?

"My lord, this is Señora Teresa Alvarez de Granada," said Tom. He pronounced the name as if he'd carefully learned the Castilian lisp. "She's a neighbor of mine. Señora, this is the Earl of Macklin."

"Earl? *De verdad*?"

Tom nodded. "I've been learning some Spanish from the señora," he informed Arthur.

"And what is an English milord doing here?" She looked around the street and back at Arthur as if she couldn't quite believe the juxtaposition. Then she looked from him to Tom, frowning.

"Señora," said Arthur with a bow. She received it with a distant nod and a twitch of her shoulder that was nearly a shrug.

He couldn't remember an occasion when he'd been received with such rudeness.

"She paints the flats I put together," Tom added.

"For the theater?" Arthur was puzzled. She didn't look like someone who would perform such tasks. "How did that come about?" he asked.

Her expression grew even cooler. "A matter of luck," she replied. Her tone was vastly unencouraging, making it clear that her doings were none of his affair.

"Indeed." Arthur could speak frostily, too. He didn't often bother, but she was acting as if he was an encroaching mushroom whose pretensions required depressing.

"Lord Macklin found me my job," said Tom. He looked amused.

"Mrs. Thorpe was the prime mover," Arthur said.

This earl knew Mrs. Thorpe. Teresa found that almost as odd as his apparent ease in Tom's company. She gazed up at the tall man before her. There was no denying his square-jawed, athletic attractiveness. Perhaps ten years her senior, she judged, more or less. His handsome face showed few lines, and those seemed scored by good humor. *Seemed* indeed, she thought with contempt. Charm was the mask aristocratic gentlemen used to hide their ruthlessness. But she knew the breed all too well. They took what they wanted and cared nothing for those without power. Indeed, they enjoyed exerting their dominance, savored it as a dark pleasure. Nothing such a man said could be trusted.

This earl's blue-gray eyes gleamed with intelligence, which made him even more dangerous. She had to suppress a shudder. The smart ones were worse. They found ways around obstacles. They set cruel traps for the unwary and relished their struggles. Her fingers tightened painfully on her cloth bag.

She reminded herself that she didn't need anything from this nobleman. She didn't have to please him. She didn't need anyone, and wouldn't, not ever again. She was free. "I must go," she said.

"I'm headed back," said Tom. "We can walk with you, can't we, my lord?"

"Of course," said the tall earl.

Teresa was amused to hear reserve in his voice. He was vexed that she hadn't bowed and scraped when told his rank. And she could afford to annoy him. How she enjoyed that. But what was he doing with young Tom? Was she obliged to warn the lad? Yes, she would, when the object of her concern wasn't looming over them like a storm cloud. "There is no necessity to accompany me," she said. She wished they wouldn't, in fact.

"We're happy to," said Tom. "Eh, my lord?"

Lord Macklin bowed, a polite acknowledgment rather than an agreement.

Tom was finding something amusing in this encounter, Teresa saw. As he did in so much of existence. She envied the boy his easygoing temperament. For her part, she wanted to get away. She did *not* require disruptive earls in any form. All was serene in her life now. Well, barring minor annoyances like Dilch. She was satisfied and settled and determined not to stray from the bounds she'd set. It had been a long, difficult road to this place. She would let nothing threaten that hard-won peace. "It is but a few steps," she said. "I won't trouble you." She nodded at Tom and said, "Good day, my lord."

The earl took his dismissal with bland grace.

Worse and worse, thought Teresa. Such smooth surfaces concealed deceit. It was much easier when this sort of man was cutting and cold. But no matter. She wouldn't ever see him again. There was no cause for concern. "Good day," she said again. And walked rapidly away with her lumpy bag of produce bumping at her knee. Though she could feel his eyes on her back, she did not rush. Prey ran; she was not prey. She would never be prey again.

"Who in the world is she?" Arthur asked Tom when the lady was gone.

"Like I said, a neighbor."

"In your lodgings?" Arthur had never seen her on his visits to Tom.

"No, she has her own house just down the street from my rooms."

"With her family? Her husband, perhaps."

Tom gave him a sidelong glance as he began to walk along the cobbles again. "No, just her and a servant girl. I think her family all died in the war. She doesn't speak of them. Turns the subject right quick if anyone asks."

"Ah." The war against Napoleon had caused a great deal of displacement on the Continent, and the Iberian Peninsula had been particularly affected. "So she lives here in London now?"

"Aye. I reckon she has a bit of money. She seems to be able to please herself."

A small income would sustain an individual in this part of town, Arthur thought. "You say she paints scenery for the theater?" He still found this odd.

"That's where I met her, at the workshop," said Tom. "She can make the flats look real as real. Like you was...were looking out over a regular vista."

"An artist then?"

"Learned watercolors as a girl, she said."

One of the accomplishments of a lady, Arthur thought. He had no doubt she was one. Was it her fall in status that made her so prickly? Or did she blame him, as an Englishman, for the depredations of the war? That seemed petty and unfair. "And who is this Dilch?"

"Him." Tom sniffed. "Our local bully."

"He hurts people?" Arthur grew concerned for Tom.

"Mostly he blusters," the lad replied. "When it starts to go beyond that, the people hereabouts band together against him. No need to worry, my lord."

Worry was only a part of what Arthur was feeling. He was remarkably unsettled, he realized. Señora Alvarez had roused and interested and annoyed him. How long had it been since he'd felt such tumult? Longer than he could recall, he thought.

He ought to simply dismiss her from his mind. She'd clearly had no interest in him. Indeed, she'd seemed eager to get away. But he did not deserve her abrupt dismissal. That was what rankled, Arthur thought. He was a...worthy person.

His face heated as he acknowledged the pomposity of that phrase. Yet it was true. Many people thought so. And for some reason, he felt a strong urge to show Señora Alvarez that she'd misjudged him. After that demonstration he would probably never see her again. They obviously did not move in the same circles.

But how then to speak with her? He couldn't call on her, a woman alone in a part of London where he didn't fit. He would be noticed; eyebrows would be raised. He had no wish to cause her difficulties. A thought occurred. Perhaps Mrs. Thorpe knew the señora? His friend seemed to be acquainted with nearly everyone in the theater world, no matter how tangential. That was it. At the first opportunity, he would find out. Mrs. Thorpe could even vouch for his character to the señora, since he seemed to require such bolstering. His brain shied away from asking whyever this should be the case.

"My lord?" asked Tom. The lad had walked on a few steps and now turned back with a quizzical expression.

He'd been standing in the middle of the street like a moonstruck calf. "Coming," said Arthur and hastened to catch up.

Two

TERESA ALVAREZ DE GRANADA TIPPED A HANDFUL OF
olives that she'd walked a good distance to purchase
from a Levantine vendor into a shallow dish, discard-
ing the twist of oily paper that had held them. She
picked out one, closed her eyes, and bit down. The
taste brought back the sunshine of her youth, the scent
of lemons, the whisper of vine leaves stirring on an
ancient pergola. Gone forever, but still remembered.
She chewed memories. If only the good ones could be
separated from the bad and kept like a casket of jewels
to be taken out and admired at will.

Teresa spit out the olive pit and put it on the edge
of the dish. Her eating habits were strange to many of
the English. She didn't much care for meat, certainly
not the thick, bloody slabs of beef they enjoyed. A
perfectly roasted chicken now and then perhaps. And
she was fond of vegetables, both raw and cooked,
which many of her new countrymen disdained as
fodder for animals. Fortunately, she could make her
own choices in this regard, as in all others now, *gracias
a Dios*.

She looked around the front room of her tiny house. Her refuge was comprised of one fair-sized chamber downstairs with an extension behind for the kitchen and a place for her maidservant. A respectable woman couldn't live all alone, here or anywhere. And she had become a respectable woman. Who would want to be solitary *en verdad*? She was no medieval hermit.

A little walled yard at the back contained the privy and a coal bin. She hoped to take up some of the cobbles in one corner for a small garden eventually.

A single bedchamber upstairs had slanted ceilings under the roof, two dormer windows, and space for little more than a bed and a wardrobe. But she owned the place; that was the important thing. And it was in good repair. The furnishings were scant but adequate and might be augmented in time. She'd managed a bit of color in the parti-colored shawl laid over the back of the drab settee and one of her own watercolors hung over the small hearth. She gazed at the sun-drenched landscape in the picture. She'd had ranks of rooms to wander through as a girl, before war came roaring over her land. If she'd known life would come down to this, she might have savored that space more.

Her home was far from the fashionable haunts where people like the Earl of Macklin attended glittering parties, Teresa thought. The tall nobleman young Tom had introduced would not find her here. He would disappear back into the ranks of English society. She'd glided through such opulent festivities in her time, long ago. She'd also had a surfeit of pain and terror—days when she had no money for food, when she had to cower in ruins to evade marching armies. She'd done things she despised. But she refused to be ashamed. She'd survived, as others had not. A plain, quiet life was just what she wanted now. It was such a magnificent luxury—that no one could give her orders or make demands.

Teresa turned away from the bitter recollection of some of those and glimpsed a flash in the mirror hanging beside the front door. Her earrings had caught the light and flung it back. She shook her head to admire the effect in the glass. Tiny sprays of emeralds glinted from chains of delicate gold filigree suspended from her earlobes. She had designed this pair herself, as she often did, and had them made, taking jewels that evoked old bad memories and turning them into something of her own, something she could cherish. Her collection of earrings was both an indulgence and a way to easily transport wealth when one might have to pick up and run without warning. Too many times she'd been forced to do that.

Those years showed in her face, Teresa thought. There were faint lines now, hints of deeper wrinkles that would come with time. Her hair was still black as night. Her figure was good. Men had called her beautiful, and that had been as much a curse as a boon. What had this Macklin thought when he looked at her?

She turned away from the mirror, rejecting the question. Whatever he had thought, she didn't need to consider it. *Gracias a Dios* once again. An earl and his opinions and whims had no place in the frugal life she'd established for herself. No man did, she repeated to herself. That was over. She was safe. She had enough set aside to live on and could make her own choices. Did she propose to forget that this was far more than she'd hoped for in those dreadful years? *Ciertamente no!* There were no reasons, no grounds, for self-pity. Only gratitude.

"Eliza," she called. "I am going to the workshop." The Drury Lane Theater was preparing for a new play, and they wanted backdrops that showed a vista of mountains. Teresa, who was more than familiar with such scenes, had been engaged to paint them through the good offices of Mrs. Thorpe.

The meeting with that gracious lady had been a true piece of luck. One did not expect to encounter such a presence in this part of London, or find that she was a friend of young Tom.

The maid appeared in the kitchen archway. Teresa had hired a sturdy, taciturn young woman to help her. Eliza offered few words but a solid presence, which came in handy when Teresa went beyond her own neighborhood. She could walk by herself in certain areas. She knew them and didn't stray into places where she might find trouble. If she had to roam farther, she took Eliza along, as well as a parasol with a stone knob well able to double as a club. Teresa's demonstration of this function a few months ago had elicited one of the maid's rare smiles.

"I'll be back in the afternoon," Teresa added. Eliza nodded and returned to the kitchen. Teresa put on her bonnet and gloves and set off.

The theater's busy workshop was nearby. She heard the pounding of hammers before she entered the large

open warehouse where carpenters constructed the flats
that created the illusion of landscapes on the stage. The
smell of paint enveloped her as she went inside. In one
corner, artisans produced the smaller objects needed
for the drama, such as bottles that broke over heads
without injury. Seamstresses worked in a room at the
back, though most actors wore their own clothes in
the plays.

Workers called out greetings, and Teresa acknowledged them on her way to her area, where a partly
painted scene waited. This shop was separate from the
hectic world of the stage, and a different kind of cama-
raderie reigned here, that of craftsmen proud of their
skills. There was some rivalry, but not the inflated
self-regard and indulgences of temperament Teresa
had seen in the casts now and then. Not all actors
were as serenely confident as her new acquaintance
Mrs. Thorpe.

Tom waved a hammer from the other side of the
space. Teresa waved back as she removed her bonnet,
gloves, and shawl and set them aside. She tied a long
apron over her gown, which had short sleeves so as
not to trail in the paint. She went to the table at the
side where her brushes had been left clean and ready,
opened paint pots, and set to work.

She had loved painting from her earliest years, and
her favorite subject was sweeping scenes—mountains,
castles, gardens, wide lawns or fertile fields, even
opulent rooms. Animals too—herds of sheep or cattle,
foxes peeking from the undergrowth, a dog or cat
sitting to the side. The vistas sometimes included
human figures in the distance as well, which was no

problem. But Teresa didn't do portraits. This was less from a lack of ability than a distaste for the process of reproducing human faces. One had to gaze so deeply into near strangers. And who knew which could be trusted? Or what incorrect message they might read into her gaze? She went back to the crag she'd begun sketching out the last time and immersed herself in the work. As usual, it occupied all her attention.

The theater provided bread and cheese and ale from a local inn around midday, which the workers supplemented with their own food. Most chose to eat in an oblong space behind the building, too rustic to be called a courtyard. It was rather a bit of ground left vacant when four buildings were constructed around it, a forgotten scrap of weedy grass. But the enclosure held the sun's heat, and on an early spring day it was a pleasant place to sit. The artisans had painted country vistas on the blank walls, and someone had planted flowers and climbing vines. A motley collection of tables and chairs were scattered about.

Tom joined Teresa for the informal nuncheon, as he often did, and she was glad. She couldn't remember when she'd met anyone easier to be friends with. He was so generally cheerful and interested in nearly any topic one could name. Surprisingly informed sometimes as well, considering the unfortunate life history he'd confided. Teresa sipped at the ale, preferring it to the thin, sour wine that could also be obtained. She knew where to procure good Spanish vintages when she wished to indulge, which was very seldom. She despised drunkenness and the disasters that came with it.

"This new play's got camels in it," Tom said.

"Does it?"

"A caravan from the mysterious East," he intoned. Tom read all the plays they worked on, and he often had comments about the stories. "You ever seen a camel?"

"Never. Except in pictures."

He nodded. "You reckon they'll dress up some actors? Front and rear, like they done for the elephant last month?"

"I suppose so. If they have the costumes."

"Huh. They'd need a few more this time. How many camels in a caravan, do you think?"

"An actual one? Many, according to paintings I've seen."

Tom nodded. "Might need a deal of players then. I reckon I could be a camel." He grinned. "Leastways the back part."

Teresa laughed as he bit off a large hunk of bread and cheese.

"Mebbe I'll ask if I can," Tom added when he'd swallowed.

"Why not? I expect you'd be good at it."

"You ever wanted to be up on the stage, 'stead of just painting for it?"

She hid a shudder. "Never." The thought of all those people staring at her—ogling—was repellent.

"His lordship says it never hurts to try a thing. If you don't like it, no need to go on."

The advice of a man who had always had free choices, Teresa thought. Typical of the aristocrats' view that the world belonged to them, to pick and choose as they pleased. But here was the opportunity she'd been looking for. "How did you come to know an earl?" she asked.

"I was walking south from Bristol when I came on a little boy running away from home," Tom replied.

As he told the story of meeting Lord Macklin and traveling with him for some months, Teresa watched Tom's face. This earl seemed to have treated the lad well, at least as far as Tom could see. There might well have been slights he didn't notice, since Tom always seemed to expect the best. Clearly, he admired the older man. It didn't occur to Tom that he had been a mere amusement, used to alleviate aristocratic boredom and continually at risk of being cast off. He had been fortunate; he'd found his own way out. Still, she felt protective. "People of that class put their own whims above all else," she said.

"Class?" asked Tom.

"The nobility."

He looked back at her with the acuity that flashed in his blue eyes at unexpected moments. "I ain't seen that, but I reckon you would know better than me."

"What do you mean?" She heard the sharpness in her voice.

"Well, I would have said you were nobility yourself, señora. Begging your pardon."

"Don't be silly." She looked away. This was not a subject she would discuss. She wished she'd never mentioned this earl, particularly since it seemed there was no need to warn Tom off him.

"Lord Macklin's coming by next week," said Tom. "I told him about that thunder machine we're building, and he wanted to see it."

This was not good news. "Which day?" Teresa asked.

Tom gave her a sidelong look. "He wasn't sure. He has lots to do."

Or, he was an earl and saw no need to consider others. He would come when he pleased, and the rest of them must adjust. Well, she would avoid him. She could do that now. She didn't have to observe every nuance of another's moods and adjust her behavior in response. She'd been purposefully becoming more of a nobody for years, and she was comfortable with obscurity. Delighted with it. When Macklin appeared, she would slip away until he was gone. It was as simple as that.

Three days later, Arthur walked into the theater workshop and stopped near the door to admire the controlled rush of activity. He greatly respected the work of skilled craftsmen, and this was evident all around the huge room. And women, he noted, seeing Tom's Spanish neighbor painting a landscape at the back.

He was here to visit Tom, of course, but he admitted now that he'd also hoped to see her again. The effect she'd had on him lingered in vivid detail. He couldn't remember when he'd met a woman—or any person really—with such presence. Nor when he'd been so definitively rejected for no reason at all. A spark of resentment rekindled at the memory of their encounter.

He'd made some discreet inquiries in diplomatic circles, and discovered no information about a woman called Teresa Alvarez de Granada. But that meant nothing. The long war against Napoleon had dislocated countless people, and not all were known to the embassy. Indeed, one of his contacts had suggested that this sounded like an assumed name. Arthur felt certain that her nom de guerre disguised a noble lineage. The lady's stance, her voice, her gaze had proclaimed it, even as she made no claims. That modesty had clinched the matter for him, actually.

He'd timed his visit for early afternoon. Tom had told him how the days went here, and he knew there was a pause for refreshment. He'd also brought a large box of Gunter's lemon tarts to share out. It occurred to him now that they were a lure for a lady, like setting out bait to trap an elusive wild creature. The idea made him smile, and as he did, she turned and met his eyes. She went still, her brush suspended in one hand. The same shock as before ran through him. What was it about this woman that stirred him so? Her gaze was certainly not welcoming. In fact, she looked quite unhappy to see him.

Tom came over to greet Arthur and led him toward the back of the workshop. He gathered up Señora Alvarez as they moved past her, even though she made an evasive gesture, and Arthur wondered at this. At both of them, really. Tom's twinkling sidelong glance was no help. They passed through a door at the back of the building into a small open space. "Ah," Arthur said. "One would never know this was here." Despite the shabbiness of the surrounding buildings, it was a pleasant area. Unmatched tables and chairs were scattered about. Tom took them to a table shaded by climbing vines and went off to fetch supplies.

Silence fell. There was no sign whatsoever that Señora Alvarez intended to break it. "Did you paint the walls?" Arthur asked her.

She looked at the country vistas that decorated the four blank walls. "Not these," she said.

Did she mean that there were other walls, somewhere, that she had painted? This seemed unlikely. Arthur placed his pastry offering on the table and opened the box.

"*Tarta de limón*," said the lady.

"Do you like them?" Arthur asked.

"One of my favorites," she replied in an odd, almost accusing tone. She started to rise. "I must go…"

Tom returned before she could slip away. "What about our picnic?" he said. "It's all planned."

"Another time. You have a visitor." She stood.

"But you must join us," said Arthur. He meant it as a cordial invitation, but she looked offended.

"*Must* I?" The phrase was nearly a growl.

What the deuce was wrong with this woman?

"But there's tarts," said Tom. He took several from the box and set them out with the bread and cheese he'd fetched. The other pastries went to a table where people could help themselves. Tom also opened the small hamper he'd brought and extracted a packet of sandwiches, a stoppered jug, and six small cups that fit into each other as a stack.

Señora Alvarez stood rigid for a long moment. She was really angry, Arthur thought. That was obvious. But why? He could see no reason for it. No credible reason. He glanced at Tom to see if the lad understood and received a bland smile in return.

The lady whirled and strode back inside the workshop. Arthur wouldn't have been surprised if she never returned, but she came back with a wedge of blue-veined cheese and a handful of olives in oiled paper. She cast these onto the table as if they were a challenge to a duel and sat down with the same defiant air.

Arthur took an olive and bit down with pleasure. "Ah."

"You like olives?" she asked.

"Very much." Her turned-down lips caused him to add, "Does that offend you somehow?" He could not help asking in a tone that implied *whyever should it*?

She shrugged. "Many Englishmen do not."

"I am not 'many Englishmen.'"

"No, you are an earl. We all know this."

Before Arthur could respond to this unwarranted remark, Tom uncorked the jug with a loud pop. Arthur turned at the sudden sound to find that Tom was grinning as he poured cups of cider. What he found to smile about, Arthur did not know, but that was often true of Tom. They portioned out the food and began to eat.

One made polite conversation over a meal, Arthur thought. But neither of his companions seemed inclined to try. He racked his brain for a likely subject. "Were you fond of the theater in Spain?" he asked the señora. "Er, Lope de Vega? Cervantes?"

She looked at him as if he'd said something very odd. "No, I never saw plays until I came to England." She sipped her cider as if it was the finest champagne. Her posture suggested that she wished he would disappear from her potential field of vision.

Arthur felt aggrieved. What the deuce was this? People did not treat him this way. Some disliked him, of course, as was their right. His life was not all ease and deference. But he could usually discover a reason for their aversion, and often amend it. Señora Alvarez had no reason. "When did you come to England?" he asked her.

"Some time ago."

Her tone said she didn't wish to talk about her life. Not to him, at least. That was very clear. "Are you enjoying London?"

"I have not been in London long."

Arthur wondered where in England she'd been before, and what she'd done before that. But she clearly didn't intend to tell him anything at all. Not one small fact about herself. Which was making this conversation ridiculous. Well, let it be then. "Did you ever meet Joseph Bonaparte?" he asked.

She stared at him, incredulous. "Of course not. Why would I?"

Her face was very expressive, Arthur thought, happy to have provoked a reaction at last. "I just thought you might have," he answered. "Living in Spain." And clearly among the nobility, he added silently.

"Joseph?" said Tom. "Is that another name for Napoleon?"

"Joseph was his brother," Arthur replied. "He was made King of Spain." And had been very unpopular with his subjects, he recalled then.

"A false king imposed on the country by a supposed 'emperor,'" said Señora Alvarez.

There was fire, Arthur thought. Her dark eyes

burned. Her lovely lips were pressed tight. He found himself wanting a real talk with her, to learn her history, her opinions, what inspired her prickly facade. "True," he said.

"He has fled to America, where he lives off the jewels he stole from Spain." She made a sound like *pfft*, coldly derisive. A flutter of fingers accompanied it.

"I didn't know that," he replied.

"It is said." She bit into one of Tom's sandwiches with elegant ferocity.

Silence returned to their group. Arthur searched for a topic to keep the conversation flowing. "You speak English very well," he said to her.

She shrugged. "One must learn, since the English do not."

It was true. Few of his countrymen bothered to acquire other tongues. But Tom said, "*No es verdad.*"

Señora Alvarez smiled at him. The effect was glorious, stunning. Arthur was reduced to wordless admiration.

"Most English people," she corrected. "You are unusual."

"I am that," replied the lad with a grin. "*Tendrás una tarta?*" He offered her a pastry, and she accepted it with regal grace.

How in heaven's name had she ended up here? Arthur marveled and sipped from his cup and reassembled his aplomb. "Good cider," he said to Tom.

"Friend of mine brings it in from Kent to sell," the lad replied.

"Everyone you meet is a *friend*," said Señora Alvarez. "You should take more care."

Arthur thought she looked sidelong at him as she said it. But that made no sense.

Tom shook his head. "Not everyone. I've met some bad 'uns. But not too many."

"You can tell the difference?" Teresa asked. She did worry about that.

"Long's I can remember," Tom answered with a grin.

It was a sad admission, but Tom's cheerful expression was irresistible. Teresa smiled back and then turned to discover that Macklin was smiling as well. Unguarded, Teresa met that smile head-on and was shaken by an inner tremor. The man was handsome at all times, but when he smiled, the effect was multiplied tenfold. More, something in his eyes seemed so benign, as if he was the soul of honor. No doubt he knew this and used the appearance to his advantage.

He and young Tom made quite the contrast, Teresa thought. Tom was a good boy, but he looked what he was, an inexperienced stripling whose lanky frame was as yet…untenanted. Despite his adventurous life, he had yet to accumulate the experiences that would define him. Macklin, on the other hand, looked thoroughly inhabited. His blue-gray eyes promised histories to recount and depths to plumb. Not to mention the prowess of his athletic body. He was unquestionably attractive. Teresa found herself wondering about his…not *earl-ess*, which would be an ugly word in any case. *Countess*… That was it, though why the English called them that when they had no counts she couldn't imagine.

She pulled herself sharply back. Macklin was a

snare, a deceit, designed to beguile before he struck. She did *not* need to learn that lesson again. Teresa rose. "I must go back to my work."

"You haven't finished your tart," said Tom.

His tone suggested that he was teasing her, though she didn't understand exactly how. She sometimes missed a nuance in her second, or really third, language. Teresa gathered all her dignity and rose. "I will take it with me."

"You don't want to get paint on it," the lad said. "I reckon that'd be bad for you."

"I will take care." Teresa made it a mild reproach. Of course she wouldn't sully her food. One of the other painters sometimes held a brush between his teeth. She never would. She picked up her pastry and walked away with a sense of making a lucky escape, and also of eyes fixed on her back as she moved.

Arthur followed her progress with an appreciative gaze. He supposed she was past thirty, but that only meant she had the lushness of maturity along with the lithe grace of youth. He couldn't remember when he'd encountered a more intriguing woman.

"I'll take another of those if you don't want 'em," Tom said.

Arthur turned back to find the lad indicating the tarts. He waved permission.

Tom ate half a pastry in one bite. "Señora Alvarez is a fine lady," he said when he'd swallowed.

"She is indeed. Though not much inclined to talk about herself."

"No." He finished the confection in another bite.

The lad would understand about such reluctance,

with the life he'd led. And he would keep any confidences he'd received, as he should. Arthur could *wish* that he was more forthcoming, however.

When Tom had consumed another tart, he said, "Shall I show you how we make thunder on the stage?"

This had been the excuse for Arthur's visit. And in fact he was interested. But he also hoped for further conversation with Tom's beguiling friend.

He never got that. Señora Alvarez had departed when they reentered the workshop. Arthur did discover that the noise of thunder was created by casting wooden balls down a wooden trough, the "thunder run." The sound was surprisingly convincing. He took care to give Tom the attention and interest he expected, even as he plotted ways to learn more about the lovely señora.

And thus it was that on the following day, Arthur paid a call on his friend Mrs. Thorpe at the lavish town house of her banker husband. He was greeted with that lady's customary aplomb—no sign of surprise despite the fact that he rarely made a personal visit. As always, Mrs. Thorpe's black hair was immaculately dressed. Her rose-silk gown was a marvel of fashion, her face a model of classic beauty. Her blue eyes gleamed with sharp intelligence.

She sat in one armchair before the drawing room fireplace and directed Arthur to another. He noted again that seeing her felt rather like an audience with the queen. She certainly was a monarch of the theatrical world. When they had exchanged pleasantries, she waited with the poise of one of the greatest actresses of her generation. Arthur, on the other hand, was not entirely sure how to begin.

"Is it something about Tom?" the lady asked finally.

"No, no. He seems to be thriving."

"He's well liked at the theater."

"As he seems to be everywhere."

"Indeed. It is his gift."

Arthur nodded. That was certainly true.

Mrs. Thorpe waited. That was *her* gift, a serene stillness.

"I wanted to ask about a lady you might know," he said.

"A lady?" His hostess raised chiseled brows and smiled. In another the expression might have been mocking. Yet there was something warm and engaging in her face. It was impossible to take offense.

"Her name is Teresa Alvarez de Granada," Arthur said. He wasn't surprised that she found his awkwardness amusing.

"Ah."

"She paints backdrops for Drury Lane, so I thought perhaps you had…encountered her."

"Yes, I am acquainted with Señora Alvarez."

Arthur felt a rush of eager curiosity.

"What is your interest in her?" Mrs. Thorpe asked.

"I met her when I was visiting Tom."

"Ah?"

The single word was weighted with implication. Chiefly, it pointed out that he hadn't answered her question. And what was the answer? "I was struck by her manner. Surely she must be a Spanish noblewoman?"

Mrs. Thorpe examined him. Arthur had seen her evaluate other people, but he'd never been the subject of such careful scrutiny. "I do not know her lineage," she said. "She has not chosen to confide it, and of course I would not pry."

Arthur's disappointment was sharp.

"Obviously that is not her position now," Mrs. Thorpe added.

"She lives near Tom's rooms, I understand. He said she has a house there."

"Yes."

"An odd choice of neighborhood for a woman of her…"

"I'm not sure you could comprehend her choices," interrupted Mrs. Thorpe. Her tone was quietly inflexible.

It was a subtle reprimand, but Arthur heard it and fell silent in surprise. He was not accustomed to being addressed so. He and Mrs. Thorpe had an established, cordial acquaintance. They had even schemed together on more than one occasion. He felt a spark of irritation. She knew he was to be trusted. He was only seeking information. "I believe I am quite capable of doing so," he replied.

He endured another searching gaze. "I like and respect you, Lord Macklin, but I don't think you can imagine what it is like to be a woman on her own, with limited means, in a foreign country. Your interest could cause difficulties for Señora Alvarez."

"My *interest* is simple curiosity about a friend of Tom's," Arthur protested.

Mrs. Thorpe's sharp eyes seemed to see right

through him, down to the reaction he'd felt when he first met the señora.

Arthur felt himself flush. "I would never do anything to inconvenience or embarrass a lady," he added. Of course not. "You know I wouldn't."

His hostess's gaze remained steady for another few moments, then she sighed. "It's never any use offering advice. So few want to hear it. I will hold you to that statement as a promise, Lord Macklin, because I like and admire Señora Alvarez."

"You may certainly do so," he answered. His voice sounded stiff, but he rather thought she deserved it. What had he ever done that she should doubt him?

Mrs. Thorpe nodded. "You are an honorable man." She folded her hands in her lap. "I met Señora Alvarez one day when I'd gone to visit Tom. We fell into conversation after repelling the advances of a bumptious fellow in the street."

"Dilch?" Arthur wondered.

"You have met him?"

"Observed only. An unattractive individual."

"As Tom would now say, a churlish canker-blossom."

They exchanged a smile, which heartened Arthur. He valued his friendship with Mrs. Thorpe.

"I enjoyed our conversation," she continued. "And found other occasions to talk with Señora Alvarez. When I discovered that she was looking for occupation and that she was a talented watercolorist, I put in a word at the workshop. For several months now, she has been painting exquisite scenery there."

Arthur nodded.

"Then recently, she was even more helpful. She

stepped in to mediate a dispute among the opera dancers." She cast him a look. "Many of them are émigrées, you know, and Señora Alvarez speaks Spanish, of course, but also French and some Portuguese and Italian."

"She's well educated then," said Arthur. He'd known she must be.

"She also has sympathy for the girls' troubles, which many do not."

"Troubles?" Arthur had never thought much about opera dancers. Beyond appreciating their performances now and then.

Mrs. Thorpe looked disappointed in him, another unaccustomed experience. "They have quite a hard time of it, Lord Macklin. Low pay, and if they're just five minutes late to rehearsal, they're fined out of that small wage. They're expected to pay for their shoes and costumes out of it, too. Many live on the verge of starvation and dangerously close to illness." She frowned as if this could somehow be his fault. "And of course there are the gentlemen who consider their backstage room at the theater a marketplace for mistresses."

Arthur knew this to be true. He had heard men joke about it. He had never been one of them, however.

"Some don't mind the offers flung at them," Mrs. Thorpe went on, as if taken by her own thoughts. "And indeed encourage them for the money they bring. But others feel forced. I do what I can to help out, and Señora Alvarez has joined me in that."

"She has a caring heart," said Arthur appreciatively.

Mrs. Thorpe raised her brows as if he'd missed an important point. "She does, but…"

"Yes?"

His hostess hesitated before adding, "The señora seems contented with her life as it is, Lord Macklin. Perhaps you should leave her alone."

"What do you mean? I don't intend to do anything to her."

"Your interest is a thing."

Rebellion stirred in his breast. "I wouldn't do her any harm."

"You won't mean to. You're a kind man. And yet, you are a man."

"And thus a blundering fool?" Arthur had never been angry at Mrs. Thorpe in the years they'd been acquainted. Until now.

"Not that. But blind to certain things. It is not your fault. You are trained so."

"Whereas you are all knowing?"

"Of course not. Yet you must admit I know more about the life of a woman than you."

He couldn't argue with that, though he wanted to. Fearing what he might say in his current mood, Arthur rose. "I shouldn't keep you any longer."

Mrs. Thorpe hesitated, then went to ring for a servant. "Further conversation does seem pointless just now," she said, which only irritated Arthur further.

Striding along the street a few minutes later, he wrestled with his annoyance. For the life of him, he could not see how he had deserved the…judgment his supposed friend had levied upon him. He could call it nothing else. And he could only see it as unfair. She was as bad as Señora Alvarez. Two of them in as many days! It was outrageous.

Three

ARTHUR WAS STILL BROODING OVER THESE ENCOUNTERS at the first great occasion of the season that year, a grand ball given by Lady Castlereagh. Standing to one side, watching the cream of society arrive, he found himself imagining Señora Alvarez here, vivid as a rose among daisies. He would like to dance with her, take her in to supper later, talk to her for more than a few minutes, and learn more about her. He wanted to show her that he was charming, he realized with chagrin. He wanted to make her smile as warmly at him as she had at Tom. But she wasn't present, and she wouldn't be at any of the festivities of the season, which suddenly seemed tedious.

She occupied his thoughts far more than any woman in his recent experience—the flash of her dark eyes, the enticing shape of her lips, the perfection of her form, and on the other hand, the…calculated impertinence of her manner. That was a good label for it. Purposefully insolent. She couldn't really *want* to offend him. Could she? He would have said certainly not, any more than Mrs. Thorpe would ever insult him. Yet these things had happened. He should simply try to forget the woman. Yet he found he couldn't.

Must he be bound by convention? Couldn't he call on Señora Alvarez even if it was improper? Rebellion stirred in Arthur once again. He could do as he liked. Who would dare question him? And as if she stood beside him, he heard Mrs. Thorpe's voice pointing out that the same wasn't true for the señora. She would bear the consequences if gossip began.

Arthur set his jaw. He'd promised not to cause the lady difficulties. And he wouldn't. He didn't wish to! But neither would he avoid all chance of seeing her. He'd visited Tom at the workshop before; he could do so again. That would rouse no talk. He would show the señora that he was a friend worth cultivating. The resolve built in him as he realized that he wanted this more than anything he'd wished for in a long time.

More than he wished to be at this ball, for example. How would Señora Alvarez look at the bedecked and bejeweled crowd? How would Mrs. Thorpe? Arthur suspected, after his recent conversations, that it would not be as he saw them. He tried to summon their different points of view as he ran his eye over the people before him. But he didn't know enough to do so, which was oddly frustrating. Most of the crowd was familiar, some of them even friends. And yet he wasn't moved to go and speak to them. He knew they would exchange commonplace phrases that they'd used many times before. Was this his thirtieth season? More than that? Had he become jaded? He didn't like that idea.

As if to illustrate the opposite end of the spectrum,

a lively party came through the archway just then. The young Duke of Compton and his fiancée, Ada Grandison, were accompanied by her three close friends. Arthur had met all of them in the autumn under far different circumstances, and he knew this was their first venture into London society. Excitement showed on all their faces. The large and stately figure of Miss Julia Grandison, Miss Ada's aunt, loomed behind them.

Compton came to join him while the ladies were detained by an acquaintance of the aunt. "My new coat," said the younger man when he reached Arthur. He turned to show it off. "Perfection, according to Ada. Thank you for the recommendation of a tailor."

"You look quite dapper."

"Yes, as long as I don't move about much," Compton replied.

Arthur raised an interrogative eyebrow.

"Dancing lessons," added the young duke in mock despair. "I keep tripping over my own feet in the quadrille. And that's only when I can remember the steps. What fiend invented that devilish dance?"

"The French."

"Some sort of revenge for Waterloo?"

"It came well before that. At the court of Louis the Fifteenth, I believe. Lady Jersey introduced it here."

"A patroness of Almack's whom I must not on any account offend," said Compton, as if repeating a rote lesson.

"I don't think you need to worry." A wealthy young duke was too attractive a parti to be spurned, even if he was already engaged.

His female companions joined them then, and Arthur smiled at the picture they presented. The four young ladies wore fashionable new dresses and sported modish haircuts. Their appearance had been polished by someone with very good taste indeed.

"Is it true that Tom is to be in a play?" asked Miss Ada Grandison when Arthur had offered his compliments on their ensembles. Miss Ada's authoritative eyebrows always hinted at a scowl even when she was smiling, as now. Arthur admired the way she wielded their expressive power. He thought she was going to make an admirable duchess.

"Yes," he replied. "Tom has a small part in the new play at the Drury Lane Theater, *Lord for a Season*."

"We must all go see it," said Miss Sarah Moran, the shortest of the four young ladies. Arthur suspected that her sandy brows and eyelashes had been subtly tinted for her debut. Her light-blue eyes sparkled with interest in the chattering crowd.

"If Harriet can spare a moment from being lionized," said Miss Charlotte Deeping. The tallest and most acerbic of the young ladies had been persuaded to wear ruffles, Arthur noted with amusement. Her black hair, pale skin, and angular frame seemed less spiky in this new guise.

Miss Harriet Finch turned on her, red-blond hair glinting in the candlelight. "Will you stop, Charlotte? I've asked you and asked you." The volume of her protest caused nearby heads to turn. The glitter in her green eyes promised retribution. Oddly, of the four young ladies, she looked most apprehensive to Arthur. Since she was a considerable heiress, and thus could expect a warm welcome from the *haut ton*, he didn't understand her stiff expression.

"I've never seen so many people in one room," said Miss Moran, in an obvious effort to smooth over the dispute. "And all strangers. Nothing at all like a country assembly. What do you do if no one asks you to dance? Sit and watch?" She eyed the rows of gilt chairs pushed against the walls with disfavor.

"You know I've promised you my brothers," replied Miss Deeping. "You won't lack partners."

Arthur thought he might have met one of her brothers last season. He recalled a lanky young sprig named Deeping among the dandy set. Even in a padded coat he'd looked rather like a toothpick.

"You mustn't *make* them ask me," said Miss Moran.

"Nonsense. What are brothers for if not to follow orders?" Miss Deeping gazed around the room. Finding what she sought, she beckoned.

A tall, slender young man approached—not the exquisite one Arthur remembered. This one looked like a male version of Miss Deeping, in plain evening dress. "What is it, Char?" he said.

"Ask Sarah to dance," was the imperious reply. "Sarah, you've met Henry."

Miss Moran murmured an embarrassed acknowledgment. The young man grinned down at her. "Honored," he said, sketching a bow.

"Where are Stanley and Cecil?" asked Miss Deeping.

Her brother gestured vaguely at the crowd. "They're about somewhere."

"Well, find them and bring them here."

"I thought you said you'd rather be a wallflower than dance with a brother," teased Henry Deeping.

"That was before I saw the walls." Miss Deeping surveyed the large ballroom with uncertainty. Not quite as assured as she liked to appear, Arthur concluded.

"Right." Her brother offered an amused salute. "I'll be back in a tic."

"And don't think you can slope off," added Miss Deeping. "You know what Mama said."

"We are to do our duty to launch our odious little sister into society."

"Beast."

"I would say beauty, but I'm an honest fellow."

"You are a pig," said his sister.

With a grin and another bow, Henry Deeping departed on his mission.

"I won't dance with Cecil," declared Miss Finch. "He looks ridiculous. His waistcoats hurt one's eyes. And all those fobs he wears *clink* when he moves. It's the most distracting thing."

"You can have Stanley," said Miss Deeping. She seemed eager to make up for her earlier comment.

But before any of Miss Deeping's brothers returned, a formidable dowager approached with a young man in tow. She introduced him to Miss Finch as a desirable partner, and he immediately asked her to dance. The beginning of a campaign to win a fortune, Arthur thought. He hoped Miss Finch might come to enjoy the process. Her demeanor suggested that so far she wasn't.

Miss Ada smiled up at her promised husband. "We

can show everyone how you have benefited from your dancing lessons," she said.

The young duke grimaced. "Would you say 'benefit'? But then, you are a generous creature." When the pair had exchanged fond glances, Compton looked at Arthur. "Will you join me in a prayer that the first dance isn't a quadrille?"

In fact, it was a country dance, to his obvious relief. Miss Deeping's brothers turned up. The young ladies joined the set, and Arthur was left standing next to Miss Julia Grandison, wondering if he was obliged to ask the formidable lady to dance. There was nothing for it. He broached the subject.

"What? Nonsense. Of course I will not dance."

Arthur was relieved. He was a good dancer. But partnering Miss Grandison must be rather like guiding a great frigate through a crowded channel. The potential for mishaps was high.

"You can do something for me, however," she added.

Her tone made Arthur wary. He knew, because Miss Grandison had told him, that she was a lady bent on revenge, itching to punish her brother for past humiliations.

"Have you seen John?" she continued, confirming his suspicion. "He's been peacocking about town bragging that his daughter is to be a duchess. As if he'd arranged the match all by himself, when in fact he did nothing. *Less than* nothing. My brother is odiously full of his own consequence."

Arthur thought this was probably a fair assessment, but that didn't mean he would be pulled into their quarrel. He was sorry that Miss Grandison had been drenched by an upended punch bowl in the year of her come-out. He was even sorrier that her brother had known of the plot to humiliate her, had done nothing to help, and had later pretended to have no connection to his beleaguered younger sister. The man was clearly an ass. Arthur actually wished Miss Grandison well in her quest to make her brother regret his sins. But he wouldn't be a party to her plot.

"I need a gentleman who can reach John inside his club," she continued. "White's, that is."

"Reach?" repeated Arthur.

"As a woman, I am barred from entry," she said. She gave him a look. "As you know." Her expression revealed what she thought of this exclusion.

Which many men saw as one of the chief benefits of their clubs, Arthur thought. Some avoided the females of their families for days on end.

"So I need an...agent to further my plans," she added.

Visions of mayhem filled Arthur's mind. What schemes would Miss Grandison require of her... henchmen? He tried to remember when a member had last been expelled from White's. Hadn't there been someone who cheated at cards?

"Well?" Miss Grandison was nearly his height and built on heroic lines. She challenged him eye to eye with a glare that might have quelled a riot.

It was best to be clear. If he hedged, the request would only rise again. "No," said Arthur. He left it at that. Any embellishment might open a path to argument.

"I see." Her tone sought to freeze him into a block of ice where he stood.

He couldn't laugh. And to walk away would be rude. "Do you remember young Tom?" he asked as a diversion.

"Of course I do," replied Miss Grandison. "There is nothing wrong with my *memory*, Macklin." Her emphasis on the word made it clear that she wouldn't forget his refusal to do her bidding.

"He's appearing in a play at the Drury Lane Theater next week."

"Is he? Well, I'm sure all his friends will be interested to see him on the stage." Miss Grandison turned away. "Excuse me, I must speak to our hostess."

Arthur hardly noticed her departure as the comment took root in his mind. All of Tom's friends would want to see him perform. Of course. And Señora Alvarez was one of Tom's friends. Ergo, she would wish to attend the play. Mightn't he make certain that she could do so? In a manner befitting her noble bearing?

If this also gave him an opportunity to be in her company, where was the harm in that? There was none. The occasion would be unexceptionable.

His mind filled with plans to make this vision come true. Everyone he needed was at the ball tonight. He would speak to them before the evening closed.

࿇

Sitting in her parlor just before going up to bed, Teresa reviewed the plans she had put in place to solve the problem of Dilch. She had grown weary of his threats and his lurking in the street to taunt her. But even more, she had hated being saved by the sudden appearance of an earl the last time Dilch had accosted her. That was not her life now. She did not rely on any man's protection, and most particularly not an annoyingly attractive nobleman. She'd vowed to take care of the neighborhood bully herself, and now she was ready to do so.

The wretched Dilch saw her as a helpless woman, an easy target. He had no idea what she'd been through in her life or what those years had taught her. He was also oblivious to the sentiment building in her neighborhood. Everyone was tired of the man's posturing and attacks. Ending them simply required some organization, which Teresa was happy to supply. And so she had proceeded—gathering information, recruiting allies, and finalizing her plans.

Dilch didn't actually live on her street. Teresa had set her maid, Eliza, to follow him home one day, and she'd discovered that he had rooms in a run-down place a little distance away. His wife and her mother lived there with him. They were not long-term residents. They'd taken the chambers less than a year ago. No one Eliza spoke to knew them well, or expressed any liking for Dilch.

The man came to their street to amuse himself, Teresa had decided, like a gentleman visiting his club. It was too bad that his idea of enjoyment was intimidating small shopkeepers into enduring his pilfering, cuffing children, and harassing any female unwise enough to enter his orbit. He liked to catch Teresa as she set out for the theater workshop at about the same time each day, walking along at her side murmuring salacious insults. And he had been even worse since she struck him with her bag of vegetables. Though not as much as one might have expected, she'd noted. At heart, he was a coward, and thoroughly despicable.

And yet he had no notion how *small* his depredations were. Teresa had seen villainy on a much larger scale. Despite his burly height, Dilch was a contemptible *little* man. Which didn't prevent him from being a menace. A number of Teresa's more vulnerable neighbors were afraid of him. One old woman who walked with two canes had stopped leaving her rooms altogether because she feared meeting him and perhaps being knocked to the ground.

And so Teresa had made a few visits, taking Eliza along to add to her consequence and wearing a gown of restrained elegance. She'd spoken to the retired prizefighter who ran a pub at the far end of the street and was endearingly passionate about justice. She'd called on a builder who lived a few doors down. Dilch had made the mistake of bullying this man's two small sons while he was out at work and then laying hands on their mother when she tried to protest. Teresa had spoken to the pugnacious wife of the greengrocer and a woman who took in laundry two houses down. All of these had passed the word to their friends. The whole of the street was aware and ready to act. They had only needed a leader, and they'd welcomed Teresa's assumption of that position.

It was rather like what Tom had told her about organizing a play, Teresa thought as she pulled on her gloves the following morning. All was ready; people were in place. She wore her costume of a widow's somber black in a cut and fabric that implied more riches than she possessed. They were ready to act in every sense of the word.

Teresa left her house and walked slowly down the street. She knew Dilch was nearby and had already extorted an apple from the fruit seller. A child had brought word of the man's arrival half an hour ago, and Eliza had been dispatched immediately to do her part. It was time to finish this.

Right on cue, she heard heavy footsteps at her back. Dilch came up to flank her, matching her steps and leering. "Looking fine as a fivepence today, see-nora," he said. It was one of his stock openings. The man had as little imagination as courtesy. He took a messy bite of his stolen apple and chewed. Then, predictably, he dropped his voice to a whisper as he sidled closer. "Not but what you'd look a deal better out of those clothes than in 'em. I could help you with *that*."

Rather than stride on, eyes on the ground, teeth gritted, as she usually did, Teresa stopped and faced the man. Dilch looked startled, and for a moment slightly daunted by the anger in her eyes. Then he grinned and came closer, leering. He even reached out as if to touch her arm. Suppressing a strong desire to hit him, Teresa moved to one side, shifting Dilch into position. She saw Eliza appear at the end of the street with Dilch's wife and mother-in-law in tow. She brought them close enough to hear, but kept them behind Dilch's back.

The builder's youngest son came by, passing much closer to Dilch than he would normally dare. Dilch gave the little boy a casual box on the ear, knocking him sideways. As agreed, the child fell to the earth and set up a howl, rather than simply fleeing.

His father shot from a narrow alleyway where he'd been waiting. The muscular builder took hold of Dilch's lapels and lifted the man onto tiptoe. "What do you mean by hitting my son?" he growled.

"And insulting respectable women with your disgusting suggestions," said Teresa in a voice meant to carry down the street.

"Stealing from honest folk who've worked hard to get what they have," cried the greengrocer's wife from the front of her shop.

The pub owner stepped from a shadow, hefting a cudgel. He looked more than capable of using it. Dilch's eyes rolled to take in the extent of his adversaries. He let the apple core fall as if hoping no one would notice it. "I don't know what you're talking about," he blustered. "This is outrageous. Unhand me, lout."

"Lout, is it?" The builder shook him a little.

Dilch's wife and mother-in-law surged forward. They were small, stoutly built women, neatly but not lavishly dressed. Their bonnets and gloves spoke of determined respectability. Here was the crux of the matter, Teresa thought. She hoped that their scene would have the desired effect. Of course it could go wrong in several ways.

"If you come into this street again, you'll suffer the same treatment you've handed out," the builder told Dilch. "Only more so!" With a final shake he released him.

"What are you doing, Mr. Dilch?" said the man's wife. She glared at Teresa.

Teresa cast her eyes down, took a step back, looked as pious as a nun, and said nothing. This was a precarious point.

"You said as how you had a job coming up," the woman added.

"He's too lazy to find work," said Mrs. Dilch's mother.

"I was just on my way to inquire about it," Dilch claimed.

"You hit a *child*," said Mrs. Dilch. Her emphasis on the last word suggested a long, sad tale.

Dilch didn't seem to notice. "A grubby street urchin," he said with a dismissive gesture.

Next to him, the builder growled. Dilch shifted quickly away from him.

"What about *her*?" asked Mrs. Dilch, indicating Teresa with a flick of her fingers.

He rolled his eyes at Teresa, ogling as if this was an irresistible reflex. "I can't help it if the women come after me," he replied.

Clearly this was a man who engineered his own doom. Teresa blinked with astonished respectability. "Come after?" called the greengrocer's wife, her voice full of outrage. "Run when they see you coming, more like. With your pinches and your filthy talk."

"Shut your mouth, slattern," replied Dilch reflexively. Then, at last seeming to take in the panorama of glares surrounding him, he hunched.

"He's doing it again, Catherine," cried his mother-in-law. "He's going to shame us. I've had my fill and more of picking up and moving, just when we're settled, because of this gormless idiot's tricks. I *told* you not to marry him." She grasped one of Dilch's sleeves, looking as if she wished it was his ear.

Dilch sputtered defiance. "Now then, dearie," he said to his wife. "You know that last move weren't my fault."

"The butcher chased you home with a cleaver because you insulted his wife!" The man's mother-in-law jerked at his coat.

Mrs. Dilch hesitated.

"Put a hand up her skirt when she turned to fetch the round of beef you *weren't* actually buying," the older woman added.

Her daughter scowled. She grabbed Dilch's free arm, and the two women began to drag him away. The older one's scolding voice could be heard all the way to the corner of the street.

Teresa watched them go. If Dilch showed defiance or a hint of retribution, she would have to plan further action. But the bully didn't look back. He cringed and whined and grew increasingly cowed. She was as sure as she could be that he wouldn't be back to *this* street, though other London thoroughfares might not be so fortunate.

The pub owner caught her eye, nodded, and tapped the palm of his empty hand with his cudgel. Teresa nodded acknowledgment. Dilch was vanquished here. They'd done it.

Eliza popped up at her side. "That was *prime*, that was," the young maid said. Her eyes shone with admiration.

Teresa wondered what had happened to make the girl savor vengeance this much. It was not the first time she'd noticed Eliza's love of rough justice.

People came up to exchange congratulations. The old woman with the canes was crying as she balanced on one of them to squeeze Teresa's hand. "Thankee, my lady," she said. "You've made some fast friends today and no mistake. If there's ever anything I can do for you, just say. Not that I'm up to much these days." She indicated her canes.

Looking around, Teresa saw the same sentiment in the faces of most of her neighbors. These were not the sort of people she had encountered in her youth, except perhaps among her parents' servants. And exchanges with them had not been the same. She would not have dreamed of joining with them to rout a petty oppressor. She hadn't known or understood them as she did these neighbors, from living among them.

Through the hard years since her girlhood, she'd rarely had the opportunity to make real friends. And the few she'd found had been swept away by circumstance. But here in her new home she'd become part of a little community. Teresa blinked back tears as she realized how glad and grateful she was to be included.

It was some time before she tore herself away and went to change her dress before going on to the theater workshop. She looked forward to telling Tom about their triumph over the odious Dilch. He'd often wanted to stand up to the bully—or, as he put it, the churlish, swag-bellied moldwarp. She smiled. Tom's expanding vocabulary entertained all the craftspeople in the shop.

Lord Macklin appreciated it, too, Teresa thought. He always smiled at Tom's sallies. She'd noticed it more than once in their three conversations in the little courtyard.

Her steps slowed. She shouldn't remember how often they'd spoken, or recall the earl's words or expressions. She did not look forward to his appearance in the busy space. She mustn't. She didn't!

Teresa stopped walking. A muddled flood of memories overtook her, bringing a queasy feeling in her stomach. What was the lesson she'd learned over and over again? Was it *really* necessary to repeat it? Men could not be trusted. Particularly, most disastrously, aristocratic men whose position gave them the power to do as they liked. They could not resist using it.

She was not a stupid woman. She'd proved that. She was proud of all that she'd learned and accomplished, and she would do nothing to risk her position.

But others seemed to find love that could be trusted, a forlorn inner voice declared. That couldn't be all illusion, could it?

A jeering laugh rang in her brain, so strong it almost seemed audible, the product of several male voices whose cold mockery she'd overheard. Love! A pathetic word, an idiot's weakness. Did little Teresa think to snare an English earl?

Teresa's hands closed into fists at her sides. "Who spoke of *snaring*?" she whispered. "*Nadie!*" She had no such idea, and she rejected, utterly repudiated, anything that threatened her hard-won triumphs.

"Are you all right, miss?"

She turned to find a draper eyeing her with concern from the doorway of his shop.

"Yes. Perfectly all right. Thank you."

Teresa moved on. No one had spoken of snaring, not even her plaintive interior murmurs, and no one ever would. Perhaps she had enjoyed some parts of her conversations with Lord Macklin. Very well. She would admit this, to herself. It was always best to face the truth. But she didn't want anything from this handsome earl. She *needed* nothing from him. And so he had no power over her. He never would. As long as she saw to that, she supposed she could talk with the gentleman now and then.

Reaching the workshop, Teresa shook off her mood, and the past, as she removed her bonnet and gloves. The earl's visits here were rare and would no doubt end now that London society had begun its annual promenade. Who knew when she would ever see him again? It might be weeks, which was *not* a disappointment of any kind. She donned her serenity with her painting apron and picked up a brush.

But some time later, when she was sitting on a bench near the carpenters telling Tom the saga of Dilch, Teresa sensed a presence behind her even before Tom's gaze strayed. She turned. Lord Macklin was there in the doorway, his eyes fixed on her.

Tom waved to him. "Come and hear how Señora Alvarez sent Dilch packing, the currish, beef-witted clotpole."

The earl came toward them, and Teresa marveled at his easy manner. By dress, bearing, and social position, the man clearly didn't belong in a workshop, and yet he had made himself welcome. Artisans greeted him like an old friend. They showed him progress on bits of theatrical paraphernalia he'd admired during past visits. And he replied with what seemed to be genuine interest. She couldn't detect a trace of condescension or impatience. Which didn't mean it wasn't there, she reminded herself. The earl might be better at dissimulation than she was at detecting it. She'd encountered such people before.

"You remember Dilch," Tom added as he joined them.

Macklin smiled at Teresa, and a shiver ran over her skin as if a length of silk had been trailed over her body. "The attempted vegetable thief," he said.

"And all-'round sheepbiter," replied Tom with the air of one agreeing. "But Señora Alvarez taught him a lesson." Tom gestured to encourage her to go on.

"I and my neighbors," she said. Though she was more self-conscious with Macklin present, she made a good story of it. Indeed, she relished her description of Dilch being hauled away by his womenfolk.

Her audience seemed to appreciate the picture. Their laughter rang through the workshop. "Bravo," said the earl.

"Right," said Tom. "Except for one thing."

"What?" Teresa wondered what she'd overlooked.

"You all did it without me," Tom complained.

"Ah." She'd expected this. "Dilch nearly always came by when you were out," she answered, indicating the busy space around them.

"Still. It don't seem fair that I missed all the action." He looked aggrieved. "I've been dying to pay off Dilch." Tom shook his fist.

And with that, Teresa realized that she'd purposely excluded Tom from the move on the bully. The lad was even more alone in the world than she was, and she hadn't wanted to risk getting him into trouble. Yes, he had friends who would help him, but why put him in that position? She saw that the earl was looking at her. There seemed to be understanding in his face, and a warmth that unsettled her. She turned away from it. "How are your rehearsals for the play going?" she asked Tom.

"Pretty well," he replied. "I've learnt all my speeches. Not that there's many. Which I'm just as glad of, to tell you the truth. I don't see how the main actors commit all them…those words to memory."

"But you are enjoying being onstage?" asked Macklin.

"I am."

When Tom grinned in that wholehearted way, you couldn't help smiling back, Teresa thought. Good humor simply shone out of him.

"I'm looking forward to seeing you," said Macklin.

"Thank you, my lord." His grin widened. "If you was moved to give me a cheer at the end, I wouldn't say no."

The earl laughed. "Certainly."

"I should get back to work," said Teresa, rising.

"You'll be coming to see me as well, won't you, señora?" asked Tom.

She hadn't considered the matter, but she realized that she'd like to.

"I reckon his lordship will be hiring a box at the theater," the lad added.

Lord Macklin gave him a sidelong glance—surprised or amused, Teresa couldn't tell. "I've engaged one for the first night of the play, in fact," the earl replied.

"There you are then." Tom looked pleased. "You should join him, señora. You wouldn't want to go alone. And you can't mill about with the rabble in the pit." He said this as if the idea was a rare joke. "It's all elbows and spitting down there."

And indignities for any woman who dared the space, Teresa thought, but she couldn't insert herself into the earl's party. "I can stand backstage and watch," she said. She was known at the theater. Surely this would be allowed.

"You'd see my back, mostly, from there," Tom objected. "You won't get the full effect."

"I'd be pleased if you'd join us," said the earl.

"That's the ticket," said Tom.

They looked at her. Teresa began to feel that she was the target of some sort of conspiracy, even though it was clear that the two hadn't discussed this idea in advance. Who was the *us* Lord Macklin had referred to?

"I've arranged an unexceptionable party," he said, as if reading her thoughts.

Teresa gazed at him. He must know, from the place where he found her, that she was not *unexceptionable*. Who was this group that could include her? How did he intend to explain her presence?

"The young ladies we met in the autumn will be there," the earl told Tom.

"Oh, good." The lad turned back to Teresa. "You'll like them," he added. "And they'll take to you, I wager." Tom turned back. "Miss Julia Grandison too? Chaperoning, like?"

The earl nodded.

"Ah. Well."

Teresa couldn't interpret Tom's expression. Was this Miss Julia a hazard? Was she important to the earl?

They exchanged a smile that explained nothing to Teresa and then went on to discuss details as if all was settled. They spoke as if her preferences mattered, as if she was the one to be considered when making arrangements. It was a novel, and admittedly pleasant, experience.

And so, although she'd intended to refuse the invitation, somehow, by the end, she'd promised to attend the theater as part of the Earl of Macklin's party. She told herself she could send regrets later, when he wasn't right here before her, compelling and persuasive, with Tom egging him on, but she knew she wasn't going to do that. Her mind had already turned to the gown she might wear and the ornaments that best set it off.

Four

It had felt as complicated as marshaling a small army, Arthur thought, but he had managed the thing. Señora Alvarez was at the play in his company. Though that was mostly due to Tom, he acknowledged. The lad had pushed the scheme before Arthur could open his mouth. An unexpected but welcome boost.

His party filled the large box he'd engaged for the performance nearly to overflowing. He'd placed the four young ladies across the front with the young Duke of Compton. Newcomers to town, they were all eager to see their first play. Their chaperone, Miss Julia Grandison, was behind them at the far end. And he and Señora Alvarez occupied the dimmest corner at the back of the box, close together, publicly private.

She wore a soberly elegant gown of dark blue, as if to fade into the shadows. A lace mantilla held in place by an ornate comb hid her face when she bent her head. She could hardly have done more to obscure her beauty. Arthur knew it was there, however, and he rather liked the idea that it was a secret they shared. At last he had a bit of time to become better acquainted with her. Some people said he possessed charm. He hoped Señora Alvarez might agree by the end of this night.

The young ladies did occasionally shoot inquiring looks in their direction, obviously curious about the foreign lady in their midst. Arthur felt a flash of uneasiness, as if he was awaiting an examination in a subject he barely understood.

Which was ridiculous. He pushed the idea aside. He knew how to make light conversation and pay a graceful compliment. Hostesses thought him an asset at any party. He was a mature man, not an awkward stripling in his first season.

And yet what he found to say to the señora was "I was in Spain once, when I was a boy." His voice even sounded younger than usual.

"Were you?" she replied. Her face was difficult to see in the depths of the box, partly shaded by the mantilla.

"Our ship stopped in Málaga after we came through Gibraltar. I remember seeing oranges hanging from trees and being astonished."

"Ah." She nodded. "There is the scent, too."

"The sweetness of the air, yes."

"Almost like tasting the fruit."

"But not quite," he said. "They let me pick it. I ate as many oranges as I could hold."

Her smile was reminiscent, as if she knew very well what he meant. Arthur enjoyed the beauty of it, and the fact that he'd evoked it. "My mother came from the south of Spain," she said. "Near Cartagena. We would go there to visit her family in the winter."

He nodded to encourage more confidences.

"The sea was so different," she went on. "Soft and blue and friendly. Not like the rough waves of Santander."

Her chagrin at mentioning this city was obvious. Clearly, she wished to reveal as little as possible about herself. It was frustrating. "Cartagena must be rather like Málaga," Arthur said to keep her story flowing.

She raised dark brows.

"Both on the Mediterranean Sea and…southern." This managed to sound both inane and naive. He gritted his teeth.

"How old were you when you made your journey?" she asked, ignoring his question.

"Ten. My father wanted us to see Greece, the whole family, that is. So he packed us up and set off."

"How original."

"He was full of ideas and enthusiasms. There were times when I chafed against his schemes, but I think now that I couldn't have had a better father."

Señora Alvarez blinked, then bent her head. The edge of her lace mantilla fell across her cheek so that he couldn't see her expression, but he knew the smile had died. He remembered that she'd lost her family in the war. He should have chosen some other topic of conversation.

"Did you enjoy your travels?" she asked.

"I did." He should have talked about the play, Arthur thought. But at the moment he couldn't remember anything about the wretched piece. He didn't usually have troubles like this.

"And did your father?"

Nothing to do but press forward. "He found that the Greek he'd learned in school was nothing like that spoken in the streets of Athens. He was quite outraged. He sent a letter of complaint to his old schoolmasters at Eton."

"Because he hadn't been taught modern Greek?"

"No. He felt that the Greeks should not have been allowed to stray from strict classical forms."

She laughed, and Arthur felt a surge of triumph. Laughter made friendships. He leaned a bit closer to her. The theater was filling, and the babble of the audience made conversation harder. He caught a hint of the sweet scent she wore, and lost his train of thought.

"And what did they reply?"

"They?"

"The schoolmasters at Eton."

"Oh. Yes. I never heard. They didn't mention the letter to me. Not even when I boasted to my school-mates, after we returned, that I had seen the world. I was quite puffed up with my own consequence."

"Did you take the, ah, the 'grand tour' after your school days like so many young English milords?"

How old did she think he was? "By the time I was of an age to do that, France had erupted in revolution," he pointed out.

"Ah. Yes." Her dark eyes grew distant. "And then the war came to our country. I was to go—" She broke off abruptly.

It seemed as if every conversational avenue led to awkwardness. Arthur wondered what journey the fighting in Spain had disrupted. He wanted to know all about her, and she didn't wish to reveal anything about her life. It was an impasse.

"It became impossible to travel," she said as if closing the subject.

He hated seeing melancholy in her face. What could he do to banish it? Arthur felt he would go to any lengths to cheer her. If only he knew how.

He hadn't meant to pry. It was natural to want to get to know a new…friend? Señora Alvarez was looking down again, hiding her face with the mantilla. Arthur struggled with unfamiliar frustration. Generally, people he met were eager to further the acquaintance. Some did it because they saw an advantage in the connection, of course. Society was full of toadeaters. But many liked him for himself. He became aware of an impulse to tell her so, and immediately felt like a preening coxcomb. He should talk of something else. Surely if he found the right words, she would respond. But none came to mind in this moment.

The beginning of the play both rescued and thwarted him as everyone's attention turned to the stage.

Lord for a Season was the story of a young man who arrived in London pretending to be a lord. Based on many years of theater attendance, Arthur suspected the young man would actually turn out to be one in the end. Tom played one of the fashionable friends the hero made in town. It was a very small part—mostly standing about as the action unfolded, Tom had said. But he was onstage a good deal and had a few speeches. It was an opportunity for the lad to show what he could do. Arthur hoped that all would go well for his debut.

Teresa leaned forward as Tom entered the play several scenes in. The theater makeup and borrowed clothes made him look older and more handsome, she thought. Tom was one of those males who would look better at forty than at sixteen.

He showed no sign of fear. In truth, she was more nervous with Lord Macklin at her side than Tom seemed to be onstage. The earl wasn't so very close to her, but somehow it felt as if he was. He was a powerful personality in every sense of those words. A fact that should *not* be forgotten, she reminded herself.

The hero of the play pranced about and made affected speeches. Other characters answered him. The ingenue simpered. Tom had little to do, but he didn't simply stand on the stage letting the action flow around him. He reacted to each line spoken with expressions and small movements. He reflected or contradicted other actors' attitudes. Teresa could see the audience noticing him. Once they laughed when he gaped in astonishment at an exchange of quips. He was certainly drawing attention. Teresa saw two other actors frown at him in ways that had nothing to do with the action of the play.

"What do you think of Tom's performance?" Lord Macklin asked her when the first interval began.

"I think he is in danger of annoying the chief actors by attracting too much attention," Teresa replied.

"I saw that. Not wise for a newcomer."

"No." Jealousy was common in the theater.

"He is rather good though."

She nodded. "He seems so much at ease on the

stage. It's as if he doesn't even notice all the people staring at him."

"Tom has a gift of ease. I've often wondered where it can come from, considering his unfortunate childhood. Some inner light that cannot be extinguished, I suppose."

The man had a brush of the poet, Teresa thought. As well as the looks of a fairy-tale hero. Those steady blue eyes urged one to drop into them and forget all else. What was that English word? *Blandishments*. Yes. That's what they were. Seductive blandishments. They promised honesty and understanding and warmth. As if eyes could not lie. Dangerous. She turned away. "That is a good way of putting it," she said.

A flurry at the doorway of the box drew her attention. It was crowded with male visitors. The young ladies were clearly attracting beaus in their bow to society. "How young they all look," she murmured without thinking. She had wondered at first if the girls might be targets of the earl's gallantry, but he'd shown no sign of interest. In fact, all the arrangements pointed to a desire to talk with *her*.

"When I was their age, I was newly on the town and thought myself vastly sophisticated," replied the earl quietly. He was smiling.

"I was…" She stopped. At seventeen, she'd been engaged to the son of a Spanish count, a marriage arranged by their parents. Her bride clothes had been sewn and the wedding date set. And then her fiancé fell ill and died. She'd mourned the young man she hardly knew and, later, the future that had expired with him. Her life would have been so different if he'd lived. His estates were outside the main battle zone. They might have lost much, but not everything, in the subsequent war.

"Is something wrong?"

This Lord Macklin was too perceptive for comfort. His open expression invited confidences. But Teresa knew that confidences nearly always led to betrayal. They would be used to manipulate or extort. "Of course," she said, making her tone dismissive. She had vowed never to be foolish again.

She should have refused this invitation. She was enjoying Tom's performance, but she was also creating a false impression. The young ladies were obviously curious, or had been before their admirers arrived. The earl's party wanted to know who she was, where she came from, and why he had invited her to sit beside him in the box. The first two were none of their affair, and the last was…a whim she ought not to have indulged. She bent her head behind the shield of her mantilla.

"Compton seems to be mounting a defense against the onslaught of visitors," said Macklin. He sounded amused.

"He is engaged to the young lady with the eyebrows," Teresa replied. She had absorbed the flurry of introductions at the beginning of the evening.

"Miss Ada Grandison," the earl said.

"She is very happy about that, I think."

"Yes, she won him in a treasure hunt."

Teresa wasn't sure she'd heard him correctly. Was this perhaps some odd English idiom? She decided to ignore it. "I think the girl with the red hair wishes she was somewhere else," she said.

"Miss Finch does look uneasy," her companion agreed. "Which is strange, since she is an heiress and much courted by society."

"For her money?" Teresa asked.

"Well, in the beginning, I suppose so."

"And you wonder that she might not like that?"

He did her the courtesy of considering her remark. "I can see that it is a two-edged sword," he replied finally. "And yet her path in society is smoothed. She is welcomed as others are not. She may not realize her luck."

"That welcome has nothing to do with her personally," said Teresa.

"I would not go so far. She is a pretty girl, and amiable."

"The pick of the heiresses, in fact. Like the ripest orange on the tree."

He cocked his head at the bitterness that had entered her voice. "She will have more choices than many young ladies are granted."

Teresa bowed her head to acknowledge his point and to shade her face. Why did she agitate herself over strangers? She had enough to do managing her own life. She was glad when the play resumed and ended the conversation.

Someone must have spoken to Tom, Arthur thought, because he was much more subdued in the later parts of the play. He did not draw attention from the main characters or add flourishes to his speeches. He was the model of a secondary actor. Arthur felt the retreat was too bad, but no doubt it was the better part of valor, and Tom would survive to act again.

The lad's part in the play ended well before the climax, and he appeared at Arthur's box as soon as the piece was finished to receive their congratulations. "I should go," began Señora Alvarez when these were done.

"Not yet." Tom took her arm with a grin. "We're having champagne to celebrate, thanks to his lordship."

In fact this had been Tom's idea. He'd arranged the whole. Really, the lad had become most enterprising in his new life.

They moved en masse to the theater entrance. There were sidelong glances as they departed with the lad, forming one of the largest groups of admirers in the place. Only the lead actors had more, and they eyed his entourage with speculative rivalry. The attention was a two-edged sword, Arthur thought. Popularity would help Tom gain more roles and build a reputation as an actor, but it might also attract retribution. If anyone could navigate those shoals, however, it was Tom.

Arthur had engaged a private parlor at a nearby inn, on Tom's instructions. The lad guided them there very much like a sheepdog whose herd included one member very eager to stray. Tom hadn't let go of Señora Alvarez's arm. Fortunately for Arthur's peace of mind, she began to look amused at the lad's enthusiasm.

At the inn, they opened champagne and toasted Tom's performance and prospects for a successful career on the stage. "Have to say I like acting," the lad said in reply. "Mebbe a bit too much, according to what was said to me during the first interval."

"I suppose the other actors were jealous because the audience liked you," said Miss Deeping.

"Do you think they did?" asked Tom.

Arthur found it touching, as well as amusing, to see that Tom wasn't immune to the desire for praise.

"Oh yes," said Miss Moran. "You were so funny."

This made Tom beam. "Mr. Bennett said it wasn't my place to draw attention, though."

"Was he the one playing the hero?" asked Miss Ada Grandison.

"That's him."

"I would call him only a passable thespian," declared Miss Julia Grandison, with the air of a seasoned critic.

"But he is well known in the theater," said Señora Alvarez. She frowned at Tom. "He could do you harm there."

"I begged his pardon and promised it wouldn't nev…ever happen again," said Tom. Under his breath he murmured, "The froward fustilarian."

That didn't bode well, Arthur thought. "Mrs. Thorpe might have some good advice for you. No one knows the London theater better."

Tom nodded.

The talk became more general. Teresa moved to the edge of the group, thinking that she might slip away and have the innkeeper find her a hackney. She felt she was here under false pretenses. She didn't belong to their society. What had Lord Macklin told these people about her? Why hadn't she asked him? But that would have been a very awkward conversation, and at any rate Tom had scarcely given her the chance. It seemed he had wanted her in the audience, and she was glad if her presence had been a support to him.

But now was the moment to go. With luck, no one would notice. Teresa turned and found the four young ladies in her path. They flowed around her like a beautifully dressed wolf pack. She could see that they were bursting with questions.

"Your headdress is lovely, Señora Alvarez," said the tallest. Miss Deeping was her name, Teresa recalled, and her eyes were acute.

"It's called a mantilla," said the smaller sandy-haired girl. That was Miss Moran, and the others were the sulky heiress Miss Finch and the engaged girl, Miss Grandison. She had remembered all the names, though it was still difficult really to tell them apart. "They wear them in Spain," Miss Moran added.

"Are you visiting from Spain?" asked Miss Ada Grandison.

The four girls gazed at her, waiting for a response. Waiting to pounce on it, Teresa thought, almost as if they were accustomed to conducting interrogations together. It might have been intimidating if they hadn't been half her age. She'd been making social conversation before they could form sentences. "No, I live in London," she replied.

"So you are a friend of Lord Macklin's," said Miss Deeping. This was not quite a question.

"I am a friend of Tom's," replied Teresa. The earl was not a friend. He was…what precisely?

"Oh, Tom." They all smiled. Clearly they liked the lad, which was a mark in their favor. "He has so many friends," said Miss Moran.

"Indeed." Teresa allowed a hint of umbrage to tinge her tone, as if being lumped in with the many was slightly insulting. Miss Moran blushed. This was beginning to be a little amusing.

"Where did you meet him?" asked Miss Grandison.

"I have a connection with the theater." Teresa watched them digest this information, or lack of it. It was a game, replying without revealing, and it seemed they knew it better than she would have expected. The girls exchanged glances as if deciding who would speak next.

"And you met Lord Macklin because of Tom," said Miss Deeping.

She was the most direct. Her dark eyes showed sharp intelligence. "I did," admitted Teresa.

"Lord Macklin is so truly the gentleman," said Miss Moran.

"He's been terribly kind to Peter," said Miss Grandison.

Peter must be the ducal fiancé, Teresa thought, judging from Miss Grandison's tender expression, which actually went well with her formidable eyebrows.

"And others as well," said the wealthy Miss Finch.

They spoke of Macklin as of a favorite uncle. One they would unite to defend... That was the message Teresa was receiving. She couldn't imagine that they would ever need to. The man seemed supremely able to take care of himself. And *she* was certainly no kind of threat. She had no designs on him. If she was glad to know that he didn't flirt with these girls or attempt to beguile them, well, that was only because this was right and proper behavior, befitting the difference in their ages. And of course the earl was hampered by their social position. These young ladies were protected creatures, not prey.

"He invited *you* to the play," said Miss Deeping.

"Because of Tom," Teresa answered, more impatient with their questions suddenly.

"Tom has so many friends. I daresay they would fill a dozen theater boxes." And yet none of those other friends were here, the angular girl's tone implied.

The debutante wolf pack waited. Teresa let them. Silence didn't intimidate her, and she didn't owe these young ladies any answers. She noticed that the large lady chaperone was looming over the young duke and looking impatient. This party was about to break up, which would be a relief. Mostly. She had enjoyed dressing in her best and going out as she had in her youth. She couldn't deny it.

"You are rather a mystery," said Miss Finch. "Very close-mouthed."

Teresa raised an eyebrow. An heiress could afford to be a little rude, she supposed. Much would be forgiven a fortune.

"We solve mysteries," said Miss Deeping.

"You?" The word was surprised out of Teresa.

Miss Deeping gestured at the four of them. "We," she repeated. Her gaze held a hint of challenge.

"We found a treasure in Shropshire," Miss Moran burst out.

Was this what Lord Macklin had meant about a fiancée won in a treasure hunt? Miss Grandison did look proudly smug. The idea was interesting, but Teresa didn't like the thought of anyone "solving" her. Her history was no one else's affair. That was a maxim of her new life, and she intended to keep it that way. "I am merely an acquaintance, not a mystery," she said in a tone that signaled this conversation was over.

"I have a puzzle for you," said Tom. He had come up behind Teresa and now joined their group. "Or worse," he added. "Happening over at the theater."

The girls' heads turned to him in unison, like a group of cats spotting a bit of dangling string. "What is it?" asked Miss Deeping.

"People disappearing," said Tom. "Dancers."

"Another?" asked Teresa before she thought. This was bad news.

"Odile," replied Tom. "Nobody's heard from her. She's not been to her lodgings." He shook his head. "She's not the only one either," he told the young ladies. "It's the same with two others."

"Are you saying something happened to them?" asked Miss Moran.

"Can't help but think so. It's too odd. Three of 'em to suddenly go off with no word."

"Perhaps they went together," said Miss Deeping.

Tom gave a humorless laugh. "That ain't it. It was at different times. And Odile and Sonia came near to hair pulling more than once. Maria didn't like either of 'em."

Teresa had to agree. She could not see these three girls banding together for any purpose.

"So three actresses have vanished," began Miss Grandison.

"Dancers," corrected Tom.

"Opera dancers?" Miss Finch looked as if she recognized, uneasily, this phrase.

Teresa almost asked Tom what the ballet master had to say about these absences, but she closed her lips on the question. She would find out later, when the inquiry would draw less attention.

"Why are you speaking of opera dancers?" inquired an indignant voice. The large lady who accompanied the girls had joined them. She loomed, every inch the fierce chaperone. She was also a Grandison, Teresa recalled from the introductions—the mother…no, the aunt, of the younger one.

"Some of them at Tom's theater have disappeared," replied Miss Deeping. "It's a mystery."

The final word seemed to irritate the older lady. She distributed a glare around the group. Teresa felt she received an extra measure of suspicion. "This is not a suitable subject for your little games," the elder Miss Grandison said to the girls.

"Not games, Aunt," replied her niece. "An investigation."

The lady snorted. "Investigation! Hoity-toity."

The earl and the young duke had come over to join them. "What's this?" asked Lord Macklin.

He looked ready to spring to someone's defense. Teresa hoped he did not imagine it was hers.

"There will be no *investigation* of opera dancers," replied the elder Miss Grandison with obvious distaste. "I'm sure they make a habit of *disappearing*. And please let that be the last mention of such…persons."

Teresa couldn't bear the contempt the older woman infused into the last word. A response burst out before she could stop it. "They are girls no older than these— many even younger—oppressed and exploited simply because of their place in society."

All eyes focused on her. Why hadn't she controlled her reaction? This was hardly the first time she'd heard that sort of remark. Tom gave her a sympathetic nod.

"We should find out what's happened to your three friends," Miss Deeping said to Tom. "Perhaps they need help."

Teresa expected the other girls to scoff, but Miss Moran and the younger Miss Grandison immediately agreed. The redheaded heiress was slower to respond, but in the end she nodded as well.

"Nonsense! I forbid it," declared their chaperone. "That sort of…female is all too likely to…wander off. No doubt they find places to go."

"But somebody knows when they do that," said Tom.

The large lady turned on him. "You hold your tongue, young man. You've caused enough trouble already."

"We won't do anything improper, Aunt," said the younger Miss Grandison.

"So you always say, and never manage," replied her aunt.

"Surely we could speak to some of these girls' friends?"

"Señora Alvarez can talk to them all in their own languages," put in Tom before Miss Julia Grandison could voice the refusal she clearly intended. "Makes things a deal easier."

"Indeed?" said the formidable chaperone. Clearly

her doubts about Teresa were growing. "And what *things* would those be?"

The four young ladies seemed simply interested. Miss Deeping spoke for them. "Perhaps you would go with us back to the theater now, Señora Alvarez, and we could…"

"No!" said Lord Macklin and Miss Julia Grandison with one voice. "The dancers will be tired after the performance," added the former.

They might well be, Teresa thought. But right now they were being ogled by amorous men in their retiring room, fending off or welcoming the sort of offers these young ladies knew nothing about. She nearly said this aloud just out of perversity, to provoke a reaction from the older woman.

"Well, tomorrow then," said Miss Deeping. She glanced at her friends and received their approval.

"I am fully occupied tomorrow," said the elder Miss Grandison. "Not to mention utterly opposed to this scheme. I shall tell your mothers what you propose, and then I wash my hands of this whole matter."

"Please don't do that, Aunt," replied her niece. "Tell them, I mean. We promise to behave with perfect propriety."

The two Grandison women faced off. The aunt was fierce, Teresa thought, but the younger one looked able to hold her own.

"Señora Alvarez could be your chaperone," said Tom. "His lordship could come along as well."

Teresa gazed at Tom in astonishment, and then found all eyes turned to her once again. She felt the weight of their attention. Lord Macklin had vouched for

her by inviting her to the play, whether he had meant to
or not. She could not deny her suitability as a chaperone
without speaking of things she didn't care for them to
know. They had no right. Well, let him solve the problem he had created. She waited for some devious denial.

"I would be most happy to escort you," said Lord
Macklin.

"I'll come as well," said the duke.

The younger nobleman clearly fell in with anything
the earl suggested. Teresa noted, for future reference,
that she couldn't expect independent opinions from
the Duke of Compton. "I don't——" she began.

"Splendid," interrupted Miss Deeping. "That's
settled then." Of the four young ladies, she was obviously the most assertive and the most interested in this
problem.

It was rather like stepping into a stream and realizing that the current was much stronger than it had
appeared, Teresa thought, feeling that she was about
to be carried away.

The young ladies smiled hopefully at her. Teresa
silently resisted. Of course she knew the duties of a
chaperone. Indeed, she might be better able to protect
young ladies from hazards than those who had never
had all the conventions of society come crashing down
around their ears. That didn't make this a good idea.
"I have obligations," she said. "I cannot." No need to
mention that they involved painting scenery in a ple-
beian workshop. She gave Lord Macklin, who knew
this very well, a sharp glance. His eyes glinted back at
her with...amusement? What was the man thinking?

But her reluctance had the unanticipated effect

of mollifying the elder Miss Grandison. She looked at Teresa as if they had become comrades with a common cause. "I suppose, if they are properly over-seen," she grumbled.

"I don't think—" Teresa tried again.

"One time only," interrupted Miss Julia Grandison. "I will *not* condone this nonsense beyond that."

Once again, everyone gazed at Teresa. Several looked ready to argue if she objected again. It didn't seem worth the trouble. "Oh, very well. One visit. I really cannot promise more than that."

"Very right." Miss Grandison began herding her charges toward the door. "And now we must go."

The party dissolved as wraps were fetched and donned. Under cover of the hubbub, Teresa quietly asked Miss Deeping, "Why do you wish to help opera dancers?" She was curious.

"Because they are in trouble. Or might be." The girl spoke as if this was obvious.

"You do not think they have 'brought it on themselves'?" That was the attitude of most of society.

"*It* being the trouble? Or some more sweeping indictment?"

This was an intelligent girl, Teresa thought. And so perhaps her friends were as well. But she expected they would lose interest in Tom's "mystery" before too long. Their sort didn't really care about the fate of the so-called lower classes.

Tom grinned at Teresa as he set her shawl around her shoulders. "I'll arrange everything," he said.

She suddenly suspected that he had already been doing so, on a larger scale than she'd realized.

Five

WHEN THE NEXT DAY CAME, ARTHUR HAD DOUBTS
about the visit between a group of sheltered young
ladies and the theater opera dancers. There seemed to
be many ways it could go wrong. It seemed that Tom
must know this, as he must have noticed that Señora
Alvarez hadn't been pleased to be named chaperone
for the outing. Her face had shown that she was being
drawn into a position she disliked.

Arthur had thought of trying to cancel the outing,
but he didn't think the young ladies would listen.
Tom had known just what to say to rouse their
interest. They would simply go anyway. In the end,
Arthur could only send his roomiest carriage to make
the rounds and fetch the feminine contingent while he
and Compton walked together to the theater where
Tom awaited them all.

At least the expedition was not unprecedented,
Arthur thought as they strode through the London
streets. The theater offered daytime tours, on formal
application, to those interested in its inner workings.
People were shown the wardrobe, the machinery

above and below the stage, provisions for preventing and extinguishing fire. This would not be quite like that, of course, but it could be made to sound so if questions arose.

"Do you think this is a good idea?" asked the young man at his side as if he had read Arthur's thoughts.

"I'm not certain," he replied.

"Ada doesn't really understand about opera dancers."

"They are not thought a fit subject for young ladies." Although Miss Julia Grandison's attitude must have given even a stupid girl a strong hint. And these four were far from stupid.

"No." The young duke frowned as they strode along. "Do you think I should have forbidden it?"

"Could you have?"

Compton considered. "If I really insisted on the point, I think Ada would do as I asked. Though she would want to know why, of course." He hesitated. "Some say a husband should command his wife?"

This was more than half a question. "Some," agreed Arthur. "And have you noticed that the men who declare that the loudest fail to see how little they actually do?"

The younger man looked confused. "So you don't think it's true?"

"I was drawn to my wife, Celia, by her beauty at first," Arthur said. "But my interest was fixed when I discovered in her an intelligent, tender, sensible person. Why then would I ignore her opinions?"

"Ah. I like that. Why indeed?" They walked through a brief silence. "But doesn't a man know more of the world?" Compton asked then.

"Parts of it. And of others, nothing."

"I don't understand."

"Childbirth, for example. It is not thought 'a fit subject' for men, but it is surely one of the most important events of our lives."

His companion looked even more bewildered.

"I think husbands and wives should consult each other and decide matters together," Arthur added, hoping he didn't sound pompous. "And there is this. What would you do if someone tried to command your every move?"

"Send them packing."

"Precisely. And if you could not, because you had no power to do so, you might turn to deception. I've seen women pretend deference and behave outrageously on the sly."

The young duke seemed shocked. The remainder of their walk passed in silence.

They reached the theater a few minutes before Arthur's carriage pulled up in front of it. The ladies descended. Señora Alvarez looked...concentrated, as if the ride had not been entirely easy. Arthur had no doubt that she'd managed whatever had occurred, however. The sense of deep presence she possessed was unshaken and so much more than simple beauty. Today, she wore a somber gown and bonnet, the dress of a staid chaperone. He offered his arm. She took it. Her fingers seemed to warm his skin, even though this was impossible through the cloth of his coat. He looked down at her, but her gaze was directed at the theater door. They all went inside together and found Tom waiting like a thoughtful host.

"The place looks so different with no audience," said Miss Moran as they walked into the vast interior. "Even emptier than it should be somehow." They had some hours until the evening performance at seven.

"And without all the lights," said Miss Ada Grandison. The powerful oil lamp that illuminated the premises for a performance was unlit, as were the central chandelier and the row of footlights. Only a few candles in covered sconces burned, leaving the place dim and cavernous.

Tom escorted them to a room in the back where they found the opera dancers he'd gathered during a break from rehearsal. They were clustered around a table that held an array of confections from Gunter's. Tom had suggested, powerfully, that Arthur should order the sorts of things served at a society ball, and he had complied. Watching the dancers revel in the food, Arthur didn't begrudge the sum.

A babble of chatter trailed off into silence when they entered, though chewing continued. Some of the girls gathered more treats as if they feared this largesse would be snatched away by the newcomers. They were all very thin, Arthur saw. One didn't notice so much when they were dancing. The ballets strove for an ethereal impression. But close up they looked too fragile, their eyes large in delicate faces. Most had wrapped shawls over their gowns as if they were cold, though the room didn't seem so to him. He was glad that he'd provided sustenance for these waifish creatures.

Tom was the only person present who was acquainted with everybody, and he naturally took charge. He chose to begin with group introductions. "These are my friends the dancers," he said to one side of the room. "And these are my friends the young ladies who solve mysteries," he told the other.

This brought a hoot of derision. Arthur didn't see which of the dancers had made it, but none of them looked impressed.

"They do and all," Tom responded. "I seen them find a treasure out in the country."

"I could use a treasure," replied a wan, yellow-haired girl.

"What about the gentlemen?" asked another dancer. "Are they looking for *treasures* as well?" She rolled her eyes at Arthur.

"I got a treasure I could show them." A girl with brown curls shook her hips. "Right popular it is with the gentlemen too."

"I'm surprised it ain't worn out with looking," said the first girl.

"Now, Bella," said Tom.

The innuendo didn't seem to unsettle him. Compton looked embarrassed, and the young ladies exhibited varying degrees of uneasiness. Arthur wondered again if this had been a good idea. The dancers were not welcoming. He glanced at Señora Alvarez. She stood to one side, observing.

"So we want to try and figure out what happened to Odile and Sonia and Maria," Tom added.

"Those cows," commented a voice from the back of the dancers' group.

"Going off and leaving us to fill in their parts," said another.

"Foreigners," declared a dancer with a London accent. "I say, let 'em go back where they came from. And good riddance."

From the glares exchanged, Arthur concluded there were two camps among the dancers—the English and the others.

"And if there is nothing to go back to, after the war?" asked Señora Alvarez. Her clear voice cut through the muttering. Her dark eyes were steady on those who had complained.

The dancers fell silent, though some heads were tossed. They obviously respected the señora, Arthur thought. No one wanted to argue with her.

"We're all the same in one way," said the yellow-haired Bella. "Nobody cares what happens to the likes of us."

"I do," said Tom. "I want to be certain Odile and Sonia and Maria are all right." He repeated the names as if reciting an incantation. "That's why I brought help. And I'd do the same for any of you who was gone with no word."

"Would you?" asked several of the dancers at the same time. The girls exchanged glances.

"'Course I would." Tom smiled. Most of the girls smiled back. They liked him as they might a younger brother, Arthur decided with a brush of relief. "So what d'you reckon?" the lad added. "Anybody know where they went? Did they say anything just before?"

The group arranged itself. Dancers settled cross-legged on the floor or leaned against a wall, fortified with more of Gunter's confections. Miss Moran opened a small notebook and poised a pencil over it.

The other young ladies ranged themselves around her, while Compton adopted them as a shield and hovered behind. Tom escorted Señora Alvarez to the lone chair as if she was royalty, and Arthur posted himself beside her.

Tom returned to the middle of the room. "All right then," the lad said. "What do we know about Odile and Sonia and Maria?"

Several dancers threw out answers. The missing girls came from France and Spain, it appeared, and none had been here more than a few months. They had gone missing over the last six weeks, at irregular intervals. Their skill with English was among the least in the ballet company. Señora Alvarez discussed this with two girls in their native languages. "They were trying to learn, but having difficulties," she translated for the others. "Why didn't they come to me? I would have helped."

"We don't have time to be schooled, do we?" replied Bella. "There's hardly a minute in the day."

"And we have to sleep sometime," said another dancer. "We can't be looking worn and tired. That's not what's wanted. They'll show a girl the door right quick if she droops." This provoked nods of agreement.

There was such a contrast between the young ladies and the dancers, Arthur noted. They were around the same age, and female, but one group was sleek and calm while the other was spiky and wary. The former exhibited a bone-deep assurance that they had a place in the world and could count on its support. The other had none of that—with good reason, Arthur supposed. The dancers were obviously scraping to survive, and they had the suspicious air of alley cats poised to evade a kick. Señora Alvarez had mentioned helping opera dancers, he remembered. He understood better now what she'd meant.

Tom presided over the chorus of voices like a concertmaster, and it emerged that the missing girls had no family or connections in England. After a long speech from one girl in Spanish, Señora Alvarez relayed the opinion that they were all a bit prickly and had made few friends. Odile had a running dispute with her landlady, whose son had been killed by Napoleon's army. Sonia had a quick temper. She'd accused another girl of stealing an earring and hadn't really apologized when the jewelry turned up in a hidden corner. Maria was quiet and standoffish; many thought she was above herself.

"They weren't liked then," said Miss Moran. The recitation seemed to have made her melancholy.

"So there was no one to inquire very closely where they'd gone," said Miss Deeping.

"If one wanted to choose dancers least likely to be missed—" began Miss Grandison.

"It would be these," finished Miss Finch.

"Choose," repeated Señora Alvarez. She looked from one young lady to another. "And who would be doing this choosing? If in fact it took place."

"We don't know yet," answered Miss Deeping. "We have to gather more information."

Arthur wondered how they would propose to do that. Miss Julia Grandison had been quite firm. He didn't think the young ladies would be allowed more than this one visit to the opera dancers.

Miss Deeping's thoughts appeared to have followed his own. She turned to the dancers. "You could help," she said.

"Us?"

"What could we do?"

"Why would we?" asked the brown-haired girl who'd wiggled her hips.

"Well, if someone is abducting opera dancers, you might be at risk," replied Miss Deeping.

"Abducting?" The word seemed unfamiliar to some.

"Stealing them away."

"Stealing," scoffed Bella. "Why steal what you can buy for pocket change?"

"What do you mean?" asked Miss Moran.

"Never mind, Sarah," said Miss Finch. "I'll tell you later." She frowned. "Or not."

"You could keep an eye out," said Miss Deeping to the dancers, refusing to be diverted. "Watch for suspicious characters hanging about the theater."

This earned her incredulous looks and harsh laughter.

"Come," said Tom. "Some are dodgier than others. Base reeky varlets. You know what I mean."

The theater was not the lad's first encounter with the seamier side of things, Arthur thought. Tom had spent his life deciding who to trust from among a motley group of persons.

The opera dancers shrugged and frowned as Tom looked from one to another. But in the end most nodded. Bella looked skeptical. "What's it going to matter if we do?"

"You can note down their names, and we will…"
Here, Miss Deeping's ingenuity failed her. Indeed,
Arthur couldn't see what the young ladies could do
with that information.

"I'll follow them about," said Tom. "Or have 'em
followed. I got friends who can help. We'll see where
they go and what they do. Something might turn up."

After some further discussion, and no better ideas,
this was decided as the plan. The gathering began to
break up, though the young ladies were clearly not
satisfied with their minor role.

Several of the opera dancers moved toward
Compton as they dispersed. They saw him as a
potential source of support, Arthur thought. That was
the only sort of meeting they were familiar with. The
young duke planted himself next to his fiancée and
took her arm as if it was a lifeline.

Arthur had begun to smile when he noticed that
dancers were converging on him from all sides. Their
narrowed eyes reminded him of a group of stockmen
appraising a prize animal. Here, he was a value to
calculate.

"I 'spect you're a lord," one said to him. "You've
got that look about you."

"Oh, looks," said another dancer. "I'd say he *looks*
ripe and ready for a bit of fun." She squeezed his arm.
The dancers clustered closer.

He could be rid of them, of course. But he
didn't wish to humiliate anyone. Arthur encountered
Compton's sympathetic gaze.

"No," said Señora Alvarez.

The entire group of opera dancers turned to gaze at

her. They were clearly intrigued as well as surprised. "Is he yours then, señora?" asked one.

They turned back to him. Arthur was suddenly the focus of a battery of female eyes. He ought to have been embarrassed. In fact, he could only feel amazement that all his senses were focused on the fervent wish that she would say yes.

"If he is, we'll keep hands off," added the dancer. "A course." The others nodded, their expressions intensely curious.

Teresa was speechless. She wondered where that *no* had come from. And why? Lord Macklin was well able to take care of himself. No man more so. He didn't need her aid. But the sight of Nancy hanging on him and the others closing in had goaded her somehow. She couldn't bear the thought of Macklin taking one of the girls as his mistress, here where she would see and know. The idea filled her with fury. It was protective anger, she decided. She wouldn't see these girls *used* by a man when she might have prevented it.

"Fair's fair," said another dancer. Nancy ran her hand provocatively down Macklin's arm.

"Yes," said Teresa.

A ripple of reaction went through the room. The dancers looked both disappointed and gratified, their eyes full of speculation. The young ladies and their escort appeared startled and then fascinated. Tom looked...smug. Was that right? The lad certainly *seemed* pleased with himself, though she didn't see why he should be.

The dancers retreated a bit, leaving Lord Macklin standing alone. He was gazing at Teresa. Who would have thought that those blue-gray eyes could hold such heat? It threatened to melt the barriers she'd set up to guard her new life. What was she doing? Had she gone mad? He was not hers, of course. She didn't want him, even if it had been possible.

Teresa's thoughts tumbled and whirled. Macklin hadn't meant to accept Nancy's invitation. His expression had made that obvious. No one had required protection. She could have—certainly should have—kept quiet, and he would have extricated himself. Why hadn't she? It could not be because she was drawn to him. She refused to be.

The room felt suddenly far too warm. The cool self-possession she'd cultivated for years was crumbling. Lord Macklin was moving toward her. He was going to speak, right here, before all these people. Why would he do that? And what might this earl expect from her now that she'd made such a foolish claim? This brought a flare of anger, and Teresa welcomed it. He had no right to expect anything. That must be made exceedingly clear. She let that determination show in her expression.

The earl stopped. Did it perhaps occur to him—too slowly—that there was nothing they could say or do with everyone looking on? They might as well be onstage here, blundering about like the hapless victims of a farce.

That was it. She'd claim her hasty word was a joke. He should think nothing of it. The English laughed about the most idiotic things. He might even believe that.

But she couldn't tell him now, with everyone

looking on. "We should go," Teresa said. She turned toward the doorway, filled with a longing for the peace of her own home, and nearly bumped into Miss Ada Grandison.

"Shouldn't we make arrangements to…" began the latter.

"We have all the arrangements we need, Miss Grandison," interrupted Teresa. This drew looks from the dancers that made her flush. They had only one definition of an arrangement. Everything she said seemed to make things worse today. She felt quite unlike herself.

"Grandison, is it?" asked Nancy. "Ain't that the name of your 'special friend,' Bella? Mr. John Grandison."

The young duke goggled. Lord Macklin raised his eyebrows.

Nancy was getting a bit of her own back, Teresa thought, having been thwarted over Macklin. She enjoyed stirring up trouble.

Miss Grandison turned to the dancer. "What? Mr. John Grandison is my father."

Well, this was an effective diversion from her own unfortunate remark. But Teresa couldn't be grateful. Miss Grandison looked distressed. Her fiancé seemed ready to spring into action and help her if only he knew how. Miss Finch's expression suggested that all her doubts about this meeting had been fulfilled.

"Is he now?" said Nancy. "Fancy that." She gave Bella a sly sidelong glance. "Course he's not near as *grand* as my viscount."

Would the dancers now begin competing over all

the society men who had been to the theater looking for mistresses? Nancy would enjoy that. So would some of the others. Teresa readied herself to put a stop to it, though part of her understood the impulse. The young ladies took so much for granted, had so much that the opera dancers would never possess. It would be satisfying to shock them out of their complacency.

"You know my father?" asked Miss Grandison.

"I have an appointment," Teresa declared in a loud voice. "I must go."

"Of course," said Lord Macklin, lending his aid. He urged Compton toward the door. Miss Finch followed, drawing Miss Moran along with her.

Teresa took Miss Grandison's arm to pull her along and herded Miss Deeping with a shooing motion. The latter seemed to be taking a satirical enjoyment in the scene, but she responded. The group began to move.

Miss Grandison was not ready to let go of the matter, however. She resisted Teresa's tug. "They know my father?" she asked her.

"Does he like the theater?" replied Tom. Teresa frowned at him. Why wasn't he helping?

"Yes, he's quite fond of plays. He comes often." Her voice wavered on the last word, as if she was seeing this situation in a new light. "That is…"

"They probably saw him here then."

"But she said special…"

"Perhaps he came around to praise the ballet," said Tom.

"Oh yes, the *ballet*," jeered Nancy. She bobbed in a plié that implied quite a different sort of movement.

"I really must go," Teresa said. Several of the dancers grinned at her, well aware of her dilemma.

"My carriage is waiting," said Macklin. "Come along."

The young people all took this as the voice of command, which annoyed Teresa even as she appreciated the result. They walked out through the empty theater and found the carriage approaching. The driver had walked the horses while they were inside. Teresa pulled Miss Grandison toward the slowing vehicle. Miss Finch brought along the other girls. Together, they chivvied the group into the vehicle.

Teresa threw Tom an admonitory glance as he said his goodbyes. The duke and the earl bowed and walked off like the cowards they were. And Teresa was left in the carriage with four *investigative* young ladies.

"One doesn't become the 'special friend' of an opera dancer by just attending plays or praising the ballets," said Miss Grandison as they started to move.

"Oh, Ada," said Miss Finch.

Teresa watched understanding come to Miss Grandison, then finally to Miss Moran. Miss Deeping had clearly seen from the beginning.

"Papa wouldn't," began the former. "Oh no."

Teresa knew nothing of Mr. Grandison, and cared less. But she understood that it was difficult to think of a parent, or a friend's parent, in these terms. "Nancy likes to talk," she said. "And not all she says is true."

"But she knew Papa's name." Miss Grandison gazed at her with wide eyes. "How would she, if he hadn't…"

"He visits the theater," put in Miss Finch. "He might have accompanied a friend to meet the dancers. Many do." This was setting aside the reason why, of course.

The other three young ladies looked at their friend. Miss Grandison wished to believe but doubted, Teresa thought. Miss Deeping expected the worst. Miss Moran was simply aghast.

A vivid memory shook Teresa. She knew what it was like to be tossed into a situation about which you knew nothing and make mistakes based on ignorance. She had begun her own disaster in that way. She wanted to help. But what could she say? It was not her responsibility to tell these young ladies what their mothers, and their society, didn't wish them to know. Indeed, she would be resented if she did. Yes, a twist of history could toss them out of their safe world and into one where no one would care, and *help* would come in detestable forms that they couldn't imagine now. But most likely that twist wouldn't happen. They would never have to learn the hard lessons she could describe. "I expect Nancy used the wrong turn of phrase," she said.

No one looked convinced. She didn't blame them. It had been a feeble effort. "She tosses out shocking remarks to start a good argument," Teresa added. Even Nancy would admit this was true. She loved a dispute, as did almost none of her cohorts.

"She wanted to argue with me?" asked Miss Grandison, looking bewildered.

As well she might.

"So you are a good friend of Lord Macklin?" put in Miss Finch.

Teresa met her cool green eyes. Miss Finch was clever, as all these young ladies seemed to be. She'd chosen the one topic that might steer the conversation away from wandering fathers. Miss Finch would sacrifice Teresa's comfort for her friends' in an instant, Teresa noted. She was an interesting girl—an heiress who didn't fit into society yet seemed to understand more about it than the others. Her question was also a challenge. Which Teresa was well able to meet. "Merely an acquaintance," Teresa said.

Miss Finch's amused expression made her look older than her years. "Yet you claim ownership?" she said. A murmur went around the carriage at her directness.

Despite everything Teresa felt a thrill at the idea. But of course the English earl did *not* belong to her. She gave Miss Finch a raised eyebrow. "A joke," she replied, trying out her excuse.

"Really? How odd."

Miss Finch certainly said whatever she pleased. Perhaps that was her difficulty in society. "Does it not fit the English sense of humor?" Teresa asked. "I do not always understand that, I admit."

"Are the Spanish so different?" asked Miss Moran.

"Perhaps we are," answered Teresa, recklessly consigning her countrymen to eccentricity.

"And you jest about owning gentlemen," said Miss Deeping. Her dark eyes were lit with amusement.

Teresa thought again of a wolf pack, hunting as a team. "It will also save Lord Macklin from being besieged backstage at the theater."

"Besieged?" asked Miss Grandison.

Which brought them back around to where they started. Why was this carriage ride taking so long? "Should we visit again about the disappearances," she added. Perhaps this was a better reason for her slip? Even though there were to be no more visits.

"We must do that," replied Miss Deeping.

"We need to know a great deal more," said Miss Moran.

Teresa felt like an angler who'd hooked a fish. She looked out the window to gauge their progress.

"Lord Macklin deserves happiness," said Miss Finch.

Really, this red-haired young lady was becoming irritating.

"He's been so kind," she added.

"Kind to you?" Teresa couldn't help asking.

"To Ada," replied Miss Moran. "She wouldn't be engaged if he hadn't helped matters along."

Miss Grandison nodded, though she still looked distracted.

"And others. He's been doing quite a bit of match-making," said Miss Deeping.

"He doesn't like to call it that," replied Miss Moran.

Miss Deeping nodded. "I know." There were giggles in the carriage. "He looks positively pained. But when you bring couples together…" She shrugged. "That is the word."

"And yet he is alone," said Miss Moran. "His wife died ten years ago."

The young ladies nodded. Miss Finch gazed at Teresa. "I wonder what would make him happy?" she said.

More than irritating, Teresa thought. A positive menace. She endured their scrutiny—cataloging, evaluating—as if she was a puzzle they were determined to solve. She could have told them that she was not the one to make any man happy, but she did not. She owed no explanations.

"He likes being of use," said Miss Moran.

Her three friends turned to gaze at her, clearly surprised.

Miss Moran seemed lost in thought. "But not all by himself," she added. "He likes having…allies." She noticed the stares. "Or so I *observe*." She made the last word sound portentous.

After a moment, Miss Deeping nodded, and then Miss Finch. Teresa wondered what the girl meant by allies. And what about love? It seemed that Lord Macklin had spent time…promoting it for others. What an unusual sort of man. Not that his nature was any of her affair.

"I must talk to Tom," said Miss Grandison, whose thoughts had clearly been taking their own course. "I think he knows more than he said about Papa."

The faces of her friends suggested that they agreed with the sentiment and were worried about the plan.

"Your earrings are beautiful," said Miss Moran to Teresa.

This one didn't like conflict, Teresa thought.

"I've never seen anything quite like them," she added. "Are they Spanish?"

"No, I design them myself." Teresa launched into a discussion of the process, in great detail. She saw to it that the topic filled the short remainder of the drive, resisting all interruption. When the young ladies got down together at the Finch house, they appeared more than ready to escape further information on metallurgy. And they'd had no chance to question her further about Lord Macklin. Now she just had to find a way to divert herself, Teresa thought as the carriage took her home.

Six

TERESA WAS NOT SURPRISED WHEN LORD MACKLIN appeared at the theater workshop the following day. She might have stayed home to avoid him, but she'd promised to complete the scenery she was painting that day. It was needed for the next night's performance and had to dry and then be installed onstage. More than that, this was her place. She wouldn't be driven out, even by her own foolishness. The earl might be a powerful man, but she was valued here; she belonged with these craftsmen who took pride in their skills.

He arrived at the time when the workers generally stopped for their nuncheon. Teresa turned her back and concentrated on a branch of autumn foliage she was tinting. Though the perfect shadings of yellow and crimson didn't matter for the action of the play, she prided herself on the details of her landscapes. They added to the audience's experience even if people didn't realize how.

She heard Macklin's voice as he greeted Tom. Moments later, she felt it when the two of them came over to stand behind her. "Got a notion," Tom said. "Good one, I think."

"I must finish this," Teresa replied without turning. After yesterday, she didn't want to meet Lord Macklin's gaze.

"Looks first rate as it is to me," said Tom.

"Lovely," said the earl.

The word, his voice, set something vibrating inside her, like a plucked harp string.

"Good day, Señora Alvarez," he added.

She had never been more conscious of another person, even though she was still not looking at him. She had to turn around. And there he was—tall but not looming, elegant but not supercilious, gazing but not ogling. What was he thinking after her blurted claim? Without quite noticing, she'd worn a gown rather too fine for painting today, and earrings that sparkled with tiny sapphires. Had that been for him? Or to bolster her own confidence? "My lord," she murmured.

"Come outside for a few minutes," Tom said. He gave her one of his engaging grins.

There was no escape. Consequences must be faced. She put down her brush and followed them out to a table in the courtyard.

"Here's the thing," said Tom when they were seated. "I reckon his lordship could be a deal of help looking for Odile and Sonia and Maria." As usual, he recited all the missing dancers' names like a kind of incantation.

Teresa glanced at Macklin. He looked as surprised as she.

"He knows the base barnacles who hang about the theater to leer at the girls," the lad went on.

"I wouldn't say *know*," the earl put in.

"Their sort," amended Tom. "And you can go to the clubs and other places where we can't." He nodded at Teresa as if she'd been a party to this scheme. Would Macklin think so?

"Señora Alvarez can talk to all the girls in their own tongues," Tom continued blithely. "She knows 'em best, and they might tell her things they wouldn't say with a feller around. And me, I can sneak about with the best of them. Follow people around town and see where they go. I got friends who can do the same." He gestured around the table like a magician completing a clever trick. "I reckon we'd make a champion team to find out what happened."

"Team," said Teresa. Part of her vehemently rejected this idea. She'd vowed never to be dependent on the aid of an aristocratic patron again. The idea filled her with repugnance. But she *did* want to find Odile and Sonia and Maria, or at the least make certain they were all right. She very much feared they were not. And the earl, like all his kind, had power in the world.

"Of course I will help," said the earl. "Anything I can do."

Teresa blinked, amazed that he agreed so easily. What would he demand in exchange? In her experience, there was always payment. He mentioned nothing, however, and she couldn't spot the sly deception she expected on his face. How would it be to have the resources of the nobility on her side without making any promises? Revolutionary, if true. "Very well," she said, keeping her tone cool.

Tom rubbed his hands together, looking altogether pleased with himself. "Right, then. So first of all, I went back around to the lodgings of all three dancers and talked to the landladies and everybody else in the houses. Nobody knows noth…anything. Those girls walked out their doors just like usual one day and never come back. They didn't take anything with them. Not a scrap."

This made no sense. As Teresa knew from bitter experience, the less one owned the harder one clung to it. More than anything else, this convinced her that Odile and Sonia and Maria had *not* meant to leave.

"And then I heard from Nancy that Maria boasted about driving out to Richmond Park," Tom went on. "In the company of a fine gentleman. I'm thinking we should ask some questions along that road, see if anybody remembers them."

"And so you are needing a carriage," replied the earl with a smile.

"If you please, my lord."

"Tom is not fond of horses," Macklin told Teresa. "He sees riding as a form of torture." The earl offered his smile to her. "Too bad. It is a pleasant ride to Richmond, which you might have enjoyed."

Did he understand that such remarks were a bid for more information about her? As if she was a partial picture he was determined to fill in? Or was it simply the way he spoke to everyone? Well, she wasn't going to tell him that she'd loved riding as a girl nor that she'd had a spirited Arab mare she loved dearly. Her current situation must make it obvious that she could not afford to keep a horse. So she said nothing.

"Is tomorrow suitable for you?"

Her scenery would be finished by then. She had no other engagements, pressing or otherwise. Teresa nodded.

"That's settled then. We should go in the morning to allow plenty of time."

"I'll see about a day out," said Tom. He rose. "Should be all right." He walked away, leaving the two of them at the table.

"We interrupted your work," said Lord Macklin.

Irrationally, Teresa found his consideration annoying. Were they going to ignore what she'd said at the theater yesterday? Was this some new way to toy with her? Lord Macklin was disrupting her carefully ordered life. This man turned things to a muddle whenever he was near, and she hated that. They must be clear, particularly now that they were to be a *team*. "At the theater yesterday, I spoke up as a joke," she blurted out.

He looked inquiring. Or disappointed? Surely not that.

"It meant nothing," she added. "A silly jest."

"The humor being…" He let his sentence trail off to encourage explanation.

"Because the idea is so ridiculous," said Teresa.

"The idea?" His blue-gray eyes glinted with… something infuriating. Was it amusement? Or worse? How was anyone to say?

Teresa grew conscious of a wish to box his ears. "It was merely a matter of convenience," she added as carelessly as she could manage. "In case you acted as escort on other visits. So that you can come and go backstage without…irritation."

"Ah. Irritation."

"Must you keep repeating my words? You might as well be a parrot!"

"I beg your pardon. Parrots can be annoying, can't they?"

Were they actually talking about parrots?

"It was very kind of you to think of my…potential unease," he added.

A spate of words died on her lips. Teresa felt as if she'd stepped down and found a stair missing, leaving her teetering in the dark. Was that all? Was there to be no taunt or innuendo?

The earl smiled at her. The expression was warm and alluring. Remembering the anger that had shaken her at the theater, Teresa realized that she hadn't been driven by anything like kindness yesterday. Some inner part of her had leapt like a tiger on Nancy's query. To save the dancers from another exploitation, she told herself again. But honesty forced her to acknowledge that her motives had been more complicated. She hadn't wanted to see him with Nancy or any of the others—for her own sake as much as theirs. She hadn't wanted him to be like the other aristocratic men she'd known. He had to be; earls were bred so from infancy. But this one seemed so different.

She sprang up. He rose politely. Teresa started away, then turned back. He stood there beside the table, a few feet away. He didn't rake her body with his eyes or mock her with knowing smiles. She'd been prepared to stave off sly comments for as long as necessary, but none had come.

"Until tomorrow then," he said. He offered a small bow and walked away, heading for the door.

She watched him go. She couldn't help it. She had better admit straight out that she was attracted to Lord Macklin, Teresa thought, in order to guard against the feeling. The earl seemed to possess so much that one would want in a man, and that made him a very cunning trap. She'd known men who were soft-spoken, beguiling—until they got what they wanted. That was the way it went. Once the prize was won, they flaunted their victory, their dominance. They didn't care how this hurt. Hadn't she seen it often enough to learn? Men with power over others exerted it. They simply did. One's only defense was not to be under their control.

A picture flashed through Teresa's mind—the Earl of Macklin standing in her tiny, bare home, avoiding any comment on its poverty, perhaps complimenting her painting to ingratiate himself. He wouldn't mock. He was too charming, too skilled for that. Perhaps he was even too kind, actually. But hot humiliation washed over her nonetheless. She'd lost so much that he possessed—position, wealth, the respect of society. They had no real common ground.

She did, however, have her hard-won independence. Nothing would take it from her, certainly not this silly idea of a *team*. She would join Tom in using the earl's resources and influence to find the missing dancers and do whatever they could for them, and then she would have nothing more to do with Macklin. Which was not a melancholy idea, she thought as she went to pick up her paintbrush again. Not in the least.

❧

Arthur walked toward his London home with a jaunty step. He wondered if Tom realized what a great favor he'd done him with this notion of a team. Probably not. The lad was concentrated on finding the missing dancers. He was always ready to spring to the aid of friends.

But Arthur felt as if he'd won a victory with the señora's agreement to the drive. From the expression on her face, he'd feared a refusal. But she'd consented. He'd wanted to find a way to become better acquainted with her, and he now had it. There would be any number of occasions when they must meet and plan or discuss their progress. There was no need to rush back and make certain. She'd promised. He knew somehow that she was a woman of her word.

When the señora had "claimed" him at the theater, Arthur had experienced a thrill more intense than anything he'd felt in years. He'd wanted to pull her into his arms and carry her off then and there. Except— she'd looked angry, furious really, as she spoke. It had obviously been no time for tender declarations.

He still didn't see any reason for her to be angry with *him*. Their evening had gone smoothly. He was sure he hadn't offended her. But she'd been irate, and he knew as well as he knew anything that she was not a person to be pushed.

It had to be the plight of the missing opera dancers,

he decided. The possibilities were enough to make anyone angry. He was glad to aid them, particularly in the company of the lovely señora. He turned his mind to ways of making their outing to Richmond a pleasure as well as a task.

She and Tom met his carriage at the workshop early the next morning. Señora Alvarez hadn't wanted it to call at her house, which Arthur understood. Tom took the rearward-facing seat for the drive of more than ten miles, leaving Arthur and the señora side by side on the other. Her silken skirts frothed about his feet.

"What do you plan?" she asked as they set off.

"We will stop at any likely point and ask about Maria and her escort," Arthur replied. "Hoping that someone can describe the man so that we can look for him."

"Why would they remember?"

"Maria is right pretty," said Tom.

"Well, yes, but..."

"And I got Nancy to make a likeness." Tom unfolded a sheet of paper and showed them a sketch of a dark-haired girl with a haughty expression.

"That's very well done," said Señora Alvarez. "I didn't know Nancy had such talent."

"She never told you so?" Tom grinned. "She has everybody else."

"Perhaps she recognizes Señora Alvarez's superior artistic skills," said Arthur. The look he received in response made him wish he'd kept quiet. He nearly said he hadn't meant the comment as empty flattery. But he decided silence was the better part of valor in this case.

Their progress was slowed by their inquiries on the road, none of them successful, and they did not reach Richmond Park until midmorning.

"It is a wilderness," the señora exclaimed as they approached.

"It's never been farmed," said Arthur. "Not since the 1200s at least. King Edward the First established the hunting park then and stocked it with deer."

"There's some of them now," said Tom, who was hanging out the carriage window to get a better view. He pointed to a group of deer leaping away.

"Oh, how beautiful," cried Señora Alvarez. She was pointing to a glade carpeted with bluebells.

"We should go look," said Tom. "The señora loves flowers," he told Arthur.

"By all means, let us walk a bit," said Arthur.

"We have no time for that," she objected.

"There is time." He leaned out and told his coachman to pull up.

Tom jumped down first and turned to hand down the señora. Macklin followed and would have offered his arm, but she was already three steps ahead of him, moving toward the bluebell wood.

It was a lovely spot. The carpet of blue blossoms wound back into the trees like rivulets of color, beckoning one deeper into the shade of branches in new leaf. A stream ran nearby, the gurgle of water blending with birdsong. The blossoms' sweet scent filled the air.

Señora Alvarez turned in a circle to take it all in. "*Maravilloso!*" She held out her arms as if to embrace the landscape and laughed.

It was the first time Arthur had seen her really

laugh, and he found it glorious—the musical sound, the flash of her dark eyes, the joyous gesture, the curve of her lips. She seemed lit from within, as if a shadow had been whisked away and the brilliance inside revealed. This was how she should always be, he thought, glowing, carefree. To be the thing that made her happy—that would be an achievement!

"I have been meaning to take up some cobbles behind my house and make a place for a garden," she said. "Why have I put it off? I must do it at once. This is...*comida para el alma*. Food for the soul."

Removing a few cobbles sounded meager. Arthur had gardens galore at his estates. He wished he could give her one. But a garden wasn't like a jewel, to be handed over. Even if she would easily accept gifts, which she would not.

"I think Mr. Dolan would be glad to pull them out," she went on as if the plan was unfolding in her mind.

"Dolan?"

Señora Alvarez turned as if she'd forgotten he was there. "One of my neighbors is a builder."

"Ah. Friend of yours?" He was not, of course, jealous. That would be ridiculous.

The query seemed to arrest and then amuse her. "He is, along with others on my street, ever since we rid ourselves of Dilch. That *canalla* bullied Mr. Dolan's son."

And she had stopped it. Arthur had never known a woman so self-sufficient. She had a life he knew nothing of, a network of friends. He felt he wasn't quite one of them, and this galled.

"People talk and do small favors for each other now. It is pleasant." She walked deeper into the wood, looking right and left as if to drink everything in. She was enraptured, and Arthur found himself envying a swathe of flowers. The idea made him laugh.

Señora Alvarez looked over her shoulder at him. "You find this amusing? That people should be kind?"

"Not that."

She raised dark eyebrows.

"I was laughing at myself."

"*You* were?" She sounded surprised.

"Why shouldn't *I*? In particular."

"You are an earl."

"And that means I cannot be ridiculous? The title conveys no such immunity. Alas." He smiled at her.

For some reason, she looked uneasy.

"And I have found laughter the remedy for a great many ills," Arthur added. Señora Alvarez seemed mystified, or…annoyed? That couldn't be right. Why should she be? Just a moment ago she'd been delighted. "Is something wrong?"

"You puzzle me…sometimes."

"But I am the most transparent of men," he joked. He was so pleased to learn that she thought about him that he added, "What do you wish to know? I have no secrets."

Her expression revealed his mistake. Señora Alvarez didn't care to discuss secrets. She had too many of her own. "I ask nothing of you," she replied, turning to walk on.

Disappointed, with her and himself, Arthur fol-lowed. Tom had wandered off, as he tended to do. There'd been no sign of him since they left the carriage. They were alone in a world of color and birdsong and scent. Perhaps the peaceful beauty of the place would soothe her temper, Arthur thought. But he didn't know what would gain her confidence.

The gurgle of the stream grew louder, and then there it was, a thread of clear water tumbling over rocks. Bluebells, ferns, and mosses bent over the banks. Soft moisture wafted through the air. Señora Alvarez breathed it in. "*Hermosa*," she said.

She was, but Arthur was not foolish enough to voice his opinion. He could not resist stepping closer.

A partridge erupted out of the bracken with a violent whir of wings. Arthur started, twisted one bootheel on a stone, missed his footing with the other, and stumbled toward the stream.

She caught him with an arm about his waist, stopping his slide to a certain dunking. They teetered together on the bank. He held onto her shoulders to regain his balance. Though she was much smaller, her grip was strong, her footing solid. She could hold her own and more. Her body felt soft and supple against his as they came safely to rest.

Arthur looked down. Her face was inches away. Her dark eyes were wide, her lovely lips slightly parted, as if primed for a kiss. She raised her chin. He bent his head to touch them with his, an instant of exquisite pleasure.

She jerked away, nearly sending him reeling once again. Her expression had gone stark. All the beautiful animation had drained out of it. "Do not play such games with me," she said.

"Games?"

"I told you that what I said at the theater meant nothing!"

"So you did," replied Arthur, stung. "And I heard you."

"Yet you try to take advantage."

"The bird startled me. I tripped."

"Into my lips." Her tone was contemptuous.

"I beg your pardon. In the moment I thought you…"

"You know nothing about me. But I will tell you that I despise tricks like that."

"It was no such thing."

She made a derisive sound.

She had no grounds to address him with such disdain, to practically call him a liar. "Do you doubt my word?"

"I observe your actions," she answered, moving away from him. "Where has Tom gone?"

"I have no idea."

"Tom?" she called. "Where are you?"

"Here," came the reply from downstream. "Come and see. There's a waterfall."

Señora Alvarez walked away. Arthur paused to master his annoyance. It took a few minutes. Perhaps he had mistaken her reaction. Though she'd looked… But she said he had, and that was that. He was sorry. He would apologize more fully if she allowed it. But honest mistakes did not deserve such complete contempt. She must know him better than that by now. Yet it had seemed that nothing he could say would change her mind.

There was worse, however. He still wanted desperately to kiss her again. He wanted more than that. She'd set him afire, as he hadn't been for years. If she felt nothing for him, his prospects were melancholy. The situation seemed all difficulties and little hope.

When he finally made his way down the stream bank, he found her with Tom, admiring a small cascade in the stream. She did not look at him, and Arthur's spirits sank further. "I meant no insult," he murmured as they walked back toward the carriage.

"We will not speak of it again," she snapped and hastened away.

He could only follow.

At Tom's urging they went on to Penn Ponds, two small lakes in the middle of the park with water birds nesting in the reed beds and groves of massive oak trees nearby.

"This old fellow's been through a bit," said Tom, running his fingers over a lightning scar in a huge oak's bark. "How old do you reckon it is?" he asked Arthur.

"Four or five hundred years, I expect," he replied absently.

"Here before Mr. Shakespeare then?"

"I would say so. It might have witnessed the Wars of the Roses."

"Does England have fighting flowers then?" Teresa heard the anger in her voice when she spoke, but she couldn't help it. She *was* furious—with the earl, with the world, but mostly with herself. How she had wanted to kiss him! He hadn't been wrong. Pressed against him, feeling the lean length of his body on hers, she had longed to do more than that. She was still flushed with desire. The mere touch of his lips to hers had told her that lovemaking would be intoxicating with this *peligroso* earl. Intoxicating and disastrous. It would wreak havoc in her safe, settled life. This was very bad.

"Warring roses, battles among the bluebells," said Lord Macklin.

Was he *joking* about it?

"Battles?" asked Tom.

As of course he would, after that remark. And of course he would look from Macklin to her and back again, wondering. Teresa imagined pushing them both into the stream and leaving them to drip their way back to the carriage. Boots full of water, squelching. Hair streaming onto damp and bewildered faces. An image *muy agradable*. But then Tom would want to know why she had done *that*.

"A duel at least," said the earl.

What was he going to say?

"I came upon one, in a bluebell wood a bit like this, when I was nineteen," he continued. "I'd almost forgotten." He glanced at Teresa as if she'd made him remember.

"With pistols?" asked Tom.

Naturally he would want all the gory details. Men loved such things. *Idiotas*.

"Swords," replied the earl. "Though neither of the fellows really knew how to use them. They were dancing about, waving cavalry sabers like carriage whips. I've always wondered where they got the weapons. Because those two were definitely *not* army officers."

Yes, that was the important thing, thought Teresa. Where had the sabers come from?

"Their seconds were twittering about in the most distracting way. Obviously they'd never been present at a fight before, but they all looked even younger than I was. I never learned their names."

"Oh, everyone didn't pause to exchange bows and visiting cards?" Teresa asked.

Her companions looked at her. "I was on horse-back," said the earl, as if this actually answered her question.

A thread of amusement snaked through her anger.

"What was the affair about?" asked Tom.

"From the taunting, I gathered that the taller one had compared the other's new hat to an antique chimney pot."

And so the young man had to skewer him, Teresa thought. Of course that made sense. None. At all.

"Would that be a matter of honor?" Tom asked. "Don't seem so to me."

"Well, I didn't see the hat," replied Lord Macklin.

Teresa burst out laughing. "*Imbéciles*," she said. Their blank looks made her snort. "I don't suppose you tried to stop them from hurting each other."

"You can't interfere in a duel," said Tom.

"Can't? I certainly would," she replied.

Lord Macklin gave her a half smile. "When they noticed me watching, they all ran off."

"That is something at least."

"I did worry that one of the combatants might stab himself in the leg with a saber."

"You should have taken them away."

They both looked genuinely shocked. "He couldn't do that," said Tom.

"Because it would be a great insult?" asked Teresa.

Tom nodded as the earl said, "And I hadn't the assurance or presence of mind at that age to intervene. I would now, as you say."

His gaze swept over her like warm sunshine after a chill. A sharp yearning filled Teresa. Was it really so impossible? Immediately, a flood of memories assured her that it was. Hadn't she learned? Shaking her head, she turned away, and suppressed her emotions, as she knew so well how to do. She would simply make sure she was never alone with him again. "We are wasting time," she said. "We are here to look for Maria."

"Right," said Tom. "Where to next, my lord?"

As if he was the only one to ask. As if no one else could possibly be in charge.

"We will drive out through a different gate and continue our inquiries on the other side of the park," the earl replied.

He spoke with an air of command that was so familiar to Teresa. He didn't ask for other opinions. The idea didn't occur. Teresa wondered what it would be like to be a wealthy, high-born man whose orders were obeyed with deference? Did they even notice the bowing and scraping, the way people jumped to comply? Or was it simply the nature of their world, the atmosphere in which they moved?

They returned to the carriage and drove on, passing more lovely vistas. Teresa drank them in. It had been a long time since she'd walked in a forest, and who knew when she would again. Wild landscapes were not part of her life now. True, commented a cutting inner voice. Nor were many unpleasant things that she'd endured and regretted.

She gave herself a mental shake. She would speak to Mr. Dolan as soon as she got home and engage him to remove the cobbles. Then she would plant a raft of flowers in her small space, and she would be very grateful to have them.

They continued their stop-and-start journey, with no luck in their inquiries until they reached a small inn on the far side of Richmond. There, the innkeeper remembered Maria when shown her likeness. "Yes, my lord," he said to Lord Macklin. "She was here with a fashionable gentleman like yourself."

This earned the man a raised brow from the earl.

"That is, not exactly like," added the innkeeper, clearly sensitive to the reactions of his customers. "But well dressed, with fine boots and a fancy coat with a deal of capes."

"He was driving himself?"

"Yes, my lord. One of them high-perch phaetons. Back wheels up to here." The man held a hand above his shoulder.

"He had a blue waistcoat with yellow stripes," piped up the young ostler. "Bright as bright. Never seen nothing like it."

"Did he?" The earl looked thoughtful, as if this meant something.

"What about Maria?" Tom exhibited the sketch again.

"The young…lady seemed to be enjoying herself," the innkeeper replied. "I believe she had some refreshment while they were here."

The ostler spoke again despite his master's discouraging glances. "She told me, 'I'm riding high, I am.' And she laughed."

"What did he look like, the man she was with?" asked Lord Macklin.

The innkeeper grew uneasy. "Is there some trouble, my lord? I wouldn't want to—"

"The young lady is missing," the earl told him.

Teresa wondered if revealing this was the best course of action. But it was too late to protest.

"Missing." The innkeeper looked more anxious.

"We are looking for her," the earl added. "And would appreciate your aid."

There was a brief gleam, as of a gold coin, Teresa thought. Of course the earl knew the power of money. She felt both grateful for and resentful of his help.

"The gentleman didn't get down from his phaeton."

"He wore a scarf that hid most of his face," said the ostler, clearly relishing his position as informer. "He seemed in a hurry, like."

The lad might be embroidering his tale, Teresa thought. But Maria speaking to him had clearly left a strong impression.

"Was he fat, thin, tall? Dark-haired? Light?"

"I couldn't say, my lord," replied the innkeeper. "Like I mentioned, he wore a long coat. A hat too. And he didn't get down."

Lord Macklin asked a few more questions, but he discovered nothing more, and soon after this they resumed their drive back to London.

"The striped waistcoat suggests this fellow is a member of the Four-Horse Club," said the earl.

"What is that?" Teresa asked.

"A group that drives racing vehicles one behind the other to Salt Hill to have their dinners," he answered dismissively. "And then they come back."

"But why?"

"To excite admiration and envy," he answered. "They hope."

"Sounds daft to me," said Tom. "Can't they can get a better dinner in London?"

"Certainly," said the earl. "But not draw as much attention to themselves."

"Are there a great many of them?" Teresa asked.

"I do not know the exact number. I will inquire."

"They must keep a list of members."

"You could act like you want to join up," said Tom. "Say you'd like to know who's who before you decide."

The older man's expression showed his distaste for this idea. "If I must."

"We would not want you to inconvenience yourself." Teresa hadn't meant to sound so sarcastic. This man seemed to magnify all her emotions.

He acknowledged her barb with a nod. "You are right. We must do whatever is required to find out what happened to the dancers."

She felt rebuked.

"But we must also take care that our quarry doesn't notice the hunt," he added.

"Miss Deeping and the others could ask about Richmond Park at all these parties they're invited to," said Tom. "Like they want to know if it's worth a visit. Maybe find out who's been there lately. Who's also in this horse club."

"They might do that," the earl agreed. "Carefully."

"If they have not tired of their 'investigation' by this time." Everything she said was coming out caustic, Teresa thought. What had become of her serenity? It was true she had no great confidence in the young lady detectives. The many amusements of the *ton* had probably diverted them already. But she needn't have said so.

"They won't have done that," said Lord Macklin.

Tom indicated agreement.

"So you will allow these young ladies to continue?" she asked the earl.

"However would I stop them?"

"By speaking to their parents, I suppose. Wouldn't they forbid it?" English families were not so different from the one she'd grown up in; Teresa had seen this for herself.

"That'd be low," said Tom.

He was frowning at Teresa for the first time that she could remember. "I didn't mean he *should*," she added.

"I don't see why I should interfere," said Lord Macklin. "Miss Julia Grandison may do that. But what happens then will be up to the young ladies."

"They've gotten 'round her before," said Tom. He and the earl exchanged a smile.

They seemed to share a real comradeship. She had seen them together a good deal by this time, and the aristocrat never condescended to the former street urchin. It was puzzling. Teresa looked from one to the other. "You take them so seriously?"

"I do," replied the earl. "I have observed them in action. It is impressive."

Tom nodded admiringly. "You should see Miss Deeping with her charts," he said. "And Miss Moran with her books, Miss Finch 'organizing.'"

"Miss Ada Grandison is most adept at interrogation." Macklin's tone held amusement, but he also seemed to mean it.

"They are young ladies," said Teresa. She couldn't quite believe that this aristocratic man respected females' abilities.

"Older than me," said Tom. He gestured to emphasize his presence as part of their quest.

The case was completely different, and they knew it, Teresa thought.

"You don't think young ladies can have such skills?" asked Lord Macklin. "I'm surprised. I would have thought you held the opposite opinion."

"It is not a case of my opinion," Teresa answered. "Or even of abilities. They are not given the chance. They are not well educated. They are controlled, patronized, treated as exhibits rather than persons. Loved by their families, yes usually, but not allowed to undertake real actions of their own."

The earl nodded. "That is often true, I think. I admit I hadn't realized how true until I met these particular young ladies and found them very different from others I'd encountered. They are quite enterprising in using their intelligence and curiosity."

"Time will take care of that," said Teresa. "Society will wear it out of them. Unless their world falls apart, of course, and they become part of the invisible flotsam of disaster." This remark earned her a sharp look from Lord Macklin. She pressed her lips together.

She was exposing too much. And why was she bothering to argue? Did she care so greatly what he thought?

"They mean to keep on," said Tom. "They told me so."

"They will acquire husbands who will not allow this."

"They mean to find husbands who do."

Teresa shrugged at the lad's naivete. "Young men make many promises when they are wooing. But once married they expect 'proper' behavior. Why else do people say it that way—the knot is tied? That sounds like imprisonment, no?"

"You are harsh to us men," said the earl. His gaze was even more speculative.

She must stop this, Teresa thought. It was too revealing. But she couldn't seem to. "Do you claim to know of liberal husbands?"

"Only a few," he acknowledged. "And some of them have had to learn hard lessons to achieve that state." He smiled as if this was half a joke.

"I don't believe in them."

"But—"

She cut him off with a gesture. "You do not see these paragons when they are left alone with their wives. Or hear what they say to them then."

The earl hesitated. She waited for a sharp response. But he said, "That is true. I suppose I can only speak for myself as a husband."

"Yourself?" Teresa became aware of an acute interest in the nature of his marriage. The thought of Lord Macklin as a husband was riveting. She pushed on, even though she knew she should end this conversation. "I suppose you will say you allowed your wife to do as she pleased?"

"I did."

"And she also had the power to give this permission to you?"

"What?"

"Oh, it did not occur to you that she had that right?" His expression was answer enough. The idea had never entered his head.

"Perhaps it did not," said the earl slowly. "Not in those terms."

"I suppose she never wanted to do anything you thought wrong," Teresa added. "Because she was too well trained. That is what draws men. Along with beauty, of course." No doubt his wife had been lovely and serenely biddable. One of those fortunate women to whom life gave everything. She felt a ridiculous spike of envy.

The earl seemed to be pondering her words. "That is not so," he said finally. "We disagreed."

"Until you convinced her that you were right."

"No." He shook his head. "Celia was a warm, intelligent, sensible person. I admired her enthusiasm for life as much as her beauty. I listened to her opinions and often came round to them." He met her eyes. "As you have said, no one else was present in those moments. You will have to take my word for it." His tone and his face promised that his word was good.

Teresa gazed at him in confusion. The difference between what she knew to be true about the world and the scene before her was driving her distracted.

She didn't *want* to try to decipher it. But could anyone play a role all the time? Pretend to be reasonable and kind with every phrase, every action, every change of expression, even when no one seemed to be noticing? She didn't think so. She was extremely sensitive to deceit; she would have caught him. It seemed this man was not playing some deep game that she hadn't yet understood. He really was honorable and accommodating, as well as a dizzyingly handsome nobleman, a combination she had not thought possible. Her admiration, her intense attraction to him, was not foolish. It was merely madness.

"So what else can we do to catch this crook-pated varlet?" asked Tom.

Teresa started. She'd actually forgotten the lad was there. He'd been so uncharacteristically quiet. And she'd been so absorbed in the conversation. She noted a twinkle in Tom's eyes.

"We must realize that this phaeton driver has not actually been connected to the disappearances," Lord Macklin replied. "We mustn't stop looking for the kidnapper."

"I'll keep on asking questions at the theater," said Tom.

"Carefully," said the earl. "Someone who is abducting opera dancers won't appreciate scrutiny. He might take steps."

"I'll be subtle," answered Tom, as if it was a joke between them. "I can be," he told Teresa.

Lord Macklin laughed. "That was the first evidence of your acting skills, I suppose."

"I cannot come out like this again."

Teresa didn't realize she'd spoken aloud until the earl asked, "Why not?"

"It is not *apropiado*." It was ironic that she should fall back on convention, but the truth was not acceptable.

"Friends may go for a drive," said Lord Macklin.

"We are not friends."

Tom looked surprised.

"You have some objection to being friends with me?" asked the earl. His face was unreadable.

"Friends are equals. We can never be that. With the great difference in our circumstances." Her life was calm and settled. He would turn it upside down. No, he already had. And she must fight her way back to safety.

"You would find much in common with Miss Julia Grandison," he said.

Teresa blinked at this unexpected reply. She was nothing like the towering woman who had looked down her nose at everyone at the play. Was this some sort of insult?

"Tom and I are friends," Lord Macklin added.

How much longer would she be shut in this carriage, her leg inches from his? His gaze was much too acute. Teresa looked out to see where they were. The outskirts of her neighborhood streamed by. "The cases are entirely different," she said. This was true whether or not she believed in their friendship. Tom was a boy, and she was a woman on her own.

"Ah," said the earl.

Now he would argue with her, explain where she was wrong and why she really should do just as he wished. Whatever that was. What was it?

"Well, we can maintain a fiction of friendship while we pursue our inquiries," Lord Macklin continued.

"A fiction?" Teresa stared at him. Was this some English expression?

"A simple...pact. That was your idea after all, wasn't it?"

"Mine?"

"When you...claimed ownership yesterday?" Something glinted in his blue-gray eyes. Did he dare tease her about that? This man was unprecedented in her experience. Tom was watching them as if fascinated. It seemed his aristocratic friend's sly manner wasn't familiar to him either.

"No obligations implied," Lord Macklin added.

"I owe you none," she snapped.

"Precisely. So, we are in agreement?"

If this was the sort of *discussion* he'd had with his wife, he didn't know the meaning of the word, Teresa thought.

"We'll have to be out and about looking for Odile and Sonia and Maria," said Tom.

And a lord could go where they couldn't. Tom had made that point. Still, it felt as if he was siding with Lord Macklin against her. No obligations, Teresa told herself. He could expect nothing. "Yes," she said.

"What harm can it do?" the earl asked.

She didn't know, but she suspected.

An hour later, Teresa sat in her small parlor with a cup of tea and a plate of biscuits at her side and her mind in turmoil. Two sides of her were engaged in a rancorous inner battle. One was bemoaning all that she had lost. It felt constricted and sad in this limited

English life. The other was grateful and happy to be in a cozy haven and wished never to venture out again. The two seemed equally strong, and each was quite disdainful of the other's point of view.

Seven

TWO DAYS LATER THE THEATER WORKSHOP WAS
enlivened by a sudden influx of fashionable ladies. A
ripple of greetings and buzz of reaction made Teresa
turn from her painting to see the four young "investigators" come in. This bevy of well-dressed females
flowed in among the craftsmen, their dresses and bonnets and wraps a swirl of moving color in the middle
of the space.

Tom went over to welcome them and offer
introductions, which they happily accepted, and he
took them around to explain the various tasks that
were being performed. The ladies asked questions and
complimented the artisans, seeming fascinated by this
peek behind the scenes of theater production.

When they reached Teresa, she wondered if they
would think less of her because she worked here. She
was also conscious that her old muslin gown, quite
suitable for painting, was shabby compared with what
they'd seen her wear before. Not to mention the streaks
of midnight blue and crimson down her long apron.

"How lovely," said sandy-haired Miss Moran when

the newcomers clustered around the flat that Teresa had been painting. "I feel as if I could walk right into the scene and climb up the hill to that castle."

"Your use of perspective is excellent," said Miss Deeping.

"How did you capture the feeling of moonlight?" asked Miss Finch. "I have tried to paint that and made a muddle of it."

Teresa could see no sign of mockery in their faces. She relaxed a bit and explained some of her techniques. Miss Finch in particular seemed interested.

"My goodness, can you paint from the top of a ladder?" asked Miss Moran. She was gazing at the upper part of the landscape. "That must be fifteen feet high."

"The carpenters set up a platform for me when I am putting in the sky."

"Ah, that's good."

"I like this place," declared the red-haired heiress. "One can see that everyone enjoys what they're doing and is good at it." She nodded to Teresa. "I can see why you bring your talents here."

Teresa thought of mentioning that this was not some careless pastime. They were all paid, and the wages were vital to the craftsmen. But she decided not to. Miss Finch hadn't meant to be patronizing.

Miss Grandison edged closer to her. "We came to consult with you and Tom," she confided in a low voice. "Though of course it is lovely to see your painting as well. But we wanted to speak to you, and we cannot visit the theater again because my aunt has made difficulties."

"I see."

"Tom told us that you stop for a sort of luncheon," the girl continued. She held up a small box tied with string, and Teresa saw that they all carried similar offerings. "Is this the right time?"

"Near enough." Teresa untied her apron and laid it aside.

In the courtyard, the ladies brought out a positive banquet of cakes and tarts and small sandwiches, setting them out to be shared by all. Then they established themselves in one corner of the space where they could talk with some privacy.

"We are not making a great deal of progress on the opera-dancer problem," began Miss Deeping with a severity that appeared to include herself.

"We have asked everyone we meet about Richmond Park," said Miss Moran. "But quite a large number of people have visited there recently, with the spring flowers coming on."

"And none of them seemed particularly...sinister," said Miss Grandison.

"They don't," said Miss Finch. "That is how they operate. They seem just like anyone else, until the moment they turn cruel. When it is too late."

The look in her eyes and harsh tone told Teresa that she had endured some hardship. She felt an impulse of kinship.

The others waited a respectful moment. Perhaps they knew what had befallen her, or perhaps they only heard the pain in her voice.

"So we need to decide what to do next," said Miss Deeping then. "What do you think?" She looked from Tom to Teresa.

"I've asked at houses all 'round their lodgings," replied Tom. "Up and down the streets. Nothing new there."

"It's too bad one of us can't join the opera dancers," said Miss Moran. "We'd be on hand to see who approaches them and judge their intentions."

Teresa waited for exclamations of horror at this outlandish suggestion. She also concluded that Miss Moran didn't really know what the *approaches* entailed.

"Imagine me in a ballet," said Miss Deeping. "I'd look like a poorly trained elephant let loose on the stage." She thumped the tabletop with her fist. "Lumbering along."

"You aren't big enough to be an elephant," replied Miss Moran.

"An ox," said Miss Finch. "Or a donkey. Yes, like Bottom in *A Midsummer Night's Dream*. We could make you a papier-mâché headpiece."

Miss Deeping made a face at her.

"The dancing master at school was always praising you, Harriet," said Miss Moran.

"That was not ballet," Miss Finch pointed out. "And he was a…beslubbering boar-pig, as Tom would put it."

Tom gave her a nod and an understanding look.

"What do you mean?" asked Miss Moran.

"Monsieur Lagrange knew I was poor and powerless. Then. So he thought he could whisper his disgusting little compliments in my ear." She shrugged. "And I do not believe he was really French either."

The other three young ladies looked shocked. Teresa was intrigued. It seemed Miss Finch had been impoverished, and now she was rich. Perhaps this was why she seemed the most interesting of them, although all four were out of the common way.

"You never said anything," said Miss Deeping.

Miss Finch waved this aside. "There was no point. Nothing would have been done."

"You could write to your school now and tell them," said Teresa quietly.

The younger girl met her eyes. They exchanged a brief silent communication, and then Miss Finch nodded once.

"I know you are not serious about becoming opera dancers," Teresa added. "But you cannot, you know." She looked around the group.

"I wonder what my father would do if he found me there on one of his 'visits,'" said Miss Grandison, who had been uncharacteristically silent.

"Have an apoplexy?" suggested Miss Finch.

Miss Grandison muttered something inaudible.

"I've been hanging about with the dancers and keeping my eyes open," said Tom. "I'll go on with that." He gave Teresa a sidelong glance, as if suggesting she might join him.

The thought of frequenting the dancers' retiring room, watching the gentlemen prey on them, most likely receiving unwanted attentions herself, filled Teresa with repulsion. Sad distaste welled up in her, turning the food sour in her stomach. But she still longed to help. "I will talk to each dancer again. I haven't pressed as hard as I might." Their situation set up rivalries. Many were reluctant to reveal good sources of income and so would not tell which gentlemen had been particularly attentive. Her impulsive "claiming" of Lord Macklin would help her there. If any girls had considered her to be competition, perhaps they wouldn't now.

As if her thoughts had brought him to mind, Miss Deeping turned to her and said, "Are you expecting Macklin today?"

Here it was. They were not going to ignore her rash words as she had begun to hope. Teresa faced a circle of friendly, but inquisitive eyes. "No," she said.

"We thought he was often here," the angular girl said.

"No," said Teresa again. "Often" was a vague designation. Who was to say what it signified?

There was a short silence. The ladies seemed to be searching for the right phrase. Tom looked brightly interested, and gave her no help at all.

"We don't mean to pry," said Miss Moran apologetically. "It's just that we are rather protective of him."

"Why should a nobleman with his wealth and position need your protection?" The earl clearly didn't. He…oozed assurance.

"'Protection' isn't quite the word," said Miss Grandison. The other ladies all nodded. "More what he has given to us."

"Interest and…encouragement," said Miss Finch.

"An open mind," said Miss Moran.

"Acknowledgment," added Miss Deeping.

"Help when sorely needed," said Miss Grandison.

They began to exchange anecdotes about Lord Macklin's role in their autumn adventure. They made him sound like some sort of guardian angel, scattering happiness across the land. It occurred to Teresa that this description would utterly revolt him. She smiled at the thought of telling him. "And what right had he to step in?" she asked after a while.

"He worried about that," said Miss Grandison. "Peter told me they discussed the matter." She smiled. "He told me he's learned a good deal from Macklin's example."

Had the earl asked the young ladies to come here and plead his case? Teresa didn't think that was it. And it didn't matter, because there was no case. He had none. But these were intelligent women. Their opinions were of value, even though they didn't know what aristocratic men got up to when their wives and mothers were not present. Look at Miss Grandison's father. Still, they had affirmed her changing opinion of the earl. She was oddly glad about that. "I need to return to my work."

"You do like Macklin, don't you?" asked Miss Moran.

Teresa stood. Part of her yearned to be one of their carefree group and exchange girlish confidences. Another knew she never would be. "We are pretending to be friends while we search for the missing girls. Nothing more."

"Pretending?" repeated Miss Moran. The ladies all looked puzzled. They glanced at each other and then back at Teresa.

"But...why should it be a pretense?" asked Miss Deeping.

"That makes no sense," said Miss Grandison.

She couldn't have stated it better, Teresa thought. *Senseless* was just the word to describe many recent occurrences. Her careful plan for her new life had not included an earl or any of these ladies—not even Tom, who had never been so quiet through a conversation in all the time she'd known him. As she had understood life, these young ladies should not be interested in the fate of a few poor dancers. They should ignore their existence. And hers. They should look through her, turn away as if she was invisible. All of this had happened to her not so very long ago. Yet now, here, it was not. No sense indeed. A quiver of emotion ran through Teresa. She turned away to hide her expression, and discovered the subject of their conversation standing in the doorway to the warehouse. How long had Lord Macklin been there? What had he heard?

Arthur moved, shaking off his surprise at finding five ladies where he expected only one. They sat in the corner of the courtyard almost as if they'd set up headquarters here. Señora Alvarez looked unsettled. Did she think he'd invited them? Her reactions were so often a mystery to him. Until he met her, he'd thought he was rather good at understanding people. He went over to join the group.

Tom extended a laden plate. "Sandwich?" he asked.

Not for the first time, Arthur envied the lad's easygoing temperament. The young ladies looked brightly inquisitive. Very brightly. It was one of their skills as investigators, he thought. They could make one feel unprepared for an important examination. Did they think he had some news?

"We were talking of our progress," said Miss Ada Grandison. "And the fact that we've made very little."

"I spoke to the head of the Four-Horse Club. At great and boring length," Arthur replied. He liked driving and riding, but he wasn't obsessed with the minutiae of these activities. Or with the clothing he wore while engaged in them. "He was no help."

"I'm going to hang about the dancers and keep watch," said Tom. "The señora will talk with each of them again. She thinks they may know things they don't realize they noticed."

Señora Alvarez looked startled, then impressed.

The other ladies continued to eye Arthur with a marked degree of attention. As if they were waiting for him to reveal secrets. Except Señora Alvarez, who was *not* looking at him. He was suddenly certain they'd been discussing more than the opera dancers.

There was a stir from the workshop behind him. A voice boomed out an inquiry. Everyone turned, and in the next moment Miss Julia Grandison appeared in the doorway. Her formidable figure filled it completely, the feathers in her bonnet brushing the upper jamb.

She scanned the courtyard and then descended on them like a striking bird of prey. "Ada, your maid said you were coming here." She looked around as if mystified by the locale. "I must speak to you at once." She loomed over the group. Miss Moran visibly winced. "Do you *know* what has been going on?" the newcomer added.

"In what sense, Aunt?"

"What sense! There seems to be very little *sense* involved." She scanned the circle of faces. "You've been snooping around the opera dancers. Very much against my advice and inclination." They sat with the silence and stillness of rabbits under the eye of a hawk. Miss Grandison's glare settled on her niece, and bored in. "Are you aware that your *father*—" She hesitated.

Miss Ada Grandison sat straighter. She managed to look innocently inquisitive. "Yes? Papa?"

"Has been showing far too much interest in these very same opera dancers," Miss Julia Grandison replied.

"Is that not an improper topic for me to discuss, Aunt?"

"Don't speak to me of improper! As if you cared anything about that. I have gone to great lengths for you, Ada. I said nothing to your parents about your ridiculous 'investigations.' I think I am owed a debt of gratitude. You should be only too glad to help me."

"Help how?"

"By telling me the truth!"

"I don't understand what you mean. I don't know—"

"You know a great many things you shouldn't!" exclaimed Miss Julia Grandison. "Things your mother would faint to hear of. I know that…a certain opera dancer was mentioned during that theater visit I countenanced the other day. Mentioned in…association with your father."

Arthur wondered who had told her this. He couldn't believe it was anyone present. Unless someone had let it slip? Or confided in the wrong friend?

"Merely give me the name of this dancer. That is all I require. I will know what to do then."

"And what is that?" asked Miss Ada, with commendable fortitude. Arthur knew the answer—revenge. Miss Julia Grandison thought she had found the lever she'd been searching for to pay back her brother.

"I don't remember," said Miss Ada. This time she was less convincing.

"Will you thwart me?"

"I don't want to cause trouble for Papa."

"Even though he is lower than a worm?"

Miss Ada looked conflicted. "I don't think he is that."

"He is careful to show you his good side."

The girl shook her head. "I won't tell tales on my father, Aunt Julia. I don't think you should ask me to." She frowned as if caught out. "Even if I knew any."

The older lady held her gaze for a long moment. "Very well. Perhaps you're even right." She started to turn away. "I'll get the name elsewhere."

"What if I tell Papa?" asked Miss Ada.

"Do so and welcome. In fact, let us go now. I should like to see his face."

Miss Ada declined the opportunity.

"What are you doing here?" asked her aunt then. She looked around the dilapidated space. "It is hardly a pleasant spot to sit, even on a warm day."

"We're interested in the workings of the theater," replied Miss Ada.

"Indeed?" Miss Julia Grandison's keen gaze swept over them all once again. Arthur felt evaluated and dismissed. Then the lady shrugged and bid them farewell. Everyone let out a relieved breath when she was gone.

"Should I tell Papa she is asking these questions about him?" Miss Ada wondered. "How would I bring up such a subject?" She turned to Arthur. "Would you do it, sir?"

Arthur tried not to shudder as he shook his head. "We are not well acquainted. Your father would be offended." This was quite true. Mr. Grandison would certainly resent the interference, once he got over being aghast at Arthur's effrontery.

"Oh." Miss Ada considered the matter. "I'll get Peter to do it."

There were some dubious looks at this, but no objections. Arthur didn't envy the young duke, but at least Compton was, or was about to become, a family member. He might have some bare excuse to broach the matter.

The young ladies took their leave soon after this. Tom and the señora moved back toward their workplaces, and Arthur followed. "Why is Miss Grandison so angry at her brother?" the señora asked.

Arthur told her the story of the punch-bowl humiliation in their youth.

"And he has never said he was sorry?"

"I don't believe so." Miss Grandison would have mentioned that, Arthur thought.

"The churlish, dog-hearted clotpole," said Tom, more in the spirit of experiment than in anger, it seemed.

"So he deserves to pay," said the señora. "But perhaps not so dearly as the large lady seems to intend."

Arthur nodded. They paused inside the workshop door. "May I watch you paint for a while?" he asked her.

She looked surprised. "Why would you wish to?"

"I appreciate mastery in all its forms."

Her cheek reddened a bit. "Mastery is…"

"The proper word for your ability."

Tom grinned and gave them a nod before walking off. The señora looked uncertain. "I suppose," she said finally.

"I promise not to disturb you." Inside, Arthur took a seat well out of her way. The señora put on her long apron and picked up a brush. She began adding a herd of tiny cows to the distant hills of the scene before her.

"My wife liked to paint, particularly outdoors," Arthur said.

The señora's brush went still and then resumed.

"Flowers were her favorite," he added. "She used to say that if one could properly depict a rose, one could paint anything."

She seemed attentive, but perhaps that was for her work and not for him.

"This was long ago of course. Nearly twenty years."

She said nothing.

"Did your husband like your paintings?"

This time her brush stopped. She glanced at him and away. "I don't care to talk about this." She went back to painting.

"It *is* painful to think of them gone," Arthur replied. "I've thought a good deal about grief lately. It never really ends, does it? But it changes over the years. My wife's death was very hard—a long, bitter illness. It was years before I could speak of her easily. Then, gradually, the bad ending grew less vivid, and good memories came drifting back. There were many more of those, after all. I'm grateful for that."

She said nothing. The rigidity of her back told him she rejected this topic. He'd wanted to share with her, felt she might have endured similar things. He'd hoped she might say so. And yes, he remained curious about the shadowy figure of her dead husband. More than curious. The fellow haunted his imagination. But he should have listened and changed the subject. Now they were afflicted with an awkward silence.

It would have been interesting to discuss grief with the earl, Teresa thought. He was surprisingly thoughtful. She'd agreed with some of his points and not with others. Her grief over her family had been quite different.

But she couldn't talk with him honestly. And that had begun to rankle more and more. Calling herself a widow had been so much easier in this new life she'd created. That status smoothed over many things, deflected a variety of questions. Even as it created more, she thought now. And she had no gift for fiction.

No, call it what it was—lying. She'd told a lie, and now she had to live with it. Lord Macklin expected a tale of her past to match the one he'd told, and she had none about her imaginary husband. Nor much inclination to invent one.

"Have you gone forward with your plan to remove cobbles from your yard?"

She turned to look at him over her shoulder. "You remember that?"

"Why wouldn't I?"

Why? How many people—most particularly men—would do so? "Yes, it was done yesterday."

"Ah, that's good. I spoke to my gardener, and he has some plants you might like for starting your garden."

"For me?" She gazed at him, astonished.

"He's very good with roses," the earl added. "And lilies. Of course he doesn't have as many plants here as he would in the country. But he said he has some fine ones to spare."

"You asked your gardener to find flowers for me?"

Arthur nodded. "He can send them over as soon your soil is ready for planting. He suggested you might benefit from the services of an undergardener in that regard."

"Regard," she repeated.

"Preparing the soil. He thought that ground that had been under cobbles would need extensive cultivation." She was staring at him as if he'd suddenly sprouted horns. Had he offended her? Did she see the offer of a few plants as interference? Really, that was unreasonable. He knew that enthusiastic gardeners exchanged specimens all the time. It was the done thing.

A wavering silvery sound rang through the workshop, like an audible expression of the feelings running through Teresa. She had to admit it; she was utterly charmed. This aristocratic Englishman had not only remembered a small detail she'd told him about her plans, but he'd gone out of his way to help her accomplish them. Even his prim way of making the offer—"in that regard"—was endearing. This was a rare man indeed.

The sound came again. On the other side of the workshop, Tom stood with a large wooden mallet in his hand. For a third time, he struck a thin sheet of metal that had been hung in a frame. The shivery warble followed. "That's done it," he called. A number of the other workers cheered. Tom grinned and took a bow.

"What an unusual gong," said Lord Macklin.

"It's a chime for the fairy kingdom in a new play," replied Teresa. "They wanted an 'otherworldly' sound, and Tom offered to invent one."

"Naturally." The earl smiled. "He is an irrepressibly creative spirit. I have so enjoyed watching him bloom."

"Have you?"

"Yes. As you do gardens perhaps."

"Why?"

"Doesn't everyone like seeing young people come into their own?"

"No. Many people never notice. And some are envious or annoyed."

"Annoyed?" He looked bewildered.

"Have you not observed that there are many petty, mean-spirited individuals in the world?"

"Of course, but..." He considered. "Even they will benefit from new ideas and...youthful energies. People who are encouraged to use their skills are happier, and that makes society more pleasant." He shook his head. "And I sound insufferably pompous."

"No." Something in his manner—perhaps the way he treated all people as equals—kept him from pomposity. He was proper, yes. Good manners and the rules of society fit him like his perfectly cut coats. But he was never stuffy or narrow.

"I think perhaps I do," he replied with a rueful smile. "But I thank you for making me think. I shall try to find ways to say it better."

She was in love with him, Teresa realized. The knowledge seemed to burst over her, like an ocean wave that knocked one tumbling and then pulled irresistibly toward the depths. But it wasn't really sudden. The sentiment had been building, bit by bit, over these last weeks. He had added to the flood with each thing he said or did.

Madre de Dios. She'd renounced everything to do with *amor* years ago. That haunted word was just another term for oppression. It was a deception, a cheat, made you commit all sorts of stupidities and then broke your heart.

But this man wasn't like the others she'd known. Perhaps he could love in the way the poets imagined. Or was that simply a sad rationalization for her weakness?

She was staring up at him. She saw an arrested expression rising in his eyes. The smoldering heat of the kiss she'd denied him was flowing back. With it came a question she had no idea how to answer. What was she going to do? She had to stop this.

Teresa turned back to her painting. She raised her brush but did not touch the surface. What could it even mean—to be in love? For her, here and now? She had fought to find safety, to take control of her life. Would she throw all that away? Wasn't that what love would require?

Tom struck his gong again. A signal, Teresa thought, but the message was a mystery. Was it a harbinger of change? Did it urge her toward some... indulgence? Or warn her of doom? Abruptly, fiercely, she longed for the first choice. But she couldn't do that. She couldn't go under.

"Señora Alvarez?"

His voice was like the touch of seductive fingers. "I must finish this painting today," she said. "I have promised."

There was a pause. Her heart teetered in the balance. Then he said, "Of course."

She heard his footsteps move away. She'd saved herself from the clutches of that overwhelming wave. And she was not in the least relieved.

Eight

TERESA WAS MORE TIRED THAN USUAL WHEN SHE reached home that afternoon. Lord Macklin had left the workshop soon after their conversation, but he might as well have been standing close behind her, looking over her shoulder the whole day. With every stroke she'd painted, her mind had wavered back and forth, vibrating between words like *independence* and *ruin*, *prudence* and *daring*, *discipline* and *desire*. Her thoughts had grown more and more jumbled as time passed without her coming near any resolution. She was still trembling.

Eliza appeared in the kitchen doorway as Teresa was taking off her bonnet. "A fellow called while you were out, ma'am," she said.

"Fellow?" No one visited her here.

"He wanted to wait, but I told him he couldn't come in."

So Eliza hadn't liked this man's looks. Who could it have been? "Not someone from the neighborhood?"

"No, ma'am. I never saw him before. He was a foreigner." Eliza held out a square of pasteboard, using only the tips of her fingers as if the object was distasteful. "He left a card."

Not a thug then, Teresa thought. They didn't leave cards. But not a gentleman, if Eliza's judgment was correct.

"He said he'd come back this evening," added the maid, clearly not happy about the prospect.

Teresa took the card and read it. "Conde Alessandro de la Cerda. I don't know who this is." The man sounded Spanish, but she recalled no one of that name. Why had he sought her out? A visitor from Spain was unlikely to be good news. And how had he found her?

"Is *conde* some kind of title?" asked the maid.

"It is the same as a count." Which England did not have, Teresa remembered, though it had countesses. The wives of earls. As *todos los caminos* led to Rome, all her thoughts seemed to circle back to Lord Macklin.

Eliza sniffed. "He weren't like any nobleman I've ever seen."

Wondering if Eliza had seen any, Teresa put the card down. "He said nothing about what he wanted?"

"He only said he'd be back, ma'am." She frowned. "I didn't like the way he looked at me."

A threatening Spaniard was not coincidence, Teresa thought. It was her fate, the doom that had dogged her existence since she was a girl. Today, she'd dared to dream just a little, and now her dream was to be shattered. She didn't know precisely how, but she had no doubt it would be. A host of bitter experiences told her so.

She sat down. A Spaniard most likely brought word

of her past. There was so little of that Teresa wished to revisit. She would have avoided it if she could. But she didn't have the means to repel this caller. And it was probably best that she discover who he was and what he wanted.

The knock came at seven that evening. Teresa let Eliza answer it, but there was nowhere for her to wait but the main room. Lurking upstairs and then coming down seemed silly in this tiny house.

A slender man of medium height entered her home. His clothes were rich, though not quite fashionable, his smile sleek and self-satisfied. Black hair, dark eyes, smooth tan skin, an aquiline nose, she recognized him at once. He was no count. His name *was* Alessandro, but an entirely common Alessandro Peron. The last time she'd seen him he'd been a member of the household of a Spanish duke. More than a servant, but not really a friend of the grandee. A hanger-on. There was an English word she'd come across—a toady. That fit him. He was rather like a *sapo*, a toad.

Teresa greeted him in Spanish. This was likely to be a difficult conversation, and she preferred that Eliza have no idea what they said.

"Teresa," he replied.

She felt a spurt of rage at his disrespectful use of her name and the caressing tone he used to speak it. She hid this. He would want her to react.

"I was so happy to learn that you were living in London. Though surprised at the address." He looked around the room with a mixture of derision and pity.

"How did you learn?"

He raised one eyebrow.

He had learned that trick from the duke. He did it less well. She began to lose patience. "How did you find me?" She knew no Spanish people here.

"The embassy told me."

She didn't believe him. She'd had no contact with the Spanish embassy. Wanted none.

"Shall we sit down?" he asked.

She acceded with a gesture, taking the armchair while he settled on the small sofa.

"A glass of wine perhaps?"

"I have none," she lied. "What do you want?"

"A cold welcome for an old friend, Teresa."

"We were never friends."

He put a hand to his chest as if wounded. "Was I not always pleasant to you?"

Outwardly, with a running undertone of insolence. He was the sort who fawned over those above him on the social scale and spurned those below. She had been a bit of both, so he had indulged in ambiguity. "What do you want?" she repeated.

"I have come to live in England," he said, spreading his hands. "I wish to establish myself here."

"As a *conde*?" Teresa indicated his visiting card, lying on a small table at her side.

"But I am, my dear Teresa. I recently inherited the title from a distant cousin."

She gritted her teeth at his form of address. He was probably lying about the legacy, but the point wasn't worth an argument. She didn't care.

"Sadly, there was no property to go with honor." He shrugged and smiled. "So I still must make my fortune. I heard that foreign titles impress the English, and so I have arrived." He made an openhanded gesture meant to be charming.

"I know no one who would be of use to you," Teresa said. Peron would be looking to attach himself to a rich man and benefit from the connection. That was his method.

He pretended surprise. "Have I asked?"

"You would, sooner or later. I saw no point in waiting. I tell you again, I have no connections."

"That is hard to believe."

"Why?" Teresa gestured at the room. "I live a frugal life. I do not go into society. How would I?"

Her unwelcome caller surveyed the place again. He appeared to find the sight distasteful. "I assumed you were simply waiting for your next...opportunity. Your charms have hardly faded." He offered her a small bow.

Rage kept Teresa silent. It nearly choked her.

"If we joined forces," he continued. "I'm sure we could...penetrate the upper reaches of—what do they call it here—the *haut ton*? Odd how they use a French phrase when they were fighting them for so long." He tried a smile.

"No." She bit off the word.

He drew back. "You are angry?"

He had the instincts of a toady, Teresa thought. He knew when he had offended.

"But this would be a great help to you," he added. "Take you out of *here*."

His disdain for her small home was infuriating.

"The lovely Teresa should be surrounded by luxury and adulation. I would like to see that restored to you."

Did he actually believe this would sway her? If she had needed evidence that he understood nothing, this would have provided it. "You care only for your own advantage," she replied.

"Mostly that," he conceded. "Like anyone else." His smile was meant to be self-deprecating, endearing. Teresa had seen it succeed. Today, it did not.

"I cannot help you," she said.

His expression hardened. "Will not, you mean."

Teresa shook her head.

"If I shared certain stories of the past, it could make things difficult for you."

This, she had expected. The threat had hung in the air from his first appearance at her door. "With whom?" she asked. "I have told you I take no part in society."

"Even your small, crude neighbors might be… surprised."

She wasn't sure how they would feel. But she knew that showing this man the least weakness was fatal. "Tell anyone anything you like. I don't care." She rose to show that this visit was over.

He remained seated. "I spoke too hastily. I beg your pardon."

"There is no need." She shrugged. "We simply have nothing to talk about."

"You would throw away the chance…"

"Freely and utterly. And now I will bid you farewell. Conde."

Eliza, who had clearly been listening if not comprehending, came out of the kitchen. She held a broom as if it was a weapon.

Frowning, the man stood. "If you oppose me…" he said to Teresa.

"I will not think of you again once you have gone. I hope you will extend the same courtesy to me. And do not come back here."

"*Cortesía*? You appear to have forgotten anything you ever knew of it."

"Perhaps I have." She walked over to the front door and opened it. Eliza swept her broom over the floorboards, a homely movement that somehow suggested a guardian repelling invaders as well.

The visitor looked from one stony face to the other. With a muttered oath he strode out. Teresa closed the door behind him and shot the bolt. She resisted putting her back to the panels.

"What did *he* want?" asked Eliza.

"He is an acquaintance from Spain. He called to say hello."

The maid's expression was skeptical. "Didn't sound like hello. Seemed like you had an argument."

"We knew each other…before under different circumstances. He thought I could be helpful to him here in England. I told him I cannot. He was…disappointed." It was only the truth, after all.

"So he ain't coming back?"

Teresa had to be honest with her. "He may. I cannot stop him. But when he finds I mean what I say, he will give up."

"I won't let him in!"

Teresa was touched by the fierce loyalty on the girl's face. "There is no need to worry. I can deal with this man."

"Like you did Dilch."

"As thoroughly, though not quite in the same way, I imagine."

Satisfied, Eliza retreated with her broom. Teresa sat down again, wondering who had told Alessandro Peron she was here, down to her very address. She had thought herself anonymous, which was a good way to be hidden. But lately she had made new acquaintances, she noted, and people chattered. There need be no malice involved. Everyone loved a story, and perhaps she had become one. The idea made her grimace, but as she'd told the purported *conde*, it didn't matter. She didn't care about the polite world's opinion. How could she?

As for Alessandro, he was a nuisance, but he *would* go away when he accepted the fact that there was no advantage to gain from her. He was not dangerous; he was only a leech.

And then she remembered Lord Macklin. He had the rank and wealth Alessandro was seeking. And if her Spanish acquaintance stuck his nose further into her life, he would discover that she knew an earl. He would find a way to make use of that without any help from her.

Teresa cringed. Lord Macklin had shown no sign of enjoying flattery. He certainly had no entourage to inflate his consequence. But Alessandro Peron was a very good toady. He could be beguiling when he exerted himself. He would scrape an acquaintance, particularly because Lord Macklin was curious about her. She was aware of this. And Alessandro could tell him things, some of which would change the earl's opinion of her. No, be honest. They would destroy it.

Teresa felt a wash of despair. Was change not possible? Did the past never let go? She clenched her fists in her lap and fought an onslaught of memories. It was a long while before she subdued them.

❧

He wanted to visit the theater workshop every day, Arthur thought, as his feet took him in that direction the following afternoon. Even though the people there were beginning to find his constant attendance odd. He was gaining an increasing reputation for oddities. His impulse, a year ago, to help a set of young men oppressed by grief had surprised everyone who knew anything about it and mystified countless others who didn't. A hostess whose renowned summer house party he'd skipped this year was convinced he was concealing a scandalous intrigue. One old friend had asked if he was ill; another had posed oblique questions about financial reverses. Arthur's "disappearance" from his customary haunts had tongues wagging even now.

And increasingly, of all the places he might have gone in London during the height of the season, he was most drawn to a room full of artisans. Or, in truth, to just one of them, the fascinating Señora Alvarez. He had come to care a great deal about her. It had progressed from his first admiration of her form and manner to something much deeper. He saw no need to deny it; he didn't wish to.

Just lately, he'd thought that perhaps she felt the same. He'd glimpsed flashes of response, hints of encouragement, he believed. But when he tried to find out, she evaded. He had to talk to her. He was not some green boy, to moon about in silence. He wanted to know what she thought, what she felt. He had timed his visit today with that goal in mind.

He found her putting on her bonnet, preparing to leave her painting, just as he had planned. But she said, "I'm going to the theater to talk with the opera dancers. I've arranged time to speak to each of them alone."

This wasn't ideal, but the walk might offer a bit of time alone. He moved with her toward the door. "I will go with you."

"No, thank you. I don't require an escort. And your presence at the theater would be a distraction."

She didn't sound cold, only determined. Disappointed, Arthur watched her walk off down the street. He returned to talk with Tom, who was assembling the frame for one of the flats that would become scenery for a play. He'd become very skilled at this, Arthur noted. His hammer fell with rhythmic precision. "The señora off to the theater?" Tom asked.

"Yes."

"I hope she finds something. I haven't had much luck hanging about the dancers' room after the performances. Too many 'gentlemen' to sort out."

"You know why they are there," said Arthur, curious about the lad's point of view.

"Looking for what they can get. With the least cost. You see a good bit of that in the streets. Men trying to take advantage. A right bad lot, mostly."

Arthur nodded. It always saddened him to think of Tom's life as a child.

"And there's women using men to keep 'em, when they don't care a fig," the lad added. "Toss 'em out like rubbish when something better comes along. A right mess. And families can muck it up even more. Look at that Romeo and Juliet."

"There is happiness as well."

Tom nodded. "You showed me that, this last year. Playing matchmaker." He grinned to show he knew Arthur didn't care for that word. "And now mebbe it's your turn?" This came with a sly look.

Arthur did not reply.

"The señora, I mean," Tom said.

"I gathered."

"I thought you liked her."

Arthur decided to admit it. "I do."

"But you ain't...haven't told her so?"

"I shall."

"Need any more help?" asked Tom with a grin.

"More?"

"I been giving things a little push when I could. I learned a deal watching you."

"You have." It wasn't a question. Arthur saw it all in that moment. He was mostly amused, and a touch appalled, at Tom's efforts.

"Just give me a sign if you need another." Tom made an airy gesture with his hammer.

Tables turning, thought Arthur. Not a comfortable sensation. He shook his head.

"It's a bit harder, eh?" asked Tom.

"What is?"

"This matchmaking stuff. You've been backstage, like, but now you're out front. And it's trickier."

"There's no question of matchmaking here."

"There never was, with any of the fellows," replied Tom with a grin. "Until, all of a sudden, the question was popped."

His case was entirely different, Arthur thought. And then he remembered the idea that had occurred to him before he came down to London this year—a new happiness. Was this the result? Had that impulse moved him to…here? He hadn't gotten that far.

Tom was watching him with open amusement.

Arthur wondered where he'd thought he was going when he decided to talk to the señora. If she *was* offering encouragement, what then? He examined the idea of Teresa Alvarez as a wife. His wife. And found it enormously appealing.

Tom was called to help with another man's project. As it was clearly going to take some time, Arthur waved a farewell and left the workshop. His mind was so full of new thoughts that he nearly collided with a small man outside the door. The fellow offered him a bow, and said, "Good day, sir. I noticed you were speaking with the lady who left a few minutes ago."

Arthur stopped, surprised. "Señora Alvarez?"

"Alv…ah, yes. I was coming up the street just now to pay her a visit. But she was away before I could speak."

How then did he know that Arthur had been talking to her?

"I was acquainted with her in Spain, you see," the man added.

Arthur examined him—slender, inches shorter than he. His clothes were foreign, as was his face with its dark eyes and aquiline nose. He realized that those eyes were making a thorough evaluation of him as well. They held a subtle gleam of cunning. "Indeed?" he said.

The man smiled. "Indeed. I am Conde Alessandro de la Cerda."

"Macklin." Arthur knew this was not enough information for a foreigner to identify him, but he found he didn't care to say more. There was something about the man that he didn't quite like. He was rather...professionally ingratiating. Arthur's position in life made the type familiar. Though this fellow was quite good at it.

"You are also a friend of...Señora Alvarez?"

"I met her recently."

"Ah, a most charming lady, as all her old friends would attest."

A jumble of curiosity and caution, along with a lamentable tinge of jealousy, unsettled Arthur.

"Such an odd place to find her though," the man added.

"Is it?"

The *conde* looked up and down the shabby street. "So very...primitive."

"As opposed to?"

"I beg your pardon?"

"Where would you expect to find her? If not this sort of place."

"Ah." The man's smile this time was satisfied, like a fisherman who felt a tug on his line. "A noble household with all of its...luxuries. Of course."

There was definitely something off about this

fellow. All Arthur's instincts told him so. He was ready to walk away. Yet he couldn't help asking, "Were you a friend of her husband?"

"Her...? Oh. No. Not her husband."

Something badly off. The Spaniard had been oddly surprised by that question.

"I did know many others very...close to her."

He wanted Arthur to draw him out. He wanted to dole out bits of gossip and be courted for more. And certainly rewarded for his knowledge. He was that sort of weasel. This exchange was feeling deeply distasteful. But Arthur's protective impulses had also been roused. "How did you find her here?"

The Spaniard was off-balance for only a moment. Then he made an airy gesture. "I have been asking about old friends at the embassy."

The señora had shown no sign of being in communication with Spanish diplomats, Arthur thought. His own inquiries had confirmed that. He wondered suddenly if he had alerted them to her presence by asking.

"His Excellency was very accommodating," the other man added.

Immediately certain that the fellow was *not* acquainted with the Spanish ambassador, Arthur turned away. "I have an engagement," he said. "I must go."

"I will walk with you, if you permit. I am not familiar with London and often find myself quite lost." A self-deprecating gesture and smile accompanied this admission.

Arthur could not refuse such a request without a degree of rudeness he was unwilling to employ.

As yet. It might be that he would eventually. No, undoubtedly he would. This sort of toadeater required definitive discouragement.

"Perhaps you could recommend to me the best ways to make acquaintances in English society," the *conde* continued as they walked.

If he thought to wangle an invitation from Arthur, he was fair and far off. "I'm sure your friend the ambassador could help you," he replied.

"Of course. But I would not wish to take too much of his time."

Arthur amused himself by deflecting the man's sallies for the remainder of the walk. It was rather like a game of tennis in which he declined every serve. As he shed the man's unwanted company at the door of his club, he determined to warn Señora Alvarez about this insinuating *conde*. He suspected she would not think much of him.

❧

Teresa met Tom at the workshop early the next morning, by arrangement, to compare notes on their inquiries at the theater. She had managed to talk with each opera dancer alone about recent happenings, and she knew Tom had made close observations in their retiring room. They shared the tidbits they'd gathered and tried to put them in order. "We should get Miss Deeping to make one of her charts," Tom said.

"We shall do our own." Teresa found paper and ink and drew a grid with the name of the dancers, including those who were gone, along one side and a list of characteristics across the top.

"You're every bit as good as Miss Deeping," said Tom admiringly.

She accepted his praise with a smile. "We know that Odile, Sonia, and Maria had certain things in common."

"From away," said Tom. "Didn't speak English well, not many friends, and no family to ask about them."

Teresa put check marks on her grid for these things. "After my talks, I think there are other girls in the same case." She ticked off two names.

"Jeanne and Elena? I seen a fellow talking to each of them. A goodish while. On different nights."

"What sort of fellow?"

"English," Tom replied. "Nobleman, I'd say. Fine clothes but didn't seem to set much store by them. Expected people to make way, that sort of thing."

Teresa nodded. She knew the type well. "We must find out his name and see what we can discover about him."

"Right," said Tom. "I can get some of my friends to keep an eye out for him. See where he goes outside the theater. Mebbe they can overhear a bit of conversation."

"Good." Teresa folded the page and put it in her reticule. At last they seemed to be making progress.

With the air of one turning to the next order of business, Tom said, "There's been somebody asking questions about you outside here, last couple of days." He gestured at the door of the workshop.

"Me?"

"Dark fellow with an arched nose," Tom added.

"He catches folks as they're leaving. Makes up to them. He took Sanders for a mug of beer. Sanders likes to talk, y' know."

Teresa's heart sank. She had no doubt this visitor was Alessandro Peron, the supposed *conde*. She had not expected him to be so persistent.

"I saw him talking to Lord Macklin."

Any triumph Teresa had felt at the progress of their investigation faded. What had Peron said to the earl? "He is someone I knew in Spain."

"Not a friend."

"No."

"Enemy?" asked Tom.

She had not thought so. She had never done anything to Peron. Except refuse to help him in England. Perhaps this was his revenge. "He is one of those who takes joy in malice," she said.

Tom nodded. "Want me to run him off?"

He did not ask for reasons to take her side, still less excuses. His faith warmed her heart, even as his careless confidence worried her. Alessandro Peron would see Tom as a worthless underling. His response would be vicious. "No."

"You think I can't?"

She did have doubts, but more, she didn't want to risk him. "I will take care of this matter." She would find some means, though this was not as simple as routing Dilch.

Tom gazed at her with an understanding beyond his years. "Blackmailer?" he asked.

Startled, Teresa drew back. So much of the time Tom seemed just a jolly lad, ready with a fantastical phrase or a joke. It was easy to forget that beneath that surface he was acutely, in this moment alarmingly, observant. And he knew as much about the seamier side of the world as she—perhaps even more. With all this, he was a staunch friend. He would never disdain her choices. Teresa nodded. "I have done things in my life, in order to survive, of which I'm not proud."

"So have I," said Tom, looking not the least disturbed. Nor did he ask for details, as some might have.

"This man knows of those things."

"And he'll tell 'em, to anybody, if it gets him anything he wants."

"Yes."

"Even just a bit of revenge. To hurt you, like."

She acknowledged that with another nod.

Tom spat out a curse that had no Shakespearean elegance.

They sat in silence. The first artisans began to trickle into the workshop.

"His lordship won't care," said Tom, once again cutting to the crux of the matter.

Teresa turned so that new arrivals could not see her face.

"He knows I stole and told a heap of lies back in Bristol," the lad added.

"Like so many things in this world, matters are rather different for a woman."

Consciousness of the truth of this showed in Tom's face. "I'll get rid of the bastard."

One of the arriving workers called a greeting. They acknowledged it. "You must concentrate on helping the dancers," Teresa said. "I think we're coming close there."

Tom hesitated. He looked torn.

"I can manage my own affairs." Teresa rose.

More people were entering. There could be no more private conversation, and Teresa found this a relief. She went to her customary place and put on her apron. She would paint, and she would think, and some plan would come to her. Because it had to.

Thus it was that on her way home that day, Teresa stopped in at the pub at the far end of her street. She had never been inside, but today she ventured through the door and stood blinking in the dimness after the sunshine outside. She was met by a sudden silence from the scatter of patrons. "Mr. Rigby," she said to the owner. "May I speak to you for a moment?"

"Certainly, ma'am." The retired prizefighter led her to the far end of the bar, out of earshot of his customers, who resumed their low conversations.

This scarred man had been most helpful in the matter of Dilch. Teresa knew his fearsome appearance covered a fierce sense of justice. "I wondered if you knew where I might procure a pistol?" she asked him.

This earned her a long look. "Beg pardon, but why would you be wanting such a thing, ma'am?"

"As a precaution, Mr. Rigby."

"If somebody's bothering—"

"A precaution only," Teresa interrupted.

"And would you know how to use a pistol, ma'am?"

"Yes. Quite well. It...amused a gentleman of my acquaintance to teach me."

"I see."

The look in his eyes told her that he probably did, more than she might wish.

"Well then, yes, ma'am, I expect I do know."

Nine

THE WEDDING OF MISS ADA GRANDISON TO PETER Rathbone, Duke of Compton, took place on a glorious May morning at St. George's Church in Hanover Square. The bride's family had done their utmost to make it a glittering occasion, and the church was crowded with their friends and the cream of the *haut ton*.

The young duke, who had no close family left, had asked Arthur to stand up with him at the altar, and Arthur was touched and pleased to do so. The bride looked lovely in a pale-blue gown and flowered bonnet. The couple spoke their vows in clear, confident voices and beamed with happiness when they greeted the waiting crowd after signing the register.

The wedding breakfast at the Grandison house overflowed with more guests than the church could hold. Arthur found the crowd frustrating because he knew Señora Alvarez was in attendance, and he very much wanted to find her. He'd seen less of her in recent days as she had no project at the theater workshop. He didn't want to think that she was avoiding him, but he feared that in fact she was.

He was searching for her in the sea of faces when Compton found him. "I wanted to thank you again," said the young duke. "You made all this possible." He gestured at the celebration.

"An exaggeration," replied Arthur. "As I have said before. You won your happiness by your own efforts."

"I'd have had no chance without your—"

Arthur stopped him with a gesture. "You have thanked me enough, Peter. Too much. Let this be the last time. Look, your wife is beckoning."

The smile that broke over the younger man's face illuminated his somewhat bony features. "My wife." He moved away like a man in a happy dream.

Seeing an acquaintance nearby, Arthur went to join him.

"Has your new great-nephew or great-niece been born?" the man asked.

"She, or he, remains imminent according to the latest letter."

His companion nodded. "Say, do you know some foreign chap, name of Cerda? I was at Manton's the other day. This fellow seemingly heard me mention your name, and he came slap up to me and introduced himself. Bold as brass. Said he's a good friend of yours."

"He is not," answered Arthur. It was time to administer the setdown this fellow deserved, he decided.

The other nodded again. "Seemed like an encroaching mushroom to me."

"Precisely."

"I thought so. Town seems to be full of them. I'll be glad to be back in the North."

"You are leaving London?"

"In a few days."

The season was nearly over. He would be expected to depart as well. Arthur excused himself and went hunting for Señora Alvarez.

He slipped through the press of people, nodding to greetings on all sides. He had nearly made it to the back of the house when he was accosted by Miss Julia Grandison, large and resplendent in magenta silk. "Hullo, Macklin," she said. "A splendid event, eh?"

"Indeed. I was just going…"

"For Ada's sake, I am allowing my brother to enjoy his triumph. Before his fall. His opera dancer is called Bella, you know."

He was not about to admit that he did. He looked to see if anyone else had heard. Miss Grandison had a penetrating voice. But no one was paying them any mind.

"It is not too late to do your part," she went on.

"My part?"

"To repay me for the service I rendered your young friend."

Arthur had no idea what she meant.

"Putting him and Ada together," Miss Grandison added impatiently. "Really, everyone seems to forget my efforts in making this match."

Because they were entirely imaginary, Arthur thought. "Excuse me, I need to speak to someone." He moved on before she could reply.

He found Señora Alvarez in earnest conversation with Miss Deeping and Miss Finch. They broke off so abruptly when he approached that he wondered what they had been saying.

The two young ladies excused themselves as he came up. "What were you plotting?" he asked Señora Alvarez.

She shook her head. "They so long to join in a plot," she said. "But I see no place for them. This matter of the opera dancers is rather more serious than a thieving crow or even a hidden treasure."

"They told you about unmasking the crow."

"Each of them, in slightly different versions."

"They are proud of that."

"I admire their...*ingenio*. But the disappearances are not part of the world they know. I think they must be left out of this."

"You will not exclude me, I hope." He hadn't meant to allow so much emotion in his voice, but in the end he wasn't sorry. It seemed that he had been trying for eons to let her know how he felt.

Señora Alvarez gazed up at him. A man might fall into those dark eyes and lose himself, Arthur thought. Unless he already had. "Can we never be alone," he complained. They were constantly surrounded by people. He could not take her hand or pull her close in this chattering crowd. He couldn't sue for the right to do so.

"To speak about the dancers," she replied.

"No!" The exclamation drew a few glances. He turned his back on them. "Of course we will plan what to do about that. But there are other things I wish to say to you."

"Other?"

"You must have some hint of my feelings. I would have spoken before this, but I think you have been avoiding me." He hadn't meant to sound accusing.

There was a pause that went on far too long for Arthur's comfort. Señora Alvarez looked as if she was considering a knotty problem. Conversations washed around them while they stood like rocks in a sea of words. This was *not* the response he'd hoped for. But then she said, "I suppose your carriage is here."

"Yes."

"Perhaps you would drive me home."

"With the greatest pleasure." He thought he managed to hide his flare of triumph. Or perhaps he didn't. He didn't care.

"Very well."

She didn't take his offered arm but simply walked out beside him. Arthur saw people noticing. He was happy to let them.

His town carriage was brought around promptly, and he handed her in. As they started off, she gazed out the window, not at him. "People here drive their carriages through the park, do they not?" she said. "Perhaps we could do that."

Surprised and pleased, Arthur gave the order to his coachman. Now he just had to find the right words to woo her. "Your company is a rare treat," he said.

Teresa glanced at him and away. Lord Macklin had a touch of arrogance, as was only to be expected from an English lord. But other emotions moved in his blue-gray eyes. He was going to say things that should not be. She didn't know exactly what things, but she knew that she had to speak before he made some impossible declaration. He was a man of honor. He would feel bound by his words, and she would not have him so.

She had thought of *her* earl for many hours since the arrival of the false Conde de la Cerda, while waiting for the Spaniard's malicious tongue to begin to wag. She had pondered love and pain and dreams and fate. She had remembered, so vividly, the feel of disaster, of a whole life sliding away—slowly at first like the tipping snows of an avalanche, building to a roar of devastation.

It was time to end this…friendship that should never have begun. She could feel the sadness already welling up in her chest. The avalanche would bury her. But she owed him this much.

"Is something wrong?" he asked.

He was a man who noticed, and cared. A rare man. Unique. She would not see his like again. The ache inside grew sharper. But there was no help for it. She would find no better opportunity, if that was the word. Here, they would not be overheard. There was no Eliza hovering nearby, no workmen, no Tom to interrupt. "I am going to tell you the truth now," she said.

"About what?" he asked.

"About me." And when she had finished, she could leave the carriage and make her way back to her small home, take up the life she had carved out for herself. The bitterness would fade in time, as all things did. She would recover, as she always did. Unless the wound was too deep this time. "I will not give you my real name," she continued. "That is dead forever. But as for the rest." She made a throwaway gesture; one could only begin. "I am not a widow. That was a lie."

"Your husband is alive?" He straightened, as if ready to square up against a rival.

She would have laughed if the pain in her heart had been less. "I never had a husband," she replied. "He was always a fiction."

"But—"

"It is best to let me speak," she interrupted. If he didn't, she would falter and perhaps fail.

Lord Macklin nodded. She could see no censure in his face. She was going to tell him everything. She'd never told anyone. But then, she'd never known anyone—else—who so deserved her confidences.

Having decided this, she found her voice frozen in her throat. Step by step, she thought. Go back to the beginning.

"I was twenty when war came to northern Spain," she said. "I was to have been married before that, but the man my father chose had died of a fever and another match was still being arranged. Rather slowly." She didn't even know what had caused the delay. Money, no doubt. Or perhaps the rising conflict had affected those negotiations as well.

"Arranged," said Lord Macklin.

"It was the way of my family." She waved this away as irrelevant. She mustn't let the look on his face shake her resolve. Sympathy was not the point. "This was before the great battles of your Wellington. Perhaps you know that the end began in 1807 when Napoleon pushed French troops through Spain to invade Portugal. More than one hundred thousand men, I have heard, only to pass through. Of course he lied. Once they were there, his troops threw out King Carlos and put in his brother Joseph Bonaparte on the throne. We have spoken of that *cabrón* before.

The royal family was not so much beloved. Prince
Ferdinand had tried to overthrow his father the year
before. But they were better than being ruled by the
French. Spain rose up. Things fell into chaos." She
pressed her hands together in her lap at the memory
of fear. "There was no organized conflict at first. It
was worse. Roving bands of men, some desperate
and hungry and more like bandits. One didn't know
where their loyalties lay."

"It must have been dreadful," said the earl.

Teresa bowed her head in acknowledgment. It had
been, but she was also aware that she had been avoiding the personal by reciting history. She took a breath
and went on. "One of these groups came across my
family's land. They claimed to be French troops, but
I think now they might have been deserters. They
seized livestock and food, terrorized the people. My
father went to order them off. He thought himself the
monarch of his acres, you see. He was so used to being
obeyed that he did not know how to expect anything
else. But these men cared nothing for his authority.
They jeered and spit at him. Papa turned his whip on
one of the officers, and a soldier shot him."

"You were not present surely?" Lord Macklin
looked deeply shocked at the idea.

"No, we heard the story from his servant, who fled."

"I am so very sorry…"

Teresa held up a hand to stop him. Compassion
now would undo her. "Once they had done this,
the men went wild. Some dark impulse was set loose
perhaps. Or they thought they must cover up the
crime, or send a warning to other landowners who

might object to their thievery. I do not know why they chose to ride after my father's man and attack our house."

"My God!"

Teresa appreciated his anger even after all these years. "War is not just ranks of soldiers facing each other. As I soon discovered."

"You… Did they—" His hand rose as if to take hers, then drew back.

"My brothers rallied every available man, and some of the women, to meet the attack, but there were far more of the Frenchmen. Diego and Roland—all the men of our household, I think—were killed giving me and a few others time to run away. Not my mother. She was already dead by then, *gracias a Dios*. The *canallas* set fire to our house when they were done. We could see the smoke as we ran."

He seemed about to speak, but then said nothing.

"We went to our nearest neighbors first, but they were afraid to take us in. They thought they might be targeted next if they helped. So we walked on. I had never been so tired in my life, up to then." Since, well, there had been other trials. The hardest part was coming up. Teresa didn't know if she had the courage to continue. She didn't want to see the earl's face change, his inevitable judgment descend. "Some of my companions found refuge in cottages or gave up. They were not…of my rank. The country people were more reluctant to hide me. I could see that. So I pushed on to the house of a good friend of my father, though it was far." Teresa had to swallow before she could go on.

"They had known each other all their lives, and…
this man had always seemed fond of me. And indeed
he welcomed me with cries of horror and ordered up
food and fresh clothes and a chamber for me. He was
my savior."

Lord Macklin watched her with grave, sympathetic
eyes. She looked away before adding, "After three
days he came to offer me even more. His protection,
as his mistress. He explained that my reputation was
ruined because I had been staying with him. He had
let word of this spread to people who knew me.
And…encouraged them to draw certain conclusions,
even though he had not touched me. But he assured
me that he would be kind to me and give me every
luxury."

The earl cursed softly.

"I refused him, of course," said Teresa. "I could not
believe the insult. I called him the worst names I knew
and flounced out as if I had somewhere to go."

Teresa paused to breathe.

"But I found I did not," she continued after a
moment. "When I appealed to another friend of my
family, I found that this man had made a great point of
saying that nothing improper had happened between
us. As your Shakespeare says, protesting too much.
And so they all thought that I had given myself to him
in exchange for my refuge. The women looked at me
with contempt. The men with…a new interest."

Lord Macklin swore again.

"They did have their own problems," Teresa
conceded. "The countryside had become perilous.
Death stalked what had been a peaceful land. No one

knew what would happen next. My fate was small in comparison."

"It should not have been!"

She was too intent on finishing this to react. The memories were rising up and threatening to overwhelm her. "You will say I should have found a way to escape."

"I say he should have been shot for what he did to you!"

"But I was…not quite myself."

"You had seen your family killed and your home destroyed!"

"Yes." She'd been exhausted and terrified and ignorant, all too conscious of having nothing when she was accustomed to plenty. She'd gone to some of her family's old servants, but they were poor and even more frightened of the future, and of the man who was holding out all the comforts she'd grown up with. He was a power in the area. "I gave in," she said. She felt the shame of it even now.

"I returned to him and hid behind his power. He knew how to deal with the troops. He placated whichever bands of soldiers swept through the region, French or Spanish or later the English." Watching that, she'd realized how much he enjoyed manipulation. More than any physical intimacies that occurred between them, in the end.

"Where is he?" said Lord Macklin. The growl in his tone made her shiver.

"He died. Just before your Waterloo. He always thought Napoleon would be coming back." He'd relished the prospect, having found many benefits in turmoil. "He had no children. There was much confusion when he was gone. And in those years with him, I had learned how to plan and persuade." As well as the hiding places of the grandee's ill-gotten valuables through the war. She'd taken her chance, purchased aid, and set off on a long, hard trek to safety. Which she had achieved, Teresa reminded herself. "There. That is all. Now you know. And you see, I am not what you thought I was."

She waited a moment, but he didn't reply. Certainly he was shocked, appalled. How could he not be? He was a most respectable man, and respectable people despised her. But there was one more thing. "The 'Conde de la Cerda' could tell much of this story," Teresa added. The man knew the general outline, if not all the details. "He will probably spread it about, since I've refused to help him worm his way into society. As if I could." And now Lord Macklin would think she had only told her story because she was about to be exposed. Perhaps that was true. Would she have made these painful admissions otherwise? It hardly mattered. Either way, his opinion of her was destroyed. And she cared nothing about the rest of society.

Still, he said nothing. The silence was unbearable.

The carriage stopped to wait for another to cross ahead. Teresa pushed open the door and jumped out, rushing across the park to a gate nearby where she could flag down a hack. The earl would not come after her. Why should he? His pride must be bruised. He was probably angry. He would never want to see her again. Teresa saw a cab and raised her hand to signal.

Arthur moved just a moment too late. His carriage pulled forward, and by the time he'd halted it again, Señora Alvarez was gone. She was not Señora Alvarez, he thought. But he had no other name to call her.

He should have spoken. He should have comforted her. He'd wanted to pull her into his arms and hold her close, shelter her from all harm. But that would have been utterly inappropriate after the story she'd told, what had been done to her. And sympathetic phrases couldn't make up for the insults she'd suffered.

Mostly, though, he'd done nothing because he was grappling with murderous rage. A protective anger that he'd felt only a few times before in his life, when those he loved were threatened, was choking him. He couldn't think, still less speak.

Arthur noticed that he was shaking with fury. He longed for action, for something to hit. If he could get his hands on the man who'd used her… His fingers curled into claws. But that villain was beyond reach. Still, there must be something he could do, some recompense he could offer her.

A thought occurred, and blossomed, more and more gratifying. That might well do. He leaned out to give his coachman new orders.

Returning to the wedding breakfast, he was pleased to find Tom still there. The press of people was thinning, however, and the lad was happy to leave with him. Back in the carriage, Arthur made automatic replies to Tom's remarks about the event. These gradually diminished, and by the time they'd reached Arthur's house, Tom said, "What's wrong, my lord?"

"Come into the library," Arthur replied. They

walked through and settled in the book-lined room. "I want to talk to you about a Spaniard who appeared in town recently."

"That fella who's been lurking about the workshop asking questions about Señora Alvarez?"

Tom was always quick, Arthur thought. A hint was enough for him. "You've seen him then?"

"He tried prying information out of me, but he didn't get no…anywhere."

Arthur wondered how much of the señora's true story Tom knew. Had she other confidants? He both hoped so and wished to be the only one. "He means her ill," he added.

"I know. The currish, half-faced scut!"

"Ah, yes." It seemed a fair description. "I intend to get rid of him."

Tom's frown deepened. "I wanted to do that, but the señora said no. She said she'd handle him herself."

"She should not have to. She deserves help." All the aid she had not been given in her youth, and more.

"She did fine with Dilch."

"This is no neighborhood dilemma."

"Well, but…"

"I know more of the true story than you do." Arthur was sure of it now.

After a moment's consideration, the lad accepted this. "So you're looking for another pair of hands for the job? I'm your man!" Tom paused and made a wry face. "But I have to say, my lord, I don't seem to have the stomach for killin'."

"Good God, I'm not planning murder!"

"Ah, that's all right then." Tom shifted in his chair. "I tried one time. With a scurvy wretch who hunted the little ones on the streets in Bristol. Set an ambush and had my chance. But I couldn't cut him down. Even low as he was. Reckon I'm hen-hearted."

"What did you do?" Arthur asked, momentarily diverted by curiosity.

"Turned him over to a magistrate. One as would listen to the truth."

"And was the creature punished?"

"Transported. Hard labor."

"So you are wise and just rather than hen-hearted, Tom."

The lad took the compliment with a duck of his head.

"I intend to send this Spaniard out of England in a way that he can't easily return."

"Transport him ourselves, you mean?"

Arthur nodded, appreciating the comparison. "I thought the Indies, one of the Spanish colonies. Puerto Rico, perhaps. He should feel at home there."

Their subject's comfort didn't appear to interest Tom. "Won't he just come right back though?"

"We'll send him off with no money. He doesn't seem to have a fortune of his own. He seems a cunning rogue and will likely accumulate funds. But it will take him some time. And by then everything will be different." Arthur didn't know how, yet he was certain it would be.

"How will we manage it?" Tom asked.

"That is the question. I considered offering a bribe, but…"

"You can't let him get a whiff of your fortune," Tom interrupted. "He's a blackmailer, and they just keep wanting more. You'd never be rid of him."

"I agree."

Tom frowned over the problem. "We'll just have to bung him onto a ship our own selves, willy-nilly. Like a press-gang."

It was a role Arthur had never expected to fill. "I expect he would object to that. Rather loudly."

"We'd have to make certain he couldn't then."

The thought of rendering the Spaniard unable to protest had its attractions. "The fellow is a toadeater. I could invite him here and then…"

"Have him walk into your house and never come out again?" objected Tom. "That's no good. What, order your butler to cosh him and the footmen to truss him up with curtain cords?"

Arthur thought of the august individual who managed his household. Chirt would be appalled at the idea. Then he recalled how ruthlessly the butler depressed the pretensions of encroaching callers. "Chirt might be up to it."

Tom, who was well acquainted with this servitor, laughed. "Mebbe so, but you don't want the man vanishin' from here. Better to invite him to go riding. I kin wait for you someplace out of the way, and we'll jump him."

"And what then? Tie him up with our neckcloths? Choose a ship at random on the docks and hand over a rebellious captive? Most captains would call in the law. And those who wouldn't…"

"Probably ain't men we want to trust. It is a puzzle."

Tom shook his head. "Be easier if we *was* going to kill him."

"Tom!"

"Beg your pardon, my lord. I ain't been called on to dispose of many people before this." He cocked his head. "Not any, actually."

"It was not included in my training either," replied Arthur ruefully. "Eton didn't go much beyond the cut direct."

"Is that sword fighting? Like a duel?"

"No, it is a public refusal to acknowledge someone. You turn your back where all of society can see."

"Oh." Tom clearly didn't think much of this. "*Could* you challenge him to a duel?"

"A cumbersome process, with inconvenient rules which would reveal matters we hope to keep private. Also, it would not dispose of the man unless I killed him. Which we have ruled out."

"He might be a good fighter, too."

"And kill *me*. Very true." Arthur began to wonder how things had come to this in his ordered, settled life. A harsh inner voice noted that Señora Alvarez had no doubt felt the same—no, far worse—when hers had fallen into ruins.

"Well, I don't think he would kill you, 'cause then he'd have to scarper, and he don't want to do that. But I can see it ain't the best plan." Tom gazed at the Turkey carpet, rubbing his hands together as if the motion promoted thought. "Ah."

"You've thought of something?"

"Somebody. Who might be able to help."

"We don't want word of this to spread."

"He knows how to keep mum."

"He being?"

"Mr. Rigby. Runs a pub down near my lodgings."

"I'm not sure a barkeep…"

"Used to be a bare-knuckle fighter," Tom interrupted. "And more besides, I reckon."

"More in what sense?"

"Late at night, when the street's gone to bed, there's some hard men visits that pub. I've seen some of 'em, when I was coming home late from the theater."

Arthur frowned at him.

Tom waved off his concern. "I steered clear. And Mr. Rigby is all right. We've had some chats. He helped the señora get rid of Dilch."

"She trusted him?"

"Aye."

"I suppose we could speak to him," Arthur said.

"Be best if I go alone, my lord."

"Easier, perhaps. But I insist on coming along." Responding to Tom's expression, Arthur added, "There may be points only I can, er, reassure him on." Mainly involving available funds. He also wanted to make his own assessment before bringing in the man.

Tom thought this over, then shrugged. "I reckon. When would you wish to go, my lord?"

"What about now? Presumably a pub keeper is generally available." And Arthur didn't feel able to sit still. He craved action.

"That's true."

They walked, as this was less likely to draw attention than a fine carriage in Tom's neighborhood. "And we should take care when we come closer," Arthur said. "I would not wish to meet Señora Alvarez."

His young companion looked dubious. "She's not to know?"

"Once all is over. Perhaps." He was not sure how to face her right now, with their ravaging conversation still fresh. And his mind had focused on one goal.

Tom considered this. "I don't think the señora is overfond of surprises."

"This is a gift," replied Arthur. Nothing could make up for what she'd suffered, but he could provide a weight on the other side of the scales.

"But she…"

"I know her better than you." As soon as he spoke, Arthur saw this for what it was—wishful thinking. But he would not be deterred.

Tom appeared to accept it, however, and they walked on.

Reaching the lad's home neighborhood, they slipped along the street and into the pub. It was low and small but clean. There were only a few patrons.

"Afternoon, Mr. Rigby," said Tom to the man behind the bar. "This here is Lord Macklin. Might we have a word?"

Rigby was probably past fifty, Arthur thought. Still well muscled, his receding red hair was cut close to his head. His face and knuckles showed the scars of his former profession. One ear had clearly been smashed by more than one fist. "What about?" Rigby asked. His voice was even. Not hostile, but not particularly welcoming either.

"Private matter," said Tom. He leaned forward and

spoke more quietly. "You remember that fella came in asking about Señora Alvarez?"

"The foreigner?"

"Aye, that one. It's about him. He's been bothering the señora."

Rigby frowned. "Come along in here," he said and led them into a small cluttered chamber behind the bar. Bottles and crates crowded shelves on three sides. There was one straight chair behind a chipped table and barely room for the three of them in the window-less space. No one sat down. Rigby faced them. "Did he lay his hands on her?" he asked with a scowl.

"No," answered Arthur. Judging from the expression on their host's face, the newcomer was fortunate that he had not. "He's threatened her, however." Arthur saw no need to explain what kind of threat. That was none of this man's business.

"We want to do something about him," Tom continued.

"Something?"

Rigby was clearly wary. Arthur wondered if he had been in trouble with the law. "I want to send him out of the country," he said. "Far enough that he cannot easily return."

The pub keeper surveyed Tom. "You're a good friend of the lady."

The lad nodded.

"And you as well?"

Under other circumstances Arthur might have been offended by a glowering inquiry from such a man. Now he simply said, "I am, and I wish to help her by removing this fellow."

Rigby considered this for so long that Arthur grew impatient. "Tom thought that perhaps you could put us onto the right sort of ship," he began.

"She asked me to find her a pistol," Rigby interrupted.

"What?" exclaimed Arthur and Tom at the same moment.

"Just a precaution, she called it. Now, I'm wondering what she means to do with it."

"So you procured a gun for her?" asked Arthur.

The scarred man nodded.

"You think she means to put a bullet into this *conday*?" asked Tom.

"That'd bring her a world of trouble," replied Rigby. He looked as if he knew about such difficulties.

On the one hand Arthur could understand the satisfaction of eliminating an enemy. On the other, the pub owner was correct. "I shall see that she does not require a pistol," he answered.

Someone in the taproom called for ale. Rigby went out to serve him.

"Would she really shoot him, do you think?" Tom asked.

"Only to defend herself, I imagine." The sooner they could be rid of this Spaniard, the better.

Rigby returned. "So what is it you're asking of me?"

"We would like to find a ship, ideally heading to the West Indies, that would take an…unauthorized passenger," Arthur replied.

This elicited a bark of laughter. "Unauthorized," repeated Rigby. "You toffs have some fine words for dark doings."

"It separates the really significant lawbreakers from the common criminals," said Arthur.

This earned him a surprised and approving glance. "I know a few people on the docks," said Rigby then. "Some as can slip an 'extra' passenger onto a ship at the right moment. Certain ships, that is."

"Like being pressed," said Tom.

Rigby grinned. He was missing a molar. "Bit more gentle than the navy perhaps. They'll want paying though."

Arthur nodded.

"And this individual would have to be kept quiet for a goodish time once he's onboard."

"Quiet," said Arthur.

"As the grave." Rigby's gaze was challenging. "Trussed up till they're well out to sea and no way back. He'll be dumped on the docks at the first port of call across the sea."

"But not harmed?" asked Arthur.

The pub owner shrugged. "Not so's you'd notice. Or so's *I* would, at any rate. I reckon he'll suffer a few clouts if he makes any trouble."

"I'd like to clout him," said Tom.

"If he starts a real fight, he'll be thrashed," Rigby added.

Arthur found he didn't care.

"And he'll be made to work for his keep, belike."

"I wish I could be there to see it," said Tom.

"You want to be tossed onboard as well?" joked Rigby.

Tom grinned and shook his head.

"One thing." Rigby held up a cautionary finger.

"You've got to lay hold of this fella yourselves. I ain't getting involved with that."

Even more certain that the man had had brushes with the law, Arthur nodded. Rigby's reluctance was understandable. Arthur wasn't keen on that part of it himself. "We are not going to tell Señora Alvarez until this is over."

Rigby appeared to find this only natural. "I'll see what ships is in port and send word with Tom about the possibles."

He looked startled when Arthur held out his hand, but he took it in a firm grasp, and they shook on the bargain.

Ten

TERESA WAS NOT SURPRISED WHEN LORD MACKLIN didn't appear at the workshop the following day, or the one after that. It was only what she'd expected. Now that he knew the truth, he wished to have nothing more to do with her. Of course. She fought off the sharp stabs of disappointment this knowledge brought. He was a leading member of society. He followed its strictures, valued them. It had been ridiculous to hope otherwise. She hadn't, really, hoped. Yet her eyes strayed to the doorway anytime there was movement from that direction. And she was downcast when the cause turned out to be someone else.

She should forget that she'd ever met the English earl. Hadn't she been continually wishing to do so? And so she would. Eventually.

Her painting went slowly, and without its usual verve, another reason for melancholy. She had decided to give up and was putting on her bonnet to return home when a note arrived for her. Writing in French, the opera dancer Jeanne informed her that she'd received a special invitation to go out driving in the country the following day. The gentleman was not among the ones they'd had suspicions about. Indeed, Teresa couldn't quite place him, which seemed a signal in itself.

He'd promised Jeanne a fine meal on the outing and a gift of coin. He'd also told her not to mention it to anyone, as he didn't care for people to know his private business. Well, he was out of luck there, Teresa thought. She'd convinced the opera dancers that secret assignations were not a good idea in the current situation, and that she, at least, should be told.

Note in hand, she looked around for Tom. He wasn't in the workshop, though he had been earlier. She checked the outside courtyard. It was empty at this time of day. Perhaps he had been given a task at the theater.

But when she went over to Drury Lane, Tom wasn't there either. This was unusual and began to concern her. It was true that he had no part in the play being presented that evening, but he was nearly always on hand to watch.

She found Jeanne preparing to dance, and they spoke together in French. Teresa discovered that the drive was to Richmond Park, which heightened her suspicions. "There are many beautiful flowers in that place," Jeanne said. "He knows I love flowers. He has brought me bouquets. We shall go early, and I will be back in time to dance. There is no problem." Nonetheless, she looked a little anxious.

"I do not think you should go," Teresa said. Under the current circumstances, it was surely not a good idea.

"I need the money. I am lacking the rent, and this would pay for a whole month." Jeanne looked stubborn. "You said that we should tell you of any invitations, and you would protect us. I have done as you asked."

That was not exactly what she'd promised, but Teresa could see that Jeanne would not be convinced. Very well. She would do her best. Tom would return, and she would enlist his aid.

But the play began, and still there was no sign of Tom. Jeanne was set to meet her escort at nine the next morning. Teresa had no more time. Lord Macklin was lost to her. She would simply have to manage this herself. She was quite good at managing, very proud of her skills. There was no reason to feel forlorn.

She decided to use some of her carefully hoarded funds to hire a carriage for the day, and she knew just the driver to engage. She had ridden with him a number of times and chatted about his family and his ambitions. His hackney, on which he lavished the greatest care, had once been a nobleman's carriage, sold when the peer had a new one built. It still looked polished and could easily be mistaken for a private vehicle.

Her plan made, Teresa went outside before the end of the play. The driver she wanted, Vining, was often to be found near the theater after a performance, on the lookout for those wanting a ride home. She found the man in his customary position and made her arrangements, telling him a good deal of the truth about their mission. Vining was moved by the plight of the dancers and was happy to follow along and make sure Jeanne came safely back. A good fare for a whole day sealed the deal.

After the play, Teresa walked home in the company of two of the actors. She paused at Tom's lodgings on the way and learned that the lad was not there. "He said he'd likely be gone till tomorrow," the landlady told her. "Has an invite from his lordship. Nice for some, to have rich friends."

Teresa couldn't suppress a pang at the thought of them enjoying some sort of expedition that hadn't been mentioned to her. But why should it be? Tom had known the earl long before she met him. They were friends. They had shared many adventures. There was no reason to suspect that Tom also had turned against her. He wouldn't, even if the earl had told the lad her story. Which *he* wouldn't. But the painful possibility that she'd lost Tom as well would intrude.

Telling herself that she had endured far worse, Teresa walked home and spent a restless night fending off loneliness and regrets.

She rose early enough to puzzle Eliza and quickly wrote out a description of what she'd learned and where she'd gone. She addressed the missive to Tom and left it sealed on the mantel shelf. Should it be needed, which she did *not* anticipate, the maid would find it and see that it was delivered.

Vining was waiting for her at the appointed spot, a place where they could watch Jeanne's lodging house without being noticed. Her supposed beau arrived on time in a showy phaeton with a restive team, and the

girl ran out to climb onboard. Jeanne had donned her
finest gown, and it made Teresa sad to see her smile
up at the jaded young aristocrat who didn't even
bother to give her a hand up. He wore a scarf about
his neck and his hat pulled low, Teresa noted, just as
the innkeeper on the Richmond road had described.
"Will we be able to keep pace with him?" she asked
Vining.

"The way that young sprig's handling the ribbons?"
Vining made a contemptuous sound. "He'll not be
rattling along with those tits. Touched in the wind, I
reckon."

Taking this as a criticism of the other's horses,
Teresa nodded.

"We'll keep back so's not to be noticed, but we
won't be losing him."

She pulled her head inside as they started off. She
trusted Vining to know best how to follow another
vehicle through London.

They threaded the city streets and headed west
toward Richmond. Teresa sat back in the carriage
and tried not to compare this journey to her last trip
along this route. She did not succeed. She wondered
how long it would take to forget Lord Macklin. And
knew at once that the answer was—forever. And with
that she lost herself in memories of the time they had
spent together.

The carriage slowed and began to turn. Teresa
roused herself and leaned out. "Where are we going?"
she called up to Vining.

"Our fellow went this way," he answered.

"But we haven't reached Richmond Park." They

had passed the inn where they'd found some answers, she noted.

"No, ma'am. Seems he weren't telling the truth about that."

And why had she expected he would? "Where does this lane go?"

"Into the countryside. I know London, not these parts. I kin follow though." Vining sounded determined.

They moved on over an increasingly rural road. Teresa wasn't certain how many miles they had covered when a tall stone wall appeared on the right. She couldn't see over it. When she asked Vining, he replied that he couldn't see anything from his higher perch either. Trees on the other side obscured the view. "I've lost sight of the phaeton," he said. He urged his horse on, and they speeded up.

The lane splashed through a shallow stream. The ford was bumpy. Teresa gripped a strap as she was jostled about.

"There he is," said Vining. "Turning in at a gate up ahead." He slowed so that they wouldn't arrive too soon, obviously following the other carriage.

A few minutes later, they came abreast of the gate. It was solidly built of wood and gave no glimpse of what lay beyond.

"Was you wishing me to knock?" asked Vining doubtfully.

Teresa thought she had found the answer to the dancers' disappearances. But was there any way to confirm this? Before she could make up her mind what to do, the gate opened just far enough for a huge, heavily muscled man to step out. He carried no weapon, but his closed fists and dark glower were clear threats. "This here's private property," he said. "No visitors."

And yet Jeanne had been taken inside. Clearly, it would *not* be a good idea to ask about her.

"Righto, my lad," said Vining. "Can you tell me if this is the road to Morbury?"

"Never heard of it."

Teresa admired her driver's quick tongue. She sat well back so as not to be seen.

"I reckon I took a wrong turning then," said Vining. "Must have been back at that last crossroad. Y'ed think they might put up signposts."

His cheery manner had no effect on the guard, for the large man could be nothing else. He made a threatening gesture. "Be off with you."

"Yes indeed. Reckon I'll try the other way." There was enough space before the gate for Vining to turn the carriage. He did so with dispatch and slapped the reins on his horse's back. They started back at a smart pace. When they had passed through the stream once more, he spoke. "Begging your pardon, ma'am, but I don't want to be going back there."

"I would not ask you to," said Teresa. "You may take me home now." Perhaps Jeanne would return from her carriage ride, she thought. She could wait and see. But Teresa didn't think she would. She'd found the source of the disappearances, and she needed to breach those walls and do something about it. For that, she had to have help, even if the idea of asking the person most able to give it made her squirm with humiliation.

Vining left Teresa at the end of her street, and she walked from there toward Tom's lodgings, hoping that he'd returned by this time. It seemed that he had. There was a coach at his door, and Lord Macklin stood beside it. This was lucky. She could give them both her news at once, though her spirit quailed at the thought of facing the earl.

He was turned away from her, looking through the carriage window at something inside when she reached him. "I believe I have found our answer," Teresa said.

He started and whirled. He looked as if she was the last thing he had hoped to see. "Oh, er, what?" he said, sounding completely unlike himself. "You've found…what?"

He had never been this awkward. Everything *was* to be different between them then. Teresa's spirits sank. "I've discovered what we were looking for."

Lord Macklin stared at her as if he had no idea what she meant. Did he mean to sever all connection with her? The knowledge cut her to the heart, but she gathered her courage. She would have to persuade him to do this one thing before that.

Tom came out of his lodging house. He was carrying a small vial, which seemed odd. He looked surprised to see her. He and the earl exchanged a look. Lord Macklin quickly shook his head. Had they in fact discussed her history? Had she misjudged Tom's reaction?

She longed to turn and walk away. But she couldn't abandon the young women she'd promised to aid. "I must tell you what I have discovered," she began. "It's—"

"We have an urgent appointment," Lord Macklin interrupted. "Perhaps we could speak tomorrow."

The two stood shoulder to shoulder in front of the carriage door, a phalanx arrayed against her.

"At the workshop perhaps," added the earl. "I will call there."

This was not a hint. He wanted her to go away.

"But we must be off now." He gestured, and Tom ran around and climbed into the other side of the carriage. Lord Macklin edged the carriage door open just enough to slip through, shutting it practically in Teresa's face. The coachman gave Teresa a quick glance, as if he was puzzled, and then the vehicle started off, leaving her alone in the street.

She hadn't quite believed that he would react in this way, Teresa realized, despite everything. And certainly not Tom. The blow was harsher than she'd anticipated. A desolation that she'd thought conquered loomed over her. In the empty street, she fought it off. Why should she mourn a thing she'd never expected to have? She hadn't really believed in a connection with the earl, had she? He was not "gone" because he had never been there in the first place.

And this was beside the point. She had to find a way to use Lord Macklin's vast resources to rescue the dancers, even if he didn't wish to be acquainted with her any longer. Perhaps a letter would do. She could explain what she'd found and assure him she was only seeking a way to get beyond those walls. She wouldn't have to see his face as he decided whether he would be associated with her this one last time. Teresa's breath caught on what was *not* tears. She turned to walk home. To her refuge, her bastion. But the idea was not nearly as comforting as it used to be.

"Shouldn't we have told her?" Tom asked Arthur quietly. He gestured at the Conde de la Cerda, lying on the floor of the carriage trussed up like a Christmas goose.

"There was no time for discussions," Arthur replied. "We can't miss the tide." Which was true. The ship was waiting. They couldn't afford the least delay, and he had no doubt that Señora Alvarez would have had a good deal to say. Not only that, he'd taken great care to keep his coachman from knowing about their captive. Arthur had sent him off on an errand while he and Tom wrestled the Spaniard into the carriage. No, this way was better.

He had everything under control, barely. Just barely. He was sticking to his mad plan and getting it over as soon as possible. "I didn't want to implicate her," he added. "She'd been seen with the *conde*."

"You implicated me," replied Tom with a wry grin.

"And that was bad enough. I wish I had not needed your help to subdue the man." The Spaniard had fought like a cornered rat. He was glaring up at them now with eyes full of fury above the handkerchief gag. Arthur longed to reach the ship Rigby had found for them, set him aboard, and watch it sail away. There was one more unpleasant task to be accomplished, however. He looked down at the vial Tom was holding. "You're sure of the dose?"

"I talked to the apothecary. It's right."

Arthur nodded. Suppressing his distaste, he pressed

the Spaniard's nostrils closed. When the man began to choke, Arthur pulled down the gag. The *conde*'s mouth gaped open as he pulled in a deep breath. Before he could do any more than that, Tom poured the laudanum into him. He swallowed convulsively. Arthur restored the gag on a stream of Spanish curses, vowing he would never do anything like this again. He was having trouble believing that he was doing it now.

They drove on toward the docks. After a bit, their captive's eyelids began to droop. By the time they reached the ship where Rigby was waiting, the Spaniard was snoring.

Arthur distracted his coachman while the fellow was transferred to the vessel. As he handed over the payment, he extracted a further promise from the ship's captain that the *conde* would not be harmed on the voyage. Both the sailor and Rigby seemed annoyed that he would doubt their word on this, and strangely enough, he did not.

⁓

As soon as she entered her house, Teresa realized that she couldn't stay. She was fully primed for action, vibrating with the need to do something. She went over to the theater and found that Jeanne had indeed not returned for the performance. The reproachful gazes of the other dancers were almost too much to bear. She couldn't offer them empty promises, any more than she could answer questions about Tom's continued absence. She departed before the play was half-done.

Back home, she sat down to write her letter to the earl, trying to find words that satisfied in her borrowed language. But writing was more difficult than speaking, and the hour grew late as she didn't find them. Finally, she shoved pen and paper aside. If he did not appear at the workshop tomorrow, she would go to his house. And she would not allow his servants to refuse her entrance. Teresa rose to seek her bed. She spent a restless night.

He did come. Lord Macklin arrived at the workshop with Tom early the next morning. And he came directly over to speak to her. "I have some news for you," he said before she could speak.

Now he wished to speak to her? When he had practically run from her yesterday? The man made no sense. "I have something to tell you," she said. "I have found…"

"May we talk privately?" He indicated the door to the courtyard with a gesture.

"No one is listening," replied Teresa impatiently. There were only a few people in the workshop, and they weren't paying attention. "Yesterday I discovered…"

The earl shook his head and beckoned as he walked toward the courtyard door. Tom shrugged and followed him. Teresa went after them.

The outside space was chilly and empty at the beginning of the day. The spring sun had not risen high enough to warm it. The earl went over to the far side, well out of earshot of the entrance into the workshop. Teresa was on the verge of clutching the lapels of his so very fashionable coat and shaking him until he heard her when he said, "I wanted to inform…to tell you that you need not worry about the Conde de la Cerda any longer."

"What?" Teresa's mind was full of her own news, and the need to plan. For a moment, she simply stared at him.

"He has been…removed from the country."

She shook her head, as if this would restart the gears in her brain.

"He was…put on a ship to the Indies. He will have no means to return."

Was it her mind or her hearing that had gone astray? She looked at Tom. He grinned as if he was proud of himself.

"I realize this is a bit of a surprise," the earl continued.

"Do you think so?"

"A shock," he amended. "You should sit down." He moved as if to help her into one of the courtyard chairs.

Teresa stepped away from him. She did not wish to sit. "*Put* on a ship. And you know this. Did you do it?"

He nodded. So did Tom. Oh so very proud, this smug pair. "For you," added Lord Macklin.

"*For* me. Without saying a word? For example, asking me if I wished it?"

"I wanted to save you…"

"Save?" She was shaken by a storm of anger. That word had been something of a refrain for her former "protector." Along with gratitude, which he thought she should continually feel for his magnanimity in giving her refuge.

"To prevent trouble from coming to you," replied Lord Macklin.

"Because I am incapable of solving my own problems."

"No."

"Like a child, really. With no power of rational judgment." The grandee had said that about her too. Time and again.

"Not at all. You are putting words in my mouth." The earl was beginning to sound annoyed. Tom looked uneasy.

Teresa felt a savage satisfaction at that. "You throw a man onto a ship."

"It was a better plan than shooting the fellow," the earl interrupted. "That sort of thing gets you sent to the gallows."

"Shooting? You were going to shoot him?"

"Not I!"

"Who then? Tom?"

The latter made warding-off gestures.

"Rigby told us you asked him to get you a pistol," said the earl sternly.

"Is no man on Earth to be trusted to keep his mouth shut?" Teresa exclaimed.

"He simply mentioned it when we were…"

"Agreeing with each other what was to be done! Of course he did. All the men planning, in their gracious arrogance, how to *save* me." When Teresa saw Tom flinch, she realized that she'd shouted. She clenched her teeth and paced across the courtyard and back, regaining control of her temper. "I was not going to shoot him," she said more quietly. "I am not a fool.

I thought it might be necessary to threaten him." Or satisfying, at the least.

"That would not have gone well," Lord Macklin replied. "When you start waving pistols about, some-one usually is shot."

"I was not going to 'wave' it about. And I am quite able to use a pistol." She wished she had her pistol now. She would show him she could hit a pip in a playing card from ten paces.

"Even the most skilled…"

"Oh, do be quiet."

He looked startled.

As her emotions caught up with events, Teresa silently admitted it was a relief to know that Alessandro Peron was far away. She wasn't yet ready to say that to the earl, however. "Is this why you acted so strangely yesterday?" She turned on Tom. "Is this where you have been? Everyone at the theater was wondering." The lad backed up a step.

"We had him tied up in the coach," said Lord Macklin. "And I didn't want…"

"In your carriage? In a public street? Right there where I was standing!"

"Yes. And I didn't want my coachman to find out. The fewer people who know anything about this, the better."

"As you have learned from your extensive experience of spiriting people out of the country against their will."

"More a matter of common sense."

She gazed up at him. Something was clogging her throat. Amazement? Laughter? "Are you really so calm about this deed?"

"I spring from a long line of ruthless marauders, you know. Came over with William the Conqueror to grab whatever they could, and continued to do so for quite some time."

"Ruthless." Teresa no longer felt like laughing.

"A joke. Actually I found it…unsettling." The earl looked at her. "I was promised the *conde* would not be injured on the voyage. And I believed the man who gave his word on that." He held her gaze. "There are many…opportunities for a clever man in the Indies. I think this will occupy the *conde* for quite a time."

He was probably right. Alessandro Peron would find it easier to impersonate a grandee there than in London. He would most likely prosper and remain. Her relief became a more settled thing.

"So that he won't come back," Lord Macklin added, as if she might not have understood.

"Yes, I see that." Only then did Teresa realize that the earl's absence and his behavior yesterday had been due to this—admittedly unrequested—service he had done her. He had not been avoiding her because of her history. In fact, he had been moved to help. But where did this leave them? "So," she said.

"So," he said at the same moment.

Teresa felt as if her confidences came to hover in the space between them. Things were *not* the same.

"That's that then," the earl said.

Tom nodded.

What was what?

Lord Macklin cleared his throat. "Did you say there was something you wished to tell us?"

"Ah, we are going to be English," Teresa said.

"Eh?"

What else could he be, after all? Any more than she could help what life had made of her? He had been raised to be *estoico*. And did she not love him for what he was—upright, steadfast, kind? And so they would not speak of what lay between them. Not now, at any rate. Later, then they would see. "I believe I know where the missing dancers have been taken," she said.

This drew a gratifying reaction from both her companions, which only grew as she told them her tale.

"You could find this place again?" Lord Macklin asked when she was done.

"Of course."

"We gotta go after them," said Tom, looking as if he was ready to race away immediately.

The earl nodded. "Indeed. We must make a plan to get in and discover what is inside that house."

"*We*," repeated Teresa with emphasis.

"The three of us and others," Lord Macklin answered. "We will require help and unfortunately some little time."

Teresa was as eager as Tom to move. She hated thinking of what might be happening to the dancers. But she knew he was right.

"We should get hold of that dismal scut who took Jeanne there," said Tom.

"Yes." The earl looked grim. "I will undertake that task. What is his name?"

"He didn't give it at the theater," Teresa replied. "He told Jeanne just to call him John."

"Not his name then," said Tom.

"No." The earl's expression didn't bode well

for the man. "But he must have been there before. Perhaps he let something drop."

"I will ask the other dancers and send word to you," said Teresa. Now that she had a specific target, she was certain she could learn more.

"I'll scout out that house in the country," added Tom. "See what's what."

"You shouldn't go there alone. It is too dangerous." Teresa would not see Tom hurt as well.

"I know how to do it," the lad replied.

"He does, actually," said Lord Macklin before Teresa could argue. "He's proved that before."

"I kin be a right sneak," said Tom with a shadow of his old grin. "And I'm good at not being noticed."

"You will be careful," replied Teresa. It was not a question.

Tom put his hand on his heart and bowed.

"I will speak to Mr. Rigby," she went on. When the others looked inquiring, she added, "The man at the gate looked like someone he might know."

"Good thought," said Tom.

All this was agreed. And then it was time for the earl to go. He took his leave with his customary courtesy and no sign of any change in his opinion of her.

"Thank you," said Teresa. She offered her hand.

He brought it to his lips, and the look he gave her then shook her to the depths of her being.

Eleven

ARTHUR WALKED WITH TOM UP TO THE DOOR OF Señora Alvarez's house, all his senses sharp with anticipation. It had been only two days since he'd seen her, but it seemed much longer. This was what he'd come to; the hours felt empty if she was not near. And now he would see her home, the place she had made for herself. It felt like a privilege.

They knocked and were admitted by their hostess. As he took off his hat and gloves, Arthur absorbed the feel of the single large room. Clearly there had not been much money to spend on it, but the place had a simple elegance that did not surprise him in the least.

"I have sent my maid to visit her family," said the señora. "I did not wish her to be involved."

"Eliza'd probably like to be," replied Tom. "She took a real pleasure in cozening Dilch."

"She did, but this matter is more serious, and she is a young woman. Like those who were taken."

"Right. Probably for the best, because there's something going on in that house you found that they don't want nobody to see."

Señora Alvarez led them to seats. "Tell us," she said.

"I found the place just where you said," Tom continued with a nod to her. "And I went sneaking around the walls in the dark." He grimaced. "They're closed up tight as a drum. Not so high you can't climb 'em, mind. But whoever lives there has dogs. Meanest looking dogs I've ever seen. They were onto me soon as I put a leg over the top of that wall. I had to jump and run."

"You promised to be careful!" exclaimed the señora.

"I was. Nobody saw me."

"They might have chased after you. You can't outrun dogs."

Tom shook his head. "They stay behind the walls. I asked at the nearest villages the next day. Just like I was wanting work, you know. Offering to lend a hand with deliveries and such, so's I could get a look inside that way. But the grocer told me they unload everything at the back gate and carry it onward theirselves. It's made the neighborhood right curious about 'em."

"So it's not going to be easy to get in," said Arthur.

"We have to find a way past the guards *and* the dogs," Tom replied.

"Mr. Rigby made some inquiries," said Señora Alvarez. "He has heard of men, from among the sort of people he knows, hired for a job in the country. Men with few scruples, he said."

"Rigby said 'scruples'?" Tom asked, raising his eyebrows.

It didn't sound like the pub keeper, Arthur thought.

"Well, no," said their hostess with a slight smile. "But his meaning was clear."

"Not men you want to cross," said Tom.

She nodded. "And according to what Mr. Rigby heard, the pay is very good."

"Some'll do just about anything for money. Whatever they're ordered."

"Those who care only for money can be...repurchased," Arthur pointed out.

"That's so." Tom looked more cheerful.

"I have put a name to the man you followed," said Arthur to Señora Alvarez. "The clues you gathered from the other dancers and the redoubled efforts of Tom's friends led me to a young sprig called Lord Simon Farange."

"Bella sneaked a look at him after you sent me word," Tom put in. "He's the one took Jeanne out driving."

Arthur nodded; he had already heard this. "He is the third son of the Duke of Yarbridge," he continued. "I am acquainted with his father. A harsh man. Perhaps because the family is in decline. They have lost most of their lands to gambling and poor management. Lord Simon is not prominent in society. He receives few invitations because his behavior cannot be...relied upon."

"And because he doesn't have a fortune to make all smooth," said Señora Alvarez.

"Indeed," Arthur acknowledged. "He is renowned for his ill temper and dissipation. Many wonder how he can afford his current indulgences. It is assumed that he is heavily in debt."

"Ripe for mischief then," said Tom.

"In many different ways." Arthur pressed his lips together in distaste. "I tracked him down at a gaming hell last night. He was well into his cups and quite surprised to be addressed by me. I doubt he will remember much of our conversation, which I found most unpleasant."

"Did you ask him about that house?" Tom wondered.

"I couldn't trust he was *that* drunk," Arthur replied. "Our exchange was more general, an effort to feel him out. I judge Lord Simon to be utterly self-centered. He cares nothing for others, and he treats those below him on the social scale as scarcely human. Opera dancers are no more than playthings for men like him. He feels that he has the right to do whatever he pleases with them or indeed anyone he can gain power over."

"I am familiar with the type," the señora said.

Arthur could hear the disgust in her voice. "Fortunately, I did not find him very intelligent," he added.

Tom gave a snort of laughter.

"I don't think he will be any use to us," Arthur went on. "Any overtures from me would bewilder him and rouse suspicions even in his thick head. I am of his father's generation, and they are bitterly at odds."

"Don't sound like he would think much of me neither," said Tom.

"He has all a weak man's contempt for the 'lower orders.'"

"The venomed varlet," said the lad. He frowned.

"If one of the other opera dancers was willing to make up to him…"

"No!" Señora Alvarez sounded adamant. "Enough of them have suffered already. We will not bring any more into this."

Arthur understood her reluctance.

Tom nodded. "No, you're right. That ain't fair. Can't we just gather a gang and storm that place? My friends would come along. Mr. Rigby too, mebbe. And he'd know others. Good fighters."

Teresa shook her head. She'd hinted at something like this when she talked to the pub keeper. "He won't. Join in or try to recruit anyone to do so. He is very wary of breaking the law."

"I suppose he has reason," said Lord Macklin. "I couldn't ask my servants or employees to take part in that sort of direct assault either. People might be hurt. And attacking a private residence without any proof of crimes would land us all in trouble."

"But if we was to find the crimes when we got inside…" Tom began.

"Against opera dancers," said Teresa. Anger and despair coursed through her. "No one cares about them, as this Lord Simon person showed. Owners of great walled estates bribe and persuade their way around the law when no one else of their class is involved."

Silence greeted her outburst. Tom started to speak, and then did not.

A thought came to Teresa. It filled her with fear so strong that her hands began to shake. Nonetheless, she voiced it. "A woman might be able to get inside."

"No," said Lord Macklin.

"They take women there," she continued.

"No," said Lord Macklin again.

"And once in, she could find a way to admit others."

"Absolutely not," said the earl. "I forbid it!" He looked as if he knew he couldn't, really, and that the knowledge enraged him.

"There's them dogs," said Tom.

"They might be given sleeping powders," Teresa went on, speaking quickly before she could think too much. "And perhaps some of the people could be also."

"How, precisely, would you go about giving a fierce guard dog a sleeping powder?" asked Lord Macklin in a harsh, clipped tone.

"Put it in some meat?"

"Because you would be moving freely around this sinister place, and no one would notice you interfering with the creatures' food?"

Teresa understood that his sarcasm came from concern, but it was difficult to hear nonetheless.

"The idea is ridiculous," he added. "Impossible."

It was much worse than that. He could not know how it terrified her—the idea of going back into captivity.

Or perhaps he did. His eyes were full of sympathy. "You cannot do this," he said.

She looked away from that compassionate gaze before it could overset her. "What do you propose then? That we simply let this—whatever it is—go on?"

"Now that we have identified Lord Simon, we can warn the dancers to have nothing to do with him."

"And the ones who are already gone?" Teresa felt a moment of hope. Lord Macklin sounded so authoritative. Might he have some other solution? But the earl said nothing. "We leave them to their fate?"

"We don't know what they are…" But he couldn't complete the sentence. They all knew the four dancers had not been spirited away for benign purposes.

All her history rose up and beat at her. *She* had been oppressed. No one had cared, still less tried to help her. She could not turn away, no matter how strong the fear. Her hands were shaking harder than ever. "I will not abandon them."

"I won't let you go—" began Lord Macklin.

"It is not your decision," she interrupted.

"Alone," he added. "I won't let you go alone."

This silenced Teresa. She stared at him.

"I will take you there," he continued.

"Take me?"

"As Lord Simon did Jeanne. I will drive up to the gate with you at my side…"

"And simply demand admission?" Teresa asked.

"I will assume a right to it," said the earl. "The thought that I could be refused will not enter my mind. Or anyone else's. I can play the arrogant ass if I have to."

"Oh, really?"

The earl gave her a slight smile. "I can also slip the guard a hefty bribe if necessary. Between the two things, I *will* get in."

"We will," she answered. His expression showed

how little he liked that idea. "You might be recognized," she added.

"Not by the sort of ruffian hired to man a gate."

"Inside though."

"We will deal with that if we must. But if you try to go alone, I will prevent you."

"How? Shut me away yourself?" She knew he wouldn't, but his insistence was rousing more bad memories.

"I will camp on your doorstep and follow you everywhere you go. Like a faithful dog."

The picture was so silly she had to smile. "You have other things to do with your days."

"Nothing more important."

In her secret heart, Teresa had to admit that having him at her side would make all the difference.

Tom, who had been looking back and forth like an observer of a tennis match, said, "You ain...aren't leaving me out of this."

"On the contrary," said Lord Macklin. "But since it seems this is not the sort of place you can enter, despite your skills, you will remain outside watching. We will need someone who knows where we are and can bring aid if necessary."

"I don't want to stand about doing nothing!"

"This is far from nothing. If things...go wrong, all our reliance will be on you."

"You will rescue us," said Teresa.

This seemed to mollify the lad. "So I'll be waiting for a signal, like?"

"Precisely," replied the earl.

Tom considered, frowning. "There's a clump of

trees not too far from one of the side walls. Room for me and my friends to lurk."

"That is what you will do then. Lurk."

"What'll the signal be?"

"You will know it when you see it," declared Lord Macklin.

"Meaning you have no idea?" Tom replied. "I don't like that."

"I don't know what we will find inside that place. Or how we might reach you."

This silenced them all for some moments. Then they gathered their resolve and carried on.

The rest of that day was spent making plans. Teresa's eagerness to move vied with a sick dread. She wondered if she would actually have done this without the earl's aid. In truth, she didn't see how.

With all their arrangements put in place, they set off the following morning in Lord Macklin's curricle with no groom up behind them. Ironically, it was a lovely warm day, with the country on either side of the road full of flowers and birdsong.

Teresa fingered the gun in a deep pocket of her gown. She had created the hiding place with needle and thread overnight. "I still think it was a mistake not to bring your pistols," she said to the earl.

"I don't have to reload a sword stick," he replied.

They followed the route Teresa had taken before. Her unease grew the closer they came to the place. Just before they reached the wall around the isolated house, they passed a small copse off to the right. She knew that Tom and some of his apprentice friends had sneaked into those trees in the darkness last night. She saw no sign of them, which was good. She turned to look at Lord Macklin's handsome profile. "Are you sorry to be doing this mad thing?" she asked him.

"I have done very few mad things in my life." He paused. "Aside from the recent matter of the *conde*, none at all, I think."

She had brought this disruption to him. Teresa didn't like the notion. "A life without mad things to do sounds very peaceful."

"I suppose it has been mostly that. But a thing that is not mad is also not necessarily pleasant. Perhaps it was time for something different."

They began to drive along the wall around the house. Teresa's discomfort rose.

And then they were at the entrance, and the curricle was slowing. The gate was a little open, and a different guard lounged beside it, she was glad to see. She was fairly certain the previous one had not glimpsed her, but she was glad not to take that chance.

The earl turned the carriage and drew to a stop. "Open up," he said to the rough-looking man.

"No one's allowed in," was the reply.

"Nonsense. Lord Simon was here just a few days ago."

"Ye're a friend of his lordship?"

"Would I be here otherwise?"

His tone was careless, arrogant, cold, everything Teresa hated about powerful men.

The guard peered up at him. "His lordship's to send word beforehand. Them's the rules."

Lord Macklin's whip stirred as if he might strike the guard with it. "Rules," he answered, as if the word was completely unfamiliar to him. "You forget yourself. If you have made some mistake, it is not my problem."

He sounded so like her old patron, as if he might actually be a man who always got his way and crushed anyone who opposed it. Teresa swayed a little in her seat.

"Rules is rules," said the guard. "That's what I was told, and I ain't going to lose a place pays as good this one."

"You will certainly do so when I complain of your behavior," replied Lord Macklin, his voice icy with contempt. "And worse than that."

This was the way of the world, Teresa thought. The men at the top cut down those who dared challenge them. There was no recourse.

"Yer honor's got to understand…"

"I understand that you are in my way. And that Lord Simon will be very angry when he hears I've been stopped." The whip twitched. At the same time gold flashed in the air between them. It was a sovereign, Teresa thought, a treasure for such a man. The guard snatched the coin out of the air. He hesitated for one more moment, then went to the gate. "Ye'll tell 'em, up at the house that Lord Simon sent you."

"Certainly."

The gate swung open. Looking back, Teresa saw the man biting the coin to make sure it was real gold. "I suppose he'll get into trouble," she said.

"If we are successful, there will be little trouble left over for him. I expect he'll take to his heels at the first sign."

He sounded tense. Teresa didn't blame him. She was even more so.

The gate closed behind them. Four large dogs appeared, two on either side of the gravel drive they drove along. The animals didn't bark or offer to attack. They simply flanked the curricle in silent menace. They had black coats and sharp, gleaming teeth.

The drive passed through a band of trees. They couldn't see anything until they rounded a curve and came upon a sizable house built of stone. It looked deceptively normal under the sunny sky. There were flowers in ornamental beds.

"The upper windows are barred," said Lord Macklin.

Teresa's blood chilled.

He drove on. A tall wrought-iron fence surrounded the house, its gate closed. Inside it, a graveled area surrounded the building.

The dogs stopped along the spiked fence, sitting on their haunches and watching them, but not moving closer. Arthur pointed this out to the señora. "We can hope they don't venture in there."

"Yes," she said. She looked very pale.

He handed her the reins. "Just hold them steady. They will not bolt."

"Where are you going?" Her voice rose near a wail.

"To open the gate. As we are not expected."

"But the dogs!"

"I trust they know their territory. Or the rules, as the guard put it." Hiding his own unease, Arthur climbed down from the curricle. The dogs stood up, their eyes following his every move, but they did not run at him. He unlatched the gate and pushed it open. There was no lock. Grasping the bridles of his leaders, he led them through the fence. With measured steps he went back to close the gate.

"*Gracias a Dios,*" said the señora.

"Indeed." Arthur returned to his seat and took the reins again. He pulled up before the front door. No groom appeared to take the carriage. It seemed they had not yet been noticed.

"Should I go and knock?" asked Señora Alvarez.

Her voice did not tremble, but Arthur could see the effort she was making to control it. "Let us wait a moment," he answered.

They waited several, and then the door opened and a woman emerged. She was finely dressed, but her square face showed the bitter lines of a hard life. Her hair was gray, her frame stocky. Arthur guessed she was around sixty. "What the devil do you mean by keeping me waiting?" he said before she could speak.

"We had no word…"

"Have you no one to care for my horses?" The key was to keep these people off-balance, goaded to obey by the voice of command. Arthur had heard such arrogance from others. "I do not see why Lord Simon spoke well of this place," he added.

"His lordship never said anyone was…"

"What has that to say to anything?"

"Everything's to be by appointment."

"And I have one."

"I never heard…"

"I could not be less interested in what you have or have not heard." Arthur debated whether to climb down from the curricle. His team was well trained and would stand. No, better to loom over this woman from above. He twitched his whip. "Do you intend to keep me waiting here?" He thought he managed threatening incredulity rather well.

After a brief inner debate, visible on her seamed face, the woman bobbed a perfunctory curtsy. She turned to the open door. "Fetch Joe," she called to someone unseen.

A groom appeared a few minutes later and took charge of the vehicle. Arthur watched where it was taken, hoping that he would soon be retrieving it and leaving this place. Then he put a hand on the señora's back to guide her. Though it wasn't noticeable at any distance, she was shaking.

They walked together into a spacious entry hall. A curving staircase rose at the back. Their—Arthur supposed she must be seen as—hostess looked Señora Alvarez up and down like a stockman evaluating cattle. Her attitude confirmed Arthur's opinion of her, and of the nature of this house. She'd certainly been a procuress of some sort. "She's a bit old," the creature said. "We have fresher meat than her in here."

"I brought her for my own reasons," Arthur replied. "No one else is to touch her."

The woman's answering grin was mocking.

"We require privacy."

The grin became a leer. "Oh yes, sir, we can give you all the privacy in the world. That's our spec-ee-ality, it is. Always supposing you've brought the fee."

"Naturally."

She held out her hand like a confident beggar.

"How much?"

Her eyes hardened with suspicion. "Lord Simon would've told you that."

"He was drunk. As he so often is. And he mumbles when he's drunk. And I am not accustomed to being kept standing."

Muttering something disparaging about toffs, the woman named a number that startled Arthur. Knowing it was probably inflated, and not caring, he opened his purse and paid her. He'd made sure to bring plenty of cash. She closed her hand over the bills and gestured. "Upstairs," she said.

They followed her to an upper hall. She threw open a door and waved them into a large luxurious bedchamber with a canopied bed.

"I was assured we would not be disturbed," said Arthur. "For any reason."

"Not until you ring," the woman replied. "That's what we do here. Nobody hears nothing. Nobody says nothing. And we can take care of things, after."

Arthur was more and more appalled with each thing he learned about this place. "I require the key to this room."

"I told you, nobody'll be botherin'…"

He silenced her with a look borrowed from his patrician grandfather in his later years and held out his hand.

Grumbling, the woman turned away. They stood in silence until she returned with the key. Then Arthur closed the door in her face and locked it. "I didn't want to discover later that they'd locked us in," he said quietly to Señora Alvarez.

"This is a bawdy house, isn't it?" she replied.

He nodded. "A very private one, apparently."

"Because here men can do whatever they like to women, and no one comes to inquire. Or cares."

"Seemingly."

She spat out a word Arthur had never heard from a lady. Her dark eyes glittered with fury, and he thought that she had a hand on the pistol in her pocket. He couldn't blame her. "We will wait a few minutes to let that creature go about her business and then search for the dancers," he said.

"I fear what we will find."

He could only agree with her.

They waited in silence. There was nothing to say; they were here to act. "That should be sufficient," Arthur said. "Will you stay here and lock the door behind me?"

"No!" Señora Alvarez gave him an impatient look. "The girls know me. They will be afraid of any man in this place. Why would they come with you?"

"Ah." He had been thinking of keeping her safe. Which was not possible. "Of course." He unlocked the door and looked into the corridor. It was empty.

They stepped out. Arthur relocked the door. "You don't think she has another key?" asked the señora.

"She may. We can only trust that she meant what she said about not returning until summoned."

"You would trust such a person?"

He shrugged. "We had best hurry."

There were several other bedchambers like the one they had been given along the hall that ran through the center of the house. They were all empty, for which

Arthur gave silent thanks. The place was eerily quiet. He was used to a household where people bustled about completing various tasks at this time of day.

They took the stairs up to the next floor. The corridor was narrower here, and the rooms smaller. Servants' quarters, Arthur thought. A glance into the first two chambers confirmed this. They were much more plainly furnished than those below.

The next door was locked, as were the five following. They heard weeping from behind the last, which stopped abruptly when Arthur tried the doorknob. He pictured a girl cowering behind the panels, praying that they did not open. He couldn't remember when he'd been so angry.

Señora Alvarez knelt and put her lips to the keyhole of the last door. "Odile?" she murmured. "Sonia? Maria? Jeanne? *Êtes-vous là?*"

"*Qui est-ce?*" came the reply.

"Shh. *Parlez trés doucement.*"

There was a stir beyond the door. Someone inside came closer. The señora conversed with her very quietly in French.

As she did, Arthur tried the key he had in one of the locks. It didn't work. He hadn't really thought it would.

After a bit, the señora came to stand beside him. "All of the dancers are here," she murmured. "As well as two other girls. They have had little chance to speak to each other. These…monsters keep them alone and afraid. Some of them are hurt as well."

Arthur's fury was mirrored in her dark eyes. "Breaking down the doors would bring them down on us," he said. "We must find the keys."

"They bring food two times each day," she replied. "We could wait and take the keys from that person."

"That could be hours. I don't want to spend so much time here. And it could be more than one person."

"We must do something!"

"I have an idea," Arthur said.

"What?"

"It is an unpleasant one," he added.

"Nothing could be worse than this!" She gestured at their surroundings.

"I could ring, from the room we were given, and ask for another girl. To…join us. I could insist upon choosing her myself."

The señora grimaced. "I suppose they would do that."

"Particularly if I offer more money."

"And then we overpower the woman and take her keys."

He nodded.

"Very well." Before they left, she whispered at all the locked doorways, addressing each dancer in her native language. The two strangers were English, wary but wild for escape.

When Arthur unlocked the door on the floor below, they found the bedchamber as they had left it. "We must set the scene," he said.

"And be certain of our plan," she replied.

A few minutes later, Arthur pulled the bell rope. When the "hostess" arrived in response he made his request, with another payment ready to tempt her. There was no difficulty. She left briefly and returned with a ring of keys to lead Lord Macklin upstairs.

Teresa waited until the sound of their footsteps had died away before slipping from the room and following. The corridor was empty. The stairway was empty. She lingered behind the door at the top, cradling the heavy vase she carried. The flowers it had held lay on the washstand in the room below. She could hear the woman speaking to the earl, but not what she said. "That one might do," said Lord Macklin in a loud voice.

This was the signal they had agreed on. Teresa surged forward. The earl stood beside an open door. He had maneuvered his companion so that her back was to the stairwell. Teresa ran forward and hit the woman on the head with the vase as hard as she could.

She fell in a heap, hitting the floor with a loud thump.

They waited, poised and tense. There was no reaction from below.

"*Espero que la hayas matado!*" said a voice from inside the room.

"*Tranquila!*" replied Teresa. At Macklin's inquiring look, she added, "Sonia hopes I have killed her." Did she care if she had? She supposed she didn't wish to kill any person, but this woman had surely deserved a knock on the head.

"Unlock the others while I bind her," said the earl. He took the ring of keys from the woman's inert hand and gave them to Teresa, then took out his pocketknife and began rapidly cutting the coverlet from the narrow bed into strips.

Teresa went from door to door, freeing the girls. The opera dancers greeted her with soft cries of gladness. The two strangers were wary at first and then grateful. Teresa would have felt triumphant, had not all of the girls showed signs of violent usage.

She asked the names of the two girls she did not know—Jill and Poppy—and then introduced all the girls to each other. "We must work together as we go." Teresa stepped back into the bedchamber, where the earl now had the hostess securely bound. She uncurled the woman's fingers, took the money Macklin had just given her, and distributed it equally among the former captives, knowing this would be a comfort and reassurance. A babble of thanks rose. "We must stay very quiet," she reminded them.

Lord Macklin emerged. "I will go and call for my curricle," he said.

"Won't they ask about *her*?" Teresa gestured at the bedchamber where the woman lay.

He assumed a haughty expression. "What has she to do with me? I am profoundly uninterested in their opinions."

"You do that manner all too well," said Teresa. She rather wished he did not.

"I have heard it often enough in my life," he replied.

"We will not all fit in your curricle."

"We couldn't think of a way around that problem," the earl reminded her. "I could not drive a coach myself."

He hadn't wanted to bring his coachman here, Teresa knew. He was careful about those who were dependent on him. It was one of the things she most admired about him.

"I will see what vehicles they have in their stables," he added. "Can you drive?"

"Well enough," answered Teresa. She had only twice handled the ribbons of a carriage, but she would do what she had to do.

"Then we will steal one," he replied.

"Yer a right one," said Poppy. She showed bruises on her face and down her arms that hurt Teresa's heart, but her blue eyes gleamed with defiance. "I know horses," she added. "I'll help ye."

A moan came from the bedchamber. Lord Macklin went to stand over their captive. The rest of them crowded into the doorway. He pulled down the strip of cloth he'd tied over her mouth. "How many people work in this house?" he asked when she blinked back to consciousness.

She glared at him, Teresa, and the huddle of girls. "Ye'll rue the day…" she began.

"I shall rue nothing," Lord Macklin interrupted. "This house will soon be receiving a visit from the local magistrate and his men, which I doubt you will enjoy. It might go easier if you answer my questions. How many people work in this house?"

She writhed in her bonds, but they were secure.

"Let me hit her," said Poppy. "I'll make her tell ye."

"*Moi aussi*," said Jeanne. All the girls but Odile crowded forward as if they would be happy to join in. Fists were raised.

"Three," said the woman. "Two maids and a cook. They stays in the kitchen unless I call for them."

"*Las criadas son muy grandes y crueles*," said Sonia.

"The maids are large and cruel," Teresa translated. The girls nodded.

"They get their licks in whenever they can," said Jill, pointing to red finger marks at her wrist.

"What about the gate guards?" the earl asked the proprietress.

"There's two of them," she responded sullenly. "One on and one off. They live in the stable with Joe."

"So they do not come into the house?"

"Not unless I need 'em for sommat and call 'em in special. Can't trust 'em with the girls."

"Who manages the dogs?"

"Them dogs'll tear you apart," she snarled. "And I'll laugh to see it."

"Who is in charge of them?" the earl repeated. When the woman didn't speak at once, Poppy rushed forward and pinched her upper arm.

"Oww!"

"You don't like how it feels?" Poppy asked. "Fancy that!" There was an angry murmur from the former captives.

"Joe feeds them," said the woman quickly.

"Joe would be the groom?"

He received an affirmative grunt in reply. "Ye'll never get away from here," she added.

Lord Macklin replaced the gag. He rechecked the bindings before leaving her on the narrow bed. Teresa locked her in. "We should secure the doors that were locked as well," he said. "In case anyone does come to check."

Teresa did so.

"You will all wait here," he began then.

But this drew a chorus of protest that made Teresa's heart leap with apprehension. "Quiet," she hissed.

They obeyed, but none of the girls would agree to stay in the house. Freed from their prisons, they wanted to run. Nothing else would do.

"We are trying to get away," Teresa told them softly.

"You didn't have no plan how to get out?" asked Poppy.

"If you don't like it, then you can stay behind, *puta!*" said Sonia.

"We will bring everyone," said Teresa, glad Poppy knew no Spanish. "It was difficult to make a plan when we knew nothing of this place."

"A moment," said the earl. He disappeared into one of the rear bedchambers down the hall. After a short time, he came back. "All right, the stables are within the inner fence," he said. "Away from the dogs. A fortunate thing for us. We will all go out there together. The garden is overgrown. There is a row of yews we can use as concealment."

"This 'concealment' is what, please?" asked Jeanne.

"Something to hide us from the house," replied Teresa. She turned to the earl. "We should find one guard, possibly sleeping, and the groom Joe in the stable."

"Yes."

"Unless that creature lied to us."

"She named all the people I've seen," said Poppy. "I watch…watched out the window."

Lord Macklin nodded. "Let us go. Carefully and quietly."

Leading them down the first flight of stairs, Arthur winced at the noise they made. No one was talking. All were trying to be quiet. But eight people simply could not move silently.

The corridor on the next floor remained empty. Arthur pointed at the door of the chamber they had been given originally, and Señora Alvarez nodded. They had agreed that she would leave it locked to throw off pursuit.

He didn't bother to look for a back stair. It would likely end near the kitchen, which they had to avoid. He would have to find another way to the rear of the house.

They edged down the stairway to the entry hall, also empty, and into a reception room on the right. This opened into a second large chamber behind and then another, smaller parlor, which had two windows looking out to the back.

There was a low fire burning here and signs of occupancy. Possibly it was the proprietress's sitting room. Arthur crossed to the rear and tried one of the windows. It opened without difficulty. The ground was not far off. He mimed climbing out and extended a hand. One of the opera dancers took it, and he helped her over the sill. He gestured for her to crouch down beside a shrub border, and she did so. Another followed her out, and another.

All was going smoothly until the girl called Poppy darted over and pushed aside the fire screen. Moving with startling speed, she raked the coals of the fire out onto the carpet, then threw a pile of papers from the writing desk over them. As flames licked up, she added the contents of the woodbin. She kicked glowing embers under the draperies of the other window. Fringe at the bottom caught fire, and more flames licked up toward the old, dry wood paneling. "That'll keep 'em busy," Poppy murmured with vindictive pleasure.

It was all over before Arthur could protest, so he didn't bother. He handed Señora Alvarez over the sill, signaled for Poppy to follow, and slipped out himself, closing the window behind them. Perhaps the fire would be an effective diversion, and not a pointer to their escape.

The señora, whose courage and resourcefulness seemed boundless, had spotted the row of yews that marched toward the wrought-iron fence at the back. She pointed to it, and he nodded. Crouching low, the group ran into its shadow.

The gardens were as oddly untenanted as the house. Certainly they looked as if no gardener had tended them for years. They moved quickly down the row of yews, keeping close to the drooping branches. Arthur didn't think they could be visible from the lower regions of the house, and indeed there was no outcry.

When the trees ended, they were not far from the stables. But a graveled yard stretched between them and the building. Arthur could see his curricle drawn up at the far side. Anyone walking across to it would be exposed. There was no choice from here.

He managed to convince his charges to wait in the shelter of the last yew tree. They were less anxious now that they were outside. Then he strode across the yard, the crunch of his boots on the gravel seeming very loud.

There was a back gate in the wrought-iron fence, he noted. Was it best to use that and not drive around to the front? It might be locked, however, and he didn't know where the lane that ran away from it led. It would have to be the front. He stopped beside his curricle. "Hello," he called.

After a moment, the groom who had taken charge of his vehicle appeared in the stable doorway.

"Joe, isn't it? Bring my team. I am leaving."

The young man looked startled. Presumably he wasn't accustomed to seeing visitors back here. But he touched the brim of his flat cap and said, "Yessir."

Arthur followed him into the stable, surprising him again. His horses were in loose boxes. Joe went to lead them out.

There was a narrow wooden stair in the back corner that surely led to rooms above. The off-duty guard would be there, Arthur concluded. He hoped the man was deeply asleep.

There were four horses in the stable other than his own. Two were clearly for riding, and two were carthorses to pull the rustic wagon that sat near the wide door. As the only choice, the wagon would have to do.

Arthur walked with Joe as he led the team out to the curricle and began to harness them. The groom looked anxious. Arthur decided to push a little. "Quite an establishment Lord Simon has here," he said.

Joe's sidelong look and twitching shrug suggested that he wasn't comfortable with the comment.

"Do you like working here?" Arthur asked him. He put a tinge of contempt in his tone.

The younger man did not look at him. "I just takes care of the horses. That's all."

"But you know what goes on inside?"

The groom finished fastening the traces. "That's nothing to do with me!"

He was so vehement that Arthur decided to take a chance. "Girls are beaten and misused in that house."

Horror flitted over Joe's face. He hunched and hurried his work on the bridles and straps.

"And since you work here, you are partly to blame for that."

"No, I ain't!"

"Perhaps you have even heard their cries," Arthur added. "And never lifted a finger."

Joe's hands dropped from the harness. He glanced fearfully up at a small window in the upper part of the stable.

Arthur noted it. That must be the guard's quarters. The frame was empty.

"I hate it here," Joe murmured to the earth at his feet. "But Harkon'll beat me within an inch of my life if I open my trap. And they said if I leave they'll hunt me down and make sure I can't squawk. I think they'd kill me. Harkon said as how he knifed a fella once."

"If you help me, I will see that they cannot harm you."

Joe finally looked up. He examined Arthur as if evaluating his power to keep his promise. "Help you how?" he asked finally.

"I am taking the girls away from here. All of them."

"Not in one curricle, you ain't. Even hanging off the sides. And the dogs wouldn't stand for that anyhow."

"Precisely. You will drive them in that cart I saw within."

The young groom looked terrified. "Harkon won't let us do that."

"I will ensure that he does."

"Begging your pardon, sir, but I don't see how. Once he sees the girls…"

"We will cover them with hay."

He took a little more convincing. But Joe really did want to leave the place, and Arthur was persuasive. At last the groom agreed.

When he'd finished harnessing Arthur's team, they went back into the stables and quickly and quietly hooked up the cart horses and half filled the farm wagon with loose hay. All the while, the passage of time beat in Arthur's veins.

"Follow my curricle over to those yews," he said to Joe when they were ready. "Stop just at the end." At the groom's nod, he climbed into his vehicle and drove it to the spot where he'd left the others huddled by the trees.

The wagon came up behind him. "Señora Alvarez will ride with me," said Arthur quietly to the group of women. "As when we arrived. The rest of you slip into the cart as fast as you can and cover yourselves with hay. Joe will drive it out."

There were uneasy murmurs and doubtful looks, but no arguments. All of them could see that this was the only choice. Arthur held out his hand, and Señora Alvarez climbed up beside him. Poppy was the first to slip into the cart and burrow into the hay.

Most of the girls were in when a hulking man came

striding out of the stables. Their luck had run out. The guard had awoken and spotted them. Arthur shoved the reins into the señora's hands and leapt down to meet him. "What the hell do you think…" began the man.

Arthur surged forward and hit him with a left to the jaw, followed by a crashing right to the man's midsection. The guard doubled over and went down, breathless but still conscious. "Joe!" called Arthur.

The groom jumped down from the wagon. "That was a right old mill there," he said.

"Rope. Now." Arthur stood over his groggy opponent as Joe ran for the stable and returned with a length of rope. They bound the man where he lay, dragged him into a tangle of yews, and returned to the vehicles.

"Mr. Rigby would be impressed," said Señora Alvarez.

"I took him by surprise. Gentleman Jackson would say it was not fair play."

This drew a snort from her. Arthur noticed that the señora had gotten out her pistol and was holding it down by her side. He did not object.

As he drove around toward the front of the house, Arthur saw smoke seeping from the back parlor windows. It seemed that Poppy's fire had taken hold.

On the other side of the building, Joe got down to open the gate in the iron fence. The dogs showed up immediately, but they seemed mollified by the groom's presence and merely paced the two vehicles as they had when Arthur arrived. No one came out of the house to question them.

They proceeded down the drive. The gate in the outer wall appeared around a curve. It was, of course, closed. "Ho, the gate," called Arthur.

There was a brief delay, and then it opened a bit. The guard who had let them in came through from outside, closing the panel behind him.

"Open the gate, man," commanded Arthur in his best sneering voice.

The guard stared. "What's Joe doing there?"

"I have no idea. Nor do I care in the least." It was a challenge to sound bored when you were vibrating with tension.

"He ain't allowed out without one of us goes with him."

"And what does this have to do with me?"

For a moment, as the guard puzzled over the question, Arthur thought they might get through. But then the man frowned. "There's somethin' havey-cavey about this." He started around the curricle toward the cart.

Señora Alvarez raised her pistol and shot the man through the calf.

"Ahh!" The guard fell to the ground, gripping the wound and yelling. The dogs went wild, slavering and barking. The señora turned her gun on them but didn't fire.

Joe, showing more speed and courage than Arthur had expected, jumped to the ground. The dogs surrounded him in a leaping mass, but they didn't bite. "Down, Rex, Faron," the groom cried. "It's all right." He pushed the gate open and leapt back to his seat on the wagon. Arthur had already set his curricle moving.

"You'll be sorry for this, Joe Crendel," said the guard as they passed. "We'll come for you."

"On the contrary," said Arthur over his shoulder. "The law will be here shortly, coming for *you*."

"So you better leg it," said Joe.

"Or hobble it," said Señora Alvarez, showing not the slightest remorse, though her voice shook.

A laugh burst from Arthur as he made the turn onto the lane outside the walls.

Joe closed the gate behind them to contain the dogs. Arthur would have left it open for the convenience of the magistrate he meant to summon as soon as possible. But he didn't want to chance canine pursuit.

They headed for the main road. Arthur slowed near the copse beyond the wall, and Tom and his group rode out to join them. "These are friends," Arthur called back to allay Joe's concern. Though he didn't really expect anyone to ride after them, he was glad of the escort.

"We was waiting for your signal," said Tom, coming up beside the curricle. "Alf thought that was it." He pointed.

Arthur turned to see a large column of smoke billowing up on the other side of the wall. The fire had not been found in time. It seemed to be a major blaze. "It is a sign of something," he said.

"*Liberación,*" replied Señora Alvarez.

Twelve

FREEDOM CAME WITH SOME COMPLICATIONS, HOWEVER. "We spent so much time planning how to enter the house," Teresa said to the earl as they drove along the lane in his curricle. "And very little thinking what to do once we succeeded."

"It does suggest a sad lack of confidence in our own abilities," he replied. He met her gaze. His eyes were bright with triumph. In fact, he looked like a mischievous boy who had pulled off an epic prank.

Teresa had to laugh. She was feeling euphoric herself. "We have the excuse that we did not know exactly what we would find."

"Or how we would manage the rescue," he agreed.

"But the girls cannot ride in that cart all the way to London."

"Of course not. Post chaises will be best, I think."

"And you will wave your hand and make them appear."

"I will go to an inn and hire them."

And he would do it with great panache, Teresa thought. He didn't seem at all concerned over their

predicament. Perhaps the awkwardness of his position
hadn't soaked in yet. "We can choose an inn where
you are not known," she began.

"Oh, I think we had better go to an establishment
where I *am* known. I can take advantage of my, ah,
privileged aristocratic position and run roughshod
over the sensibilities of those who serve me."

She had used phrases rather like that on him once
upon a time. Clearly, he had not forgotten. "But how
will you explain a cartload of young women hidden
under piles of hay?"

"Explain?" he asked, in the drawling, imperious
tone he had used on the denizens of that dreadful
house.

"I beg your pardon, *my lord*. But you must know
that tongues will wag."

"Let them." He shrugged as if it didn't matter a jot
to him.

Teresa thought it would matter when the gossip
started. He would not like being twitted by his society
friends. But she saw no other way to transport her
charges, and so she said nothing more.

Lord Macklin led their cavalcade to the nearest inn,
where he was indeed well-known. As he was engaging
a private parlor for their use, the girls began to emerge
from the piles of hay in the wagon. Naturally, this
caused a sensation. The landlord grew more and more
stiff and expressionless with each one who appeared,
particularly those who showed signs of ill usage.
Finally, he could bear it no longer. "My lord!" the
hefty, aproned man protested.

Teresa was amazed that the earl showed no sign

of embarrassment. "We have uncovered a nest of criminals not far from here," he said. "I require the direction of the nearest magistrate."

"Sir Samford Jellison lives a matter of two miles away," said the landlord. He gaped at Odile, who had a dark bruise on the left side of her elfin face.

"Ah, good, not too far." Lord Macklin turned to Teresa. "I am sorry to leave you, but I must go and speak to him at once." He set one booted foot on the step of his curricle. Then he paused, lowered it, and came over to Teresa. "You had best take this," he murmured, slipping her a thick roll of banknotes. "I intend to be back quite soon, but it's best you have the means…"

"To overawe the innkeeper?"

He smiled down at her in a way that made her heart pound. "Precisely. You will be all right?"

"Of course."

"I'll look after 'em," said Tom. The state of the dancers had eroded his usual good humor. He looked grimly determined.

The earl gave them each a nod and climbed into the curricle. "Tell me how to find this Sir Samford," he said to the innkeeper. The man did so. "I will return as soon as possible." Lord Macklin touched the brim of his hat and drove away. Teresa felt a twinge of dismay at his departure. She suppressed it ruthlessly.

Her fingers gripping more ready money than she'd possessed in a long time, Teresa put on her most authoritative manner. "Come," she said to the six girls. She took them up to the private parlor and ordered whatever refreshment they desired. The landlord seemed glad to have them out of his yard and made no difficulties. Yet.

"My friends have to go," said Tom, who had followed them upstairs. "They're due back at their work."

Teresa nodded. "Where is Joe?"

"Hiding in the stable, looking after the cart horses. He seems to think they're his now."

"Why not?" It seemed fair to Teresa.

"I'll just see Alf and the others off." Tom went out, closing the door behind him.

Maria dissolved into hysterics. Odile collapsed onto the settee and put her face in her hands. Jill clasped hers tightly as if to stop them trembling and started to cry. Sonia cursed at length, and most colorfully, in Spanish. Jeanne sat very still, as if afraid to move. "It all comes over you, like, now that we're well away," said Poppy. She plopped into a chair and bit her lower lip.

"Yes, it does," replied Teresa. She was quite familiar with aftermath. She saw them all seated, comforted Maria, and reassured the others. When the trays arrived, she distributed cups of tea with plenty of sugar along with cakes and ham sandwiches and well-buttered scones with jam. At some point during this process, Tom stuck his head around the door, approved the scene, and immediately withdrew.

The sustenance helped. The girls slowly recovered. They began picking irritating bits of hay from their gowns. From the way they moved, it was clear that the ride in the cramped cart had been a strain and that some of them were more hurt than they appeared. They would need care, and Teresa started to wonder how this could be managed. Her house was far too small. Their scattered lodgings would not do, even if they were still welcome there.

Tom reappeared and consumed all the scones that were left. "Joe's sloped off with the cart horses and wagon," he said. "Slipped out to a lane behind the inn and scarpered. You want me to ride after him?"

"Do you think he is a danger to us?" Teresa asked him.

"I think he means to run as far from here as he can and never look back."

"Well, we will let him go." She had enough people to worry about.

As if in response to this thought, Jill wailed, "What's going to become of us?"

"Do you have family?" Teresa responded. "We could help you return to them."

As Jill shook her head, Poppy said, "Neither of us has anybody close. Reckon that's why that she-devil took us on. We was at a mop fair, and she asked all about our families before she offered us work." She looked as if she wanted to spit. "Work! I wisht I *had* hit her when I had the chance. And I hope I burned that place right down."

"That's the spirit," said Tom.

From the settee, Odile moaned. She was the worst off, and Teresa wished she knew how to help her. They needed a doctor.

The sound of carriage wheels below took her to the window. Lord Macklin had returned. The sight of him filled Teresa with a burst of joy so strong she could scarcely contain it. They'd labored side by side to save the day. He'd trusted her, and fully deserved her trust in him. Now, the handsome man pulling into the inn yard seemed everything that was admirable. She hurried down to meet him.

Stepping from his curricle and turning toward the inn door, Arthur was buoyed up by the welcome in Señora Alvarez's dark eyes. "I have told the whole story to the magistrate," he said. "Sir Samford was very much shocked. He is gathering a group of men to go to the house and detain anyone who remains there."

"I suppose most of them have run away," she replied.

"Probably. But it was most important to rescue their captives."

"Yes."

Arthur didn't think that she'd ever looked at him this way before. A heady mixture of tenderness and desire surged through him. If he found the right words now would she…?

A hail from above drew his eyes to the window of the private parlor. Tom stood there with his hand raised. Arthur waved.

The señora looked up as well. "Odile is in a bad way, I think. I would like her to see a doctor."

"I have a good physician in town. Can she make it so far?"

"I'm quite worried for her, but let us go and ask what she would like to do."

When he saw the young opera dancer lying on the settee, ashen and weak, Arthur was once again filled with rage. She was such a small, fragile-looking girl, and clearly she had been treated shamefully. What sort of man could do that? What sort let it happen? Because the staff had known very well what was going on in that place. How did people come to care so little for others' pain?

When consulted by the señora, Odile begged to go home to London. The thought of staying anywhere near the house where she'd been imprisoned clearly terrified her.

Arthur moved closer. "We want to care for you."

She cowered away from him. No one had ever gazed at Arthur with such sick fear. He hated it, and hated the reason she now felt it. Those responsible should pay for this. He retreated to the other side of the room.

Señora Alvarez soon joined him. "It is clear that staying here would be worse for Odile than the drive to town. However hard that may be."

And so the arrangements were made, and they all set out—Teresa and Macklin in the curricle, the six young women in a roomy post chaise, and Tom riding beside.

"Where are we going to go?" Señora Alvarez asked after a few miles on the road. "The dancers lost their lodgings when they were taken away, and Poppy and Jill have none."

"I've been considering," Arthur replied. Six girls, most of whom showed clear signs of ill usage, would not be welcomed at an inn or hotel, even with ample funds. And after their imprisonment, they would not care to be shut into strange rooms alone. He thought they might do best if they were together. "I believe the best plan is to take them to my house for a while to recover," he answered.

Her mouth fell a little open. "Your..."

"You could stay with them there, as reassurance and as a nod to propriety." He hadn't thought of this until just now. But he found the idea of installing her in his home very appealing.

Señora Alvarez seemed to grope for words. "Have you gone mad?" she asked finally.

"Not that I'm aware."

"Nod to propriety," she muttered. "You know very well that I offer no such thing."

"Ah, well, you *appear* very proper." He was more and more pleased with his plan.

"Lord Macklin!"

He reined in his high spirits. But not his determination to convince her. "These poor girls need peace and quiet and safety," he said. "Time to see a doctor. And it seems to me best that they be kept together for a while. So that they can support each other as they heal. My house satisfies all those conditions."

"But word would spread. This would cause a great scandal."

He had thought of this, and found he didn't care a jot. "I have lived a life untouched by any hint of scandal," he replied. "Perhaps it's time to add a bit to the mix."

"Will you be serious? This is not a joke."

"I'm not joking."

She stared at him as if trying to probe the depths of his brain. Arthur endured the examination calmly. It was true that he wanted to impress her as well as help the unfortunate girls. But he *did* wish to help them. There was no deception involved. "Your house," she said.

Her heavy tone reminded Arthur of her history. He hadn't thought that an invitation to stay with him might feel like a threat. Now he remembered the grandee who had done the same and then closed her in a trap. "You will be completely free to order things as you wish. I can ask my housekeeper to give you charge of all the keys."

Her gaze at his face never wavered. "Your housekeeper would be outraged by such a request," she said. "She would probably give you her notice."

"We can explain what the girls have endured. And that they trust you. And so this temporary measure…" He trailed off. Mrs. Garting would *not* be pleased by such an arrangement. Nor was Chirt going to welcome these visitors. At first. He would come around. Probably. "My butler may be a bit…difficult. He has a rigid sense of propriety. I wonder if I should stay with friends, or at a hotel, until this is…"

"Running away and leaving me to cope with the complaints of your staff?" She seemed torn between amusement and irritation.

He had to admit the option was appealing. "I'm certain you are more than up to the task."

"Have you ever lived in a house where the servants showed their displeasure at everything they were asked to do? No matter how small?"

"No." Arthur realized that the idea shocked him, as if servants had no right to opinions. He did not believe that. Did he? Señora Alvarez always taught him things—some, about himself, that he might not have wished to learn.

"There must be some other place we can go," she said.

"Not with all they need. Not immediately."

Struggle was visible in her lovely face. "For a day or two. I suppose. After that we must think of something else."

"Certainly."

"You have an annoying way of agreeing with what I say when I know you will actually do whatever you please," she replied.

"I would do nothing you disapprove of."

"You have done all sorts of things I disapprove of."

"Ah, well, I've noticed that you are occasionally a bit overparticular."

She burst out laughing. Under the circumstances, Arthur took it as a triumph and let the subject rest. And when Tom rode closer as they neared London and asked where they were headed, he answered with bland calm. Fortunately, Tom received the information with no sign of disapproval, or surprise.

When they pulled up at the doors of Lord Macklin's town house some time later, Teresa stepped down from the curricle with a good deal of trepidation. She had informed the earl that she would not require the keys from the housekeeper. She did not want to contemplate the uproar that request would have caused. But she still expected his very superior servants to object to this invasion. And unlike him, she knew quite well what animosity from staff was like.

Tom bid them farewell, saying he would visit the next day. "I'll see about having their things brought over," he said as he went.

The earl offered Teresa his arm, and she took it. In the entry hall, the butler, Chirt, received the news that they were to host seven female houseguests with quickly hidden surprise. When the girls began to file in, and their station and battered condition grew obvious, he went utterly expressionless. Stunned, perhaps? Lord Macklin introduced only Teresa, saying she was in charge and should be given anything she asked for.

This earned her a searching look from the major-domo. She must not be cowed. That would be fatal to her future interactions with the staff. But she could assume an air of calm command nearly as well as Macklin. "We must send for the doctor first of all," she said.

"Have someone fetch Phipps," the earl confirmed. "Ask him to come as soon as he is able."

His butler gave one nod and a nearly imperceptible gesture. A footman at the back of the entry leapt forward. "Also Mrs. Garting," murmured the butler. The younger servant practically saluted before disappearing into the back premises.

The housekeeper appeared so quickly that Teresa wondered if she'd been listening at the door. She was a solid, efficient-looking woman who would no doubt have been welcoming under other circumstances. It would be best to confide in her at the first opportunity, Teresa decided. Not the entire truth, but a version of it. She could frame this visit as…a burst of eccentric philanthropy. And make its temporary nature quite clear.

"We require rooms for our guests," the earl said. He didn't make excuses, which was wise.

"Yes, my lord. If the ladies would like to sit in the blue parlor for a bit." The tiny emphasis on the word *ladies* was the closest the housekeeper would come to a reproach, Teresa thought.

"The drawing room," replied Lord Macklin, his tone a mild reprimand.

The housekeeper dropped a curtsy. Message heard and received, it said. But not greatly appreciated.

"We will be happy to do so," said Teresa, as if she customarily commanded a vast estate. "Except for Odile. She must lie down at once." She'd noted that Odile was swaying on her feet and looked ready to faint. "And perhaps we might have some tea," she added, just to show that she could. She wished she'd worn a grander gown. But how anyone could plan an ensemble for breaking into a criminal bordello and visiting an earl's London town house in the same day, she did not know.

The butler and the housekeeper looked at her, evaluating. They'd taken in her manner and way of speaking. "Yes, ma'am," the housekeeper said, and Teresa knew that she had established a measure of authority.

By the time the rooms were ready and the girls settled, the doctor had arrived. Teresa stayed with her charges for the examinations, knowing that they should not be left alone with a strange man just now. Afterward she returned to the drawing room and sat with Lord Macklin to hear the man's opinion.

"Most of the young ladies are merely bruised and weary," he said.

"Merely?" Teresa could not help but reply.

The doctor accepted the reprimand with a bow of his head. "I beg your pardon. There is nothing 'mere' about such treatment. I found no broken bones or serious injuries except for the first. Odile, isn't it? She has been hit very hard in her midsection." He touched his own torso to demonstrate the location. "Very hard. Something may have ruptured inside. With complete rest and quiet and proper care, she may heal."

"May?" asked Teresa, dismayed.

"Some recover from this sort of injury. Others do not. It is difficult to tell why."

Lord Macklin looked as grim as Teresa felt. "Leave instructions about what she requires," he said. "We will see that they are carried out."

"Yes, my lord." The doctor looked from him to Teresa and back again. "These girls have been badly treated. I hope something is being done about that."

"The matter is in the hands of a magistrate," replied Lord Macklin. "All that can be done will be."

Teresa wondered a little at the way he phrased this.

"Ah. Good," said the doctor. When it became clear that he would be told no more, he rose and took his leave, promising to send the medications he recommended with all speed.

And then Teresa was left alone in the grand drawing room with its noble owner. He sat beside her, the partner who had helped her accomplish…miracles really. And he hadn't asked for anything in return. He was a man like no other.

If she reached out, she could touch his hand, his cheek. The love she felt for him filled her. "I would like to thank you," she said. "For helping me get them out."

"As who would not?"

"So very many people. You know how girls in their position are valued by most of society."

"Not at all, you mean." He looked vexed. "I admit I never paid much heed. You have shown me so many things."

Teresa's throat was tight with emotion. "You are extraordinary."

"I hardly think so."

"That is part of what makes you so." She hadn't understood that such men existed. She hadn't believed until he proved it to her. Now he drew her irresistibly. She wanted to nestle into his arms. She wanted to throw off every scruple, forget everything but him.

"That word applies better to you," he said with one of his dizzying smiles. "But I'm pleased that you think so. I want you to think well of me."

"I?" He said this even though he knew the truth of her past? She'd fallen in love with this English earl because of the way he treated her. She'd been certain his attitude would change when she told her story. How had it not? She leaned closer. Her fingers brushed his sleeve. His lips were right *there*. She moved the last few inches and kissed him. Tentative at first, questioning, merely exploratory. At his immediate, ardent response, she slid her arms around his neck, pressed close, and lost herself in the embrace. Soft, all-encompassing, replete—a kiss like no other. She'd thought of him once as an ocean wave that knocked one tumbling and then dragged irresistibly toward the depths. Here they were, engulfing her. And she didn't care. She surrendered to that passionate tide.

Lord Macklin pulled away from her. Teresa reached

for him with a soft protest. "I cannot," he said, his voice uneven. "You are a guest in my house. Under my protection. Any… It would be quite wrong of me."

"I don't require protection from you," she replied. The truth of it rang through her as soon as she spoke, leaving her shaken. Here was the heart of the matter—trust.

But he edged farther back and then stood up. "I had better go before…"

The always immaculate earl looked mussed. His neckcloth was twisted.

"One cannot resist the irresistible," he murmured. "But I must."

The ever-articulate aristocrat spoke in disjointed phrases. Teresa reveled in it.

"When this visit is done…" With one searing look at her, he strode out.

Lord Macklin did not appear at dinner that evening. Nor in the drawing room afterward. Teresa assumed that he slept in his bedchamber, a few doors down the hall from hers, through the night. She was tempted to find out, but she knew he would not like it. So in the end she too resisted.

Rising early the next morning she found no one else in the breakfast room when she went down. The earl had gone out, she was told, and it appeared that the girls were taking advantage of the unaccustomed luxury and sleeping as long as they liked. She was glad; they needed the rest after their ordeal. Having eaten, Teresa sought out the housekeeper and talked with her as she'd planned. Mrs. Garting was stiff at first. But she gradually unbent as Teresa told her tale—all true but carefully tailored to her audience. By the time she'd finished, the atmosphere had lightened, and she thought the earl's staff would be less prickly from now on. She went to sit in the drawing room, not sure quite what to do with idleness after the recent intense activity.

The butler came to her there to report that she had callers.

"But no one knows I'm here."

"These ladies appear well informed, madam."

She hadn't expected the rumors to begin quite so soon. Teresa sighed. She didn't feel like fending off curious gossips, coming to pry all the details out of her. All alone. Then she remembered that she had a high-nosed butler at her command. "Tell them that no one is at home to receive them."

"Yes, madam." Chirt looked as if he would enjoy it.

But a few minutes later Teresa heard a chorus of voices approaching, and in the next instant three young ladies burst into the drawing room. Chirt followed on their heels with an outraged expression.

"I cannot believe you would deny us," said Miss Charlotte Deeping.

"You left us out of everything," complained Miss Sarah Moran. "It's not fair."

"Tom told us what you've been up to," said Miss Harriet Finch, in response to Teresa's startled expression. "Part of it, at any rate. I suspect he left out a good deal. No, I'm certain he must have."

"And so we have come to hear." Miss Deeping plopped down on the sofa next to Teresa. She looked as if it would take several strong footmen to remove her. "And if you think you can fob us off, you will find you are mistaken," she said, confirming this impression.

Miss Moran and Miss Finch also sat. They looked like fashionable debutantes, decked out in gowns and bonnets for morning calls, but the stares they fixed on Teresa were worthy of a wolf pack.

"It's all right, Chirt," said Teresa. "Thank you."

The butler turned away, clearly incensed. He walked out, somehow managing to express profound disapproval with his back.

"He thinks we're dreadfully rackety," said Miss Moran.

Miss Deeping made a dismissive gesture. "Tell," she said to Teresa.

She didn't care to be commanded. But more than that, she wasn't sure how much the young ladies should be told about the sinister house in the country.

A movement at the door caught her eye. The earl looked in and then ducked back out of sight. "Lord Macklin!" called Teresa.

After a moment he reappeared. His expression made it obvious that he had intended to escape. Teresa laughed at him. He smiled ruefully when he saw it.

A clamor rose from the three visitors, accusing the earl also of leaving them out of the adventure. They began to sound like children deprived of a promised treat.

"Enough!" said Teresa. She looked at Lord Macklin and pointed to an armchair. He sat down. She stood up. "You have no actual right to information, you know," she said to the young ladies. "You are not *owed* an explanation."

They looked surprised, hurt, offended, according to their various personalities. Teresa felt a mixture of weariness and compassion.

"We helped investigate," said Miss Deeping.

"We asked all sorts of questions," said Miss Moran. "How can you say that we…"

"We are not speaking of a pet raven stealing trinkets here," interrupted Teresa.

Now she had provoked them all. A row of frowns confronted her.

Teresa suddenly felt far older than these young ladies. "Evil exists in the world, you know."

"We are well aware…" began Miss Deeping.

"You don't know what real evil is, and perhaps you shouldn't have to," Teresa interrupted.

"We may be ignorant," replied Miss Finch. "It does not follow that we *should* be."

"You could consider it good luck," said Teresa. Much of a person's destiny seemed to come down to luck.

"I do not," said Miss Moran quietly.

Teresa was surprised that it should be this girl who objected.

"Knowing is always best, I think," the girl added. "One should never refuse to learn."

"But once you learn a…dreadful thing, you cannot erase it from your memory."

"Talk, talk, talk," said Miss Deeping. "The truth is you have gone off on adventures without us, and you have no intention of explaining." She looked from Teresa to the earl and back again.

Her petulance goaded Teresa. "The opera dancers we were seeking, and two other girls, were imprisoned in a place where men came to do whatever they pleased to them. Vile, unprincipled men. The girls are lying upstairs, bruised and still frightened. Odile may die from the mistreatment she received."

This brought a shocked silence. Lord Macklin, who had raised a cautionary hand, let it drop.

Miss Finch murmured a curse.

"But why would anyone…" Miss Moran began. She fell silent.

"Evil," said Teresa. "In the world." She'd achieved the effect she was looking for; she had shaken them. And now she was sorry she'd lost her temper.

"How did you…" Miss Deeping began. She stopped and shook her head. "It's not just an exciting story." Miss Moran swallowed, her blue eyes wide.

"I hate people," said Miss Finch. She was looking out the window as if she could eliminate a few passersby with her stony gaze. "Nearly all of them are despicable."

Even more, Teresa wished she hadn't spoken.

"Helping can be an adventure too," said Lord Macklin.

Everyone turned to look at him.

"The old tales are full of swordplay and derring-do, but adventure is not only physical danger. As I discovered this past year."

"Whatever it is, we are supposed to have nothing to do with it," said Miss Deeping. She sounded thoroughly disgruntled.

"Not necessarily."

Teresa was surprised by his intervention. She didn't understand what point he was making.

"Are you going to suggest that we become smug Lady Bountifuls, distributing largesse?" asked Miss Finch. "If you knew how many people have come to me for donations since I inherited! I find their attitude…"

"Grasping?" the earl interrupted. "Undeservedly entitled? Condescending?"

Miss Finch nodded, looking surprised.

"I *hate* being patronized," said Miss Deeping. "Half the *haut ton* seems to think they know better than I ever could. About *everything*!"

"I don't think anyone enjoys being treated so," said the earl.

"As if you'd know," muttered Miss Deeping.

"Charlotte!" said Miss Moran. "There's no need to be rude."

Miss Deeping murmured an apology. Lord Macklin waved it aside. "I was patronized as a boy," he said. "I admit it has been a while."

When his eyes twinkled in that way, he was irresistible, Teresa thought. What if she refused to resist? The thought was so enflaming that she nearly missed the next remarks.

"What do *you* mean by help?" asked Miss Finch. She had a gift of staying with the topic at hand. "And why do you call it an adventure?"

"The adventure comes in discovering the kind of help people really want. Not what you may believe they want, or think they *should* want. Particularly the latter. That discovery takes one in unexpected directions."

"Isn't finding out just another kind of patronizing?" asked Miss Finch.

"You are quite an intelligent young lady," the earl replied.

Miss Finch blushed with pleasure.

"And the answer is, it can be," he went on. "One must make an effort to be sure that it is not. Beginning with respect. Discussing matters as equals and not, as you said, Lady Bountifuls. And then observing behavior as well as talk. Action may not match words. People may not know their true wishes. The process is not easy."

He spoke to the young ladies as if they mattered, Teresa thought, just as he'd always treated her with respect. How had a privileged nobleman become this unusual man?

"That doesn't sound like adventure to me," said Miss Deeping. Seeing Teresa's eyes on her, she sighed. "Yes, I understand what you have said."

"The opera dancers need help," said Miss Moran slowly. "Especially the ones staying here. But all of them have a hard time of it."

"Perhaps we could find better places for them," said Miss Deeping. "Some other sort of employment."

Miss Finch shook her head.

"They like to dance," said Teresa. "Most of them love the theater. They don't wish to leave."

"Better pay?" asked Miss Moran tentatively.

"You would suggest that we ask them," said Miss Finch, with a nod to Lord Macklin.

"In doing so, you would enter another world," he said.

"And that is the adventure," said Miss Deeping. "I do understand." She didn't seem entirely reconciled to the idea.

"May we see them?" asked Miss Finch.

"When they are more fully recovered," answered Teresa.

It was agreed that she would send word when this time came, and the group started to break up. But they had scarcely pulled on their gloves when Chirt marched in with a large figure at his heels. "Miss Julia Grandison," the butler announced in a deeply aggrieved tone. Arthur had no trouble interpreting his expression. Chirt resented the chaos that had overtaken his well-ordered household. And he was just waiting for the right opportunity to express his outrage. "She did not care to wait below," the man added in sepulchral tones.

"What do you think you are doing, visiting a man's home?" boomed a familiar voice as the formidable lady sailed in behind him. She raked the young ladies with her harshest glare.

"Señora Alvarez is here," said Miss Deeping.

"Indeed? Well, she should know better. Or perhaps *be* better."

"I can only aspire," said the señora. Arthur stifled a laugh.

Not waiting for an invitation, Miss Grandison took an armchair as if it was a throne. "The most *extraordinary* rumors are flying about town," she said. She frowned at Arthur. "They are saying you have filled your home with opera dancers, Macklin. Dozens of them!"

"There are only…" began Miss Deeping, then fell silent as both Teresa's and Miss Grandison's sharp gazes swung to transfix her.

"Well," continued Miss Grandison. "What have you to say for yourself?"

"Nothing," Arthur replied. He had to keep reminding himself not to gaze at Señora Alvarez like a lovelorn boy. He could think of nothing else since that searing kiss. He ached for her, day and most particularly night. To be so near and not touch her—it was maddening. His only consolation was the conviction that she would welcome his suit when they were done with this visit. Which already felt interminable.

"I beg your pardon?" said Miss Grandison.

"I owe no one explanations," he replied.

"You will allow malicious tongues to wag?"

"I doubt I could stop them."

"How fortunate to be a man," murmured Miss Finch. Señora Alvarez gave her an appreciative sidelong glance.

Momentarily, Miss Grandison seemed at a loss. Clearly, she had expected to mow down opposition. But for what purpose? "I wish to speak to these opera dancers," she said then. "At once."

Ah, that was it. "About your brother?" Arthur asked.

"I require only a bit more information."

"No," said Señora Alvarez.

Miss Grandison turned on her. "You do not wish to make an enemy of me, my good woman."

"I would rather not. But I will not expose the girls to your interrogation."

Arthur agreed with this. They were in no shape to endure the formidable lady's questions.

"I believe I can talk civilly to anyone," said Miss Grandison.

"Your idea of civility will intimidate them," said the señora. "Find out about your brother from someone else."

Miss Grandison made a sour face. "The men close ranks, you know. And many of the women as well."

Señora Alvarez looked as if she was quite familiar with this tendency.

"Those who recall me under the overturned punch bowl seem to rather enjoy the memory. I'm sure I made a most amusing picture." The older lady's tone was bitter.

"I am sorry." The señora sounded sincere. "But would it not be better to let the past go? Is it really necessary to humiliate him? What about your brother's wife? Do you give no thought to her?"

"He treats her with contempt," replied Miss Grandison coldly. "But she is too timid to pay him back herself. He *ought* to be taken down a peg."

The three young ladies looked as if they agreed with this description, which was telling. There was a short silence. Arthur saw no need to fill it. Señora Alvarez was more than holding her own. She was the equal of anybody.

"I will ask the dancers more about your brother," she replied finally. "When I think they are up to it. I cannot predict what day that will be."

The two women's eyes held. Neither wavered. Arthur decided one would have to judge the face-off as even, ending in mutual respect.

"Very well." Miss Grandison stood and hovered at her full impressive height. "I will bid you farewell. Are you girls coming with me?"

"We will stay a bit longer, ma'am," said Miss Finch. Only to avoid Miss Grandison's company, Arthur thought.

"I am not your chaperone" was the disapproving reply. "I suppose you may behave as badly as you please." She turned and swept out of the room.

"You might have helped me," Señora Alvarez said to Arthur.

"You didn't need any help," he answered. "And I feared the intervention of a mere man would make things worse."

Miss Finch snorted a laugh.

"You were wonderful," said Miss Moran. "Ada's aunt always makes me quake in my boots."

The señora made a *pfft* sound. She was always magnificent, Arthur thought.

Thirteen

OVER THREE QUIET DAYS, THE RESCUED GIRLS RECOV-
ered. With safety, good food, rest, and care, they
regained their strength. Only Odile remained weak,
and even she was showing some improvement. Their
spirits were a different matter. These veered from tears
to rage to anxious tremors as the group sat together
in the earl's drawing room. But Teresa knew how to
comfort without discounting these reactions, allowing
them to run their course. She understood, too, that
the tales might need to be repeated more than once.
She had found this for herself, long ago. Repetition
weakened bad memories; their impact could slowly
trickle away, like sand running from an hourglass.

Visitors from the theater, including Tom, called
to cheer the dancers, and Lord Macklin, on his brief
look-ins, treated them with grave courtesy. Teresa
grew hopeful that they would be able to move on very
soon to whatever came next. She longed for that with
all her being because she was finding it maddening
to be in the earl's company but not really *with* him.
They had less conversation than during his visits to the

artisans' workshop. His sense of honor had become a barrier in his own house.

On the fourth day, she was determined to catch him and broach the subject of the future. But at mid-morning the peace of the house was broken by shouting from the lower floor. The noise brought all the girls to worried alert. Puzzled, Teresa went out to the top of the stairs and looked down into the entry hall. A man was actually grappling with the earl's butler. As she watched, he struck out and knocked Chirt to the floor. Where were the footmen?

The intruder started up the stairs, coming very fast, and then Teresa recognized him. It was Lord Simon Farange, the man behind the kidnappings. They had expected that he would hear the gossip and deduce who had raided the house, but Teresa hadn't imagined he would force his way in here. He snarled up at her, missed his footing, and caught at the stair rail to keep his balance. Teresa concluded that he'd been drinking. Surely only drunkenness would lead him to invade the earl's residence.

Chirt was struggling to his feet below. He would bring help. Until then, it was up to her to protect her charges.

Teresa rushed back into the drawing room. "Lord Simon is here," she said. Gasps around the room greeted this unwelcome news. They all knew his name by this time. "He is alone," Teresa added. "And there are seven of us." She went to the hearth and picked up the fireplace poker. She posted herself between the girls and the doorway.

Lord Simon burst in and stood swaying there.

"Here's a fine sight," he said. "A huddle of whores gone to ground." He laughed. "Even my lovely little Odile." He pointed at her. "Do you imagine I won't scoop you up the moment you pass through the front door? Did you really think to escape me?"

From the sofa, Odile made a soft frightened sound.

"Come on!" cried Poppy. With a sweeping gesture, she surged forward. There was a moment's hesitation, and then the others, except Teresa and Odile, joined her. In a mob, they threw themselves on Lord Simon, bearing him to the carpet. There they surrounded him, punching and kicking and cursing. The man seemed stunned by this response, scarcely able to defend himself.

Three footmen ran in with Chirt right behind them. Teresa held up a hand and let the pummeling continue for a little longer. Then she moved forward to pull the girls away. The footmen hauled Lord Simon to his feet and held him upright. He drooped in their grip, much worse for wear. He would have some bruises of his own, Teresa noted with satisfaction.

She turned to replace the poker and discovered Odile, sitting up shakily on the sofa and pointing Teresa's pistol at the intruder. When had she taken the gun? The last Teresa knew it was shoved into the back of a drawer in her bedchamber. Had she even mentioned that? It seemed that the girl had searched her room. "Odile," Teresa said.

"I wish to kill him dead," replied the girl.

"It will cause great trouble for you if you kill him," said Teresa.

"I don't worry. He is deserving of death."

"He may deserve it, Odile, but you do not deserve the consequences of such an act."

"No one cares about me."

"We do." Teresa looked around at the other girls. "Don't we?"

They all nodded.

"He ain't worth it," said Poppy. "He's no better than a piece of trash."

"Me, I know someone to kill him for us," said Jeanne, breathing hard, her fingers still crooked into claws.

Teresa didn't respond to this. Better not to discuss hired assassins. "We will use the law," she answered instead.

"They will not listen to the likes of us," objected Sonia.

"They will listen to *me*," said Lord Macklin from the doorway.

His sudden appearance startled Odile. The pistol jerked upward in her hand and went off. The report was shockingly loud in the closed room. The air filled with the acrid smell of gunpowder.

"*Merde!*" Odile dropped the pistol as if it had bitten her.

The footmen had flinched and ducked, but they hadn't released their captive. The earl, perhaps seeing the angle of the weapon, had stood very still. The rest of them had quailed. Slowly now, they straightened.

A chittery sound broke the silence. Bits of plaster fell from a hole high on the wall.

"Take him to a storeroom and lock him in," said the earl.

Lord Simon glared at him. "You're no better than me," he said. His voice was more slurred than before due to a bloodied lip. "You've got yourself a houseful of whores right here in London."

Teresa's fingers tightened on the poker.

Lord Macklin showed no reaction to the taunt. "I shall speak to the authorities, and your father."

"He won't care," declared Lord Simon. He rasped and spit on the carpet. His spittle was red. "Nobody will care about a bunch of light-skirts. Why should they? Worthless doxies."

The earl gestured, and the footmen pulled Lord Simon out of the room. Chirt followed them.

Teresa replaced the poker and went to pick up her gun, which she would hide far more securely from now on.

"I am very sorry for this intrusion," said Lord Macklin. "I hope you are not too shaken up." His gaze passed over them all.

"I liked kicking him," said Poppy.

"I would have preferred killing him dead," said Odile.

"Quite understandable," answered the earl. "But that would have been imprudent."

Jeanne walked over to sit beside Odile and take her hand. Teresa made a note to discover the details of their whispering and make certain they did not involve hired killers.

The earl drew Teresa aside. "*Will* anyone listen to you?" she asked him.

"After this latest outrage, I'm sure I can convince the duke to send his son away."

"No more than that?"

Lord Macklin looked grim. "All the people from that house fled before the magistrate reached it."

"Even the woman we tied up?"

He nodded. "I suppose she was found and freed. I have just heard that the hunt for them has turned up nothing. They are still being searched for. I hope some may be found."

"Because without them, it is only 'whores' accusing Lord Simon. And they must be liars, *sí*?"

He made no reply.

"There is the driver who took me into the country," Teresa exclaimed. How could she have forgotten him? "We saw Lord Simon drive through the gates with Jeanne."

"Ah. Of course. That could be helpful." His tone was doubtful.

"But not enough?" She felt bitterness well up. "Another insignificant person lining up against the son of a duke."

"A private arrangement with his father would be most likely to succeed," said Lord Macklin.

"So all goes on as before. He will not be punished. Perhaps I should let Jeanne's friend the assassin kill him."

"What?"

"Oh, of course I will tell her she mustn't. It just makes me so angry that nothing will happen to that man."

"I was thinking of suggesting a madhouse," replied the earl.

This startled her.

"This is not his only outrage. Lord Simon is subject to irrational fits of rage. He has attacked people with a whip. Incidents have been hushed up. Several promising horses were taken ill after his visit to a baron's racing stable. And he is suspected of cheating at cards. More than suspected, perhaps. I am looking into that."

"So there are offenses against *important* people to be taken into account."

He didn't deny it. "Forcing his way into my house is so far beyond the line. I think his father will listen."

"Because you are of his class and rank. And might make trouble for him among those he…values."

"I am sorry—"

Teresa cut off his apology with a gesture. "Of course I am thankful that you are willing to act. I don't know what would have become of these girls without you." That wasn't true. She had a very good idea. She only wished she didn't know.

"I am glad to do what I can," he said.

"Noblesse oblige." Teresa turned away. "We must be humbly grateful." She had been expected to appreciate so many unpalatable things in her life. At least the inequity of justice wasn't a personal slight. Though near-universal oppression was hardly any better.

"Nonsense!" The sharpness of his tone made several of the girls on the other side of the room turn to look at them. "You know I seek no such thing," he added. "I don't want your…obeisance for doing a thing that is right. What a repellent idea."

He said it as if there could be no argument. She'd forgotten his quality for a moment. If she'd found someone like him after her family was killed... Teresa cut off a rush of regrets.

Silence had fallen over the drawing room. Odile looked frightened. "I must speak to them," she said with a gesture.

"Yes. I had thought we could talk about what kind of help our guests would like, but this is not a good time."

"No." He said "our" as if they could both offer aid. But despite his attitude, the gift of largesse remained almost wholly his. And so it would always be, between them.

"Tomorrow perhaps. They must be wondering about the future."

Teresa nodded. There had been questions. It was undoubtedly time for this little fairy-tale visit to end.

⁂

When Arthur entered his drawing room the next afternoon, he found all of the rescued captives there with Señora Alvarez. Tom was present as well. The lad sat beside Poppy, and they had their heads together. Arthur had noticed that these two talked a good deal when they had the opportunity. Though Poppy was a few years older, Tom's experience of the world had given him a maturity that belied his age, and they seemed to easily find common ground. Or perhaps common spirit was a better term. They shared an innate optimism and good temper, as well as a dauntless attitude. Tom had been full of admiration when he heard that Poppy had set fire to the house where she'd been imprisoned.

Arthur sat in an armchair so that he would not seem to be lecturing the group. "I should tell you first that Lord Simon Farange has been sent away from London," he said. "He will not be returning."

"Who will stop him?" asked Odile.

"His family." Arthur had put forceful arguments to the duke, who had seen his points.

"So they say now." Odile looked wan.

"They will see to it," said Arthur. He believed the duke would keep his word. The man was unpleasant but not dishonorable. He certainly did not want his name dragged through the mud, which Lord Simon seemed hell-bent on doing.

"So nothing's going to happen to him?" asked Poppy. "He'll be living the high life on some country estate?" She scowled. "Doing what he likes with the maidservants."

"No." Arthur looked around the room. "The terms have been set out very clearly. He will reside at a small country house, yes. But he will be supervised by men under orders from his father." His suggestion of a madhouse had not been well received.

"What is this 'supervised'?" asked Odile.

"Guarded," replied Arthur. "Deprived of all his... customary amusements. The estate is up near the Scottish border, and he will not be allowed to leave there." There was muttering, which he understood. Señora Alvarez was unusually silent. "I have made my own arrangements to keep watch on the place," he added. "Should anything go wrong with this agreement, steps will be taken."

Around the room, they digested this news. "I hope this beast will be *misérable* in this place," said Odile.

"I think he will be," Arthur replied.

"Not so much as we were under his hand," muttered Sonia.

"His lordship has been very kind to act in this," said Señora Alvarez. "The punishment is worse than this *canalla* would be likely to receive if he stood before a judge."

She never called him "his lordship." Arthur pushed on in a circle of frowns. "With that settled, I thought we might talk about what comes next. What would be most helpful to you."

"You want us out of your house," said Sonia.

"You know you cannot remain here," said the señora.

She spoke more harshly than Arthur would have.

"I do not wish to," said Jeanne. "It is very dull."

"Jeanne!"

The girl tossed her head. "*Eh bien*, señora, I am grateful." She acknowledged Arthur with a curtsy. "I thank you, sir. But I want to dance. It is what I love."

"And now that you are feeling better, you would like to go back to the theater," said Arthur.

"Yes, my lord."

Several others nodded as if they felt the same.

"Poppy's going to work at the theater too," said Tom. "Mrs. Scanlon says she sews a treat, and she'll be glad to have her."

Jill gave Poppy an astonished look. "Who?"

"The woman who manages the costumes for the plays," replied Poppy.

"But… What about me?"

Jill had come to rely on Poppy for direction, Arthur

saw. Even though they had not known each other long.

"I cannot dance anymore," said Odile. "Perhaps never again." She looked frightened.

"So what would you like?" Arthur asked her.

Odile simply stared at him with wide, anxious eyes.

"Perhaps a place to stay," said Señora Alvarez. "A...refuge when needed." She said the word with a combination of reverence and melancholy.

"We might hire a house in London that could be used for such a purpose." In fact, Arthur had already sent out inquiries and unearthed several possibilities in neighborhoods that were safe but not overly fussy about their denizens' occupations.

"Is this what they call the royal *we*?" asked the señora, as if he'd mocked her.

Arthur didn't understand why she was so prickly today. He'd been careful not to seem to dictate.

"And you are to pay for this," Señora Alvarez added. "Forever?"

"I expect Miss Finch would join in to help. And her friends. We would set up a fund." He might have paid for it all himself, but that would cause talk. More talk. There was quite enough of that already. He turned to the dancers. "What do you think of this plan?"

"A place to go and stay for free?" asked Maria.

"Yes."

"For as long as we want?" asked Jill. "Without any rent?"

"There would have to be rules about that," said the señora.

Arthur nearly objected, until he saw the nods

of agreement. "You shall make them," he said to Señora Alvarez. "With others you choose to consult. Women should oversee everything about this place, I think."

Odile narrowed her eyes as if trying to see some trick in this suggestion. This was the world they navigated, Arthur thought, continually waiting for an unpredictable hammer blow to fall. He'd had no notion before he met Señora Alvarez.

His visitors all agreed that this seemed a good plan. And over the next few days, the arrangements were made. A suitable house was found and engaged. Arthur went to call on Miss Harriet Finch and ask for her help. Alone, as the señora claimed to be too busy to accompany him. Miss Finch quickly agreed to contribute. "People may wonder at your interest in such a cause," Arthur warned her.

She shrugged. "The thing I have discovered about being a great heiress is that people will accept a host of eccentricities if they come with money," she answered. "It is one of the few advantages."

"Señora Alvarez hopes that you will serve as one of the overseers of the new refuge." He had been told to ask this.

Miss Finch looked flattered and intrigued. "I will. Perhaps I can do some good in the world. At least until I am harangued into marriage and all the money is handed over to my husband."

"You can find a husband who would also like to help," he suggested.

"You are a rare breed, Lord Macklin. I don't expect to meet another like you."

He shook his head and told her she was wrong, but she had clearly not been convinced.

And then, quite suddenly it seemed, all was settled. Some of the dancers returned to lodgings near the theater and their work. Odile and others moved to the new house to recover more fully in peace. Señora Alvarez departed with the briefest of goodbyes for her own home. And Arthur's house suddenly seemed very empty. He might have felt melancholy about that, if he had not had a firm plan in mind for the future.

Fourteen

Teresa sat before the small fire in her small parlor and contemplated her narrow little life. Not long ago, this state had seemed the height of peace and contentment. Now, because she had allowed herself to venture out into another sort of existence, it felt empty. Her tranquility was spoiled. She'd let that happen.

Yet how could she have done otherwise? When the dancers began disappearing, should she have turned away and ignored this…evil? Impossible. That was how evil grew, when no one stepped forward to fight it. And she'd done well. She'd found a way to help those who needed it. She had been part of creating a refuge for women going on into the future. This was splendid. She was proud and glad. So she mustn't care if this effort had caused difficulties for her. The result was well worth the sacrifice.

If only she had not allowed herself to fall in love with an earl and then to believe, for a while, that there might be some future with him. She ought to have resisted this stupidity.

Eliza looked in from the kitchen. "Would you like some tea, ma'am? Or a glass of wine perhaps?" The maid had been delighted to have Teresa back in the house, but now she appeared concerned.

"No thank you, Eliza."

The girl frowned at her before she withdrew.

She had resisted him, of course, Teresa thought. With all her might. She had held back, doubted, rejected. It had been a long battle of will and wits. But Lord Macklin had countered every gambit and gradually made his way into her heart. So deeply into her heart. Even now her thoughts were full of his handsome figure, his wonderful smile, his many sterling qualities. Most of all she remembered the kiss—a simple act, lasting only a few moments, that had shown her how much of life she'd been missing. It still made her dizzy to think if it.

But in the last few days, as the final arrangements for the dancers' future were being made and her part in things had dwindled down to nothing, Teresa had been reminded of their inequality. He had great power in the world, and she had none. He had taken over all the helping. She had stood back and watched and remembered times when she'd been helpless. She'd hated that. And the truth of their differences didn't change because he was a good person.

Must she stop seeing the Earl of Macklin now? Because it hurt too much? If she asked him to stop visiting the theater workshop, he would want to know why. Her spirit cried out against such a loss.

Again, Eliza looked in from the kitchen. "Are you sure I can't fetch anything at all for you, ma'am?" she said.

"No thank you, Eliza." Perhaps she should leave London, Teresa thought, but she couldn't think where she would go. And she didn't want to.

"There's nothing like a nice cup of tea," said the maid.

"Not right now."

Eliza went out, looking over her shoulder as if hoping for a different answer.

The knock on the door was unexpected. Teresa rose in response even as Eliza returned and went to open it.

The Earl of Macklin stood on her doorstop. Teresa couldn't pretend not to see him. She was perfectly visible.

"I beg your pardon for calling without warning," he said. "I have something particular to say to you."

She could only invite him in. "Some tea after all, Eliza," she said.

The maid eyed their noble visitor with frank curiosity as she left.

"Has something gone wrong with our plans?" Teresa asked.

"Not at all. I'm told that everything is proceeding very well at the house, though Miss Finch would be able to give you a more detailed report. I have heard that Jill is taking a position as household assistant."

"Assistant?"

"She did not wish to be called a maid."

Teresa had to smile. She indicated the sofa as she returned to her chair. He sat down opposite her, looking uncharacteristically awkward. And like everything a woman could desire.

Eliza returned with a tray. She must have had a kettle boiling. Teresa poured tea and offered it as the maid went out again.

Lord Macklin set his cup down beside his seat. "I thought you might have some idea of what I'm going to say," he said. "After all that…has passed between us."

The heat of their kiss was in his eyes, but that told her only of desire. She shook her head.

"This is more difficult than I remembered." His smile was wry. "But it has been rather a long time."

What could he be talking about?

"Should I get down, I wonder?"

What did he mean? Down where?

"I think not. If I had difficulties rising from the floor…" He made a deprecating gesture.

"Is something wrong?" asked Teresa. She'd begun to be concerned.

"Best just to blurt it out, I suppose." Lord Macklin sat straighter. "Would you do me the honor of becoming my wife?"

Teresa discovered that there could be an astonishment so great that it drove every thought, every feeling, from her mind. *Estupefacta*, she thought. Like a person in a fairy tale frozen by a magician's spell. She blinked, parted her lips to respond, produced nothing.

The earl's brows drew together. "Señora Alvarez?"

She found her breath, drew it in, let it out.

"Teresa?"

She had to speak. Of course she could. "You would ask me this?" she managed. In another sort of world, she might have been waiting and longing for his offer, she realized.

"I have done so." He looked uneasy.

"But I have told you about my life." A surge of elation shot through her, to join the furor of emotion upsetting her inner balance. That he would ask! He cared enough, respected her enough. But that didn't change the facts.

The earl nodded. "You have."

"So you know that this is impossible. It cannot be."

"Why not?"

"Have I not caused enough scandal for you?"

"Apparently not," he said with a smile.

"How can you joke? I am ruined. I will never be accepted in your circles."

He shrugged.

Teresa was bewildered by his nonchalance. He was not stupid. "Alessandro Peron is not the only one who will remember me," she went on. "If I drew such attention…" A wedding to an English earl would bring all eyes to bear on her. There would be a flood of inquiries, all the scrutiny she'd taken pains to avoid. The Spanish embassy, the *haut ton*, the distant remains of her family perhaps! They had been happy for her to disappear. "Others will spread their stories. Society will think you mad."

Astonishingly, Lord Macklin laughed. "You know, I find I don't care in the least. Until quite recently I lived a very conventional life, you know. And much of it was pleasant. Even wonderful." He shook his head. "But lately, I've changed. I went wandering around the country. I visited near-strangers without invitation, stuck my nose into their private affairs, ignored the proprieties more than once. And I have been happier than ever before. Society can go hang for all I care."

Did he really compare these trivial transgressions to the step he was proposing? "Marriage to an...outcast is completely different."

"You are no such thing!"

Perhaps he really did not understand. He had always been respected, even revered, by the people surrounding him. And they would not cut him off completely if he did this thing. He was a man. He would still be received. "They will whisper behind your back. Point you out and pity you." She had felt the cut of those superior looks.

"Let them, if they are so small-minded. I shall enjoy my life as I choose. Do you like the country?"

"What has that to do with..."

"Of course you do. You are very fond of gardens. I remember. Those about my country house are extensive. You may do whatever you like with them."

Eliza came in with a plate of tea cakes. She wanted to know what was happening, Teresa thought, and it was difficult to hear from the kitchen. They were silent as she slowly set the plate down and went out.

"What about your family?" Teresa asked then, speaking more quietly. "Your children would not stand for this."

He shrugged. "I think they will be glad to hear that I've found a...dear companion. At Christmas, I seemed to get hints that they would prefer not to be my sole reliance. They are much occupied with their own families now, you know."

"That doesn't mean they want you to marry someone like me!"

"Well, I am putting my own happiness first in this case. They will adjust."

"Lord Macklin…"

"Won't you call me Arthur?"

"No, I will not." The man did not seem to be paying attention.

"I would be so happy if you would."

"Will you listen?"

"I have listened. You have not said anything to the point."

"The point is that I won't ruin your life," Teresa declared.

"You will only do that by refusing me. I love you, you know. I seem to have forgotten to say that." He looked rueful. "It *has* been a long time since I made an offer. And I've only done it once before. I hope you will make allowances. I love you with all my heart. You are everything I admire, and desire, in a woman."

The elation shook her again.

"I had thought that perhaps you felt something for me," he added.

He said it humbly, hopefully. Teresa felt as if *her* heart would break. "It doesn't matter."

"On the contrary. It is critical. You have talked about me, and my life. Well, that is my concern. Let me decide. But you must tell me how you feel, what you want."

"No," she said.

"You won't tell me?"

"We must stop this."

"Or do you say that you care nothing for me and do not wish to be my wife?" He actually looked anxious. "Can you say so?"

"I don't…" She tried to force out the words. But she couldn't lie to him. Of course she cared. She loved him. Couldn't he see that this was the reason she must refuse? He didn't really want to be notorious. He wasn't that sort of person. He was upright and sociable, the soul of honor. He would see that she was right when he had time to think.

"Teresa, do you say you do not care for me?" His face showed that he was growing hopeful. He reached for her hand.

She pulled it away. "Too much to let you do this."

"Me again. What of you? Would you throw away the chance at happiness? I don't wish to brag, but I have a good deal to offer."

Only everything, Teresa thought. And she had nothing to give him but trouble. But she wanted him so much. If they could avoid the censorious gaze of society… "I would be your mistress," she said.

"What?"

"You could visit me here." Some of the neighbors would frown, but many in this part of London would not care. She would not, of course, take any of his money. "We could have…"

"You want me to behave like the man in Spain who treated you so shabbily?" He was scowling at her.

"This is nothing like that."

"Is it not? I can't see a great deal of difference." She realized that he was furious. "You think I am such a man, that I would put you in that position?"

"We could be together without causing a great scandal."

"Because I am a nobleman, and I can have a mistress, and no one will care."

His eyes burned into hers. He looked magnificent. She wanted him as she had never wanted anything else in her life.

"Haven't you shown me the inequities of this? Haven't we worked together to combat some of the unfairness?"

She couldn't deny it. Yet this remained the way of the world. "I will not be the instrument of your ruin."

"But I am to be yours?"

"I'm already ruined."

"Will you stop saying this? The past is irrelevant!"

"You may believe that is true," said Teresa. "But you have no idea what disgrace really means."

He seemed to struggle with his temper. She thought perhaps he lost, because he sprang up, clapped his hat on his head and stalked out. Teresa realized that she'd been holding her breath. She released it. In relief, she told herself. Not despair.

Eliza came out of the kitchen. She stood before Teresa, frowning.

Of course she had managed to overhear. Parts of the conversation at least. It was inevitable in this tiny house, even if she hadn't tried. Which she had. "Yes, Eliza?"

"I don't understand," said the maid. "Mebbe I didn't catch it all... Did you really say no to marrying Lord Macklin, ma'am?"

Teresa could only manage a nod.

"But he's an earl!" Her maid looked bewildered. "You'd be a grand lady and have gowns and carriages and anything you wanted. A big house. More than one, I expect. Would you take me along if you go? I can be a proper housemaid. I promise I can!"

"I'm not going anywhere, Eliza."

She clearly could not comprehend this decision. "There'd be a load of others above me, I know," said the girl. "But that doesn't matter. I can learn. I'd like to."

"We are not going anywhere," Teresa repeated. "I said no. The matter is closed."

Eliza stared at her as if she had well and truly lost her mind.

Teresa went up to her room to wrestle with the tears that threatened to overwhelm her. She would not cry! But of course she did.

❧

Arthur walked. He was unaware of where he was walking for quite some time as he struggled with anger and disappointment and outrage. He was still arguing with the señora in his mind.

No.

Teresa, he was going to think of her as Teresa from now on, he decided. She couldn't prevent that! At least it was a real name. Wasn't it? He didn't even know that for sure. He ground his teeth.

He went over the visit, wondering what he could have done or said to change the outcome. Nothing! She'd been blindly stubborn and unfair. She hadn't really listened to him. She just refused and refused until she decided to insult him by classing him with that blackguard who'd mistreated her. By God, he was nothing like that wretched man! How could she imagine... She'd practically offered *him* a slip on the shoulder!

A harsh laugh escaped him. There could be no other woman like her in the world. He loved everything about her—except her ridiculous reasons for refusing to marry him. She thought they were telling, yes. He saw that. But he did *not* agree.

Arthur looked around and found that he'd reached familiar precincts. He was not too far from home. He turned toward it.

An acquaintance passed and greeted him with a nod and a touch to his hat brim. Arthur strove for his habitual calm as he returned the salutation. And in that commonplace moment, it occurred to him that Teresa must care a great deal for him. She would never have offered to return to the position she'd hated in Spain, of her own free will, for anything less than...love?

The relief that coursed through him then nearly tripped him up. She loved him! She wanted him so much she was willing to offer this! Rather than plodding along the pavement, he suddenly felt as if he was floating.

Then he came back down to Earth. If she truly loved him, why not just marry him? Couldn't she see... But she couldn't. Arthur stood still as things she'd told him, reactions he'd observed, a whole panoply that made up her point of view came together in his mind. It was like turning from a panoramic view and finding a chasm inches from one's toes.

This fear she had of ruining him was ground into her soul. She'd been a sheltered girl, reeling from the murders of her family, when that thrice-damned blackguard had taken her. He'd played on her grief and terror, made her plight seem worse than it was perhaps. Yet it was true that there was no human creature more easily disgraced than an unprotected young lady, as society saw things. The strictures that hemmed them round!

But he was a mature man with a prominent position in the world, and a peer to boot. It was not fair, but he was not nearly so easy to ruin. Nearly impossible in fact. What could the gossips do to him? They might titter and whisper, but he would still be among them. His life would be comfortable and effective even with a scandalous wife. And if people tried to snub her, he would make them sorry. He'd enjoy it! Arthur imagined crushing the pretentions of anyone who offered to snub Teresa. If one had position and power one could…

He felt a brush of shame. That would be acting like the kind of nobleman she despised. He would not do it. He wanted to make her proud.

People were glancing at him as they passed, wondering why he was standing stock-still on the cobbles. Arthur started walking again. And thinking. Teresa was transfixed by this idea of ruin. She thought he would feel it as keenly as she had, when it came to him. But he wouldn't. And it wouldn't. How could he convince her of this?

His love was not a woman to be talked around. He knew that. So, it would have to be actions. He would have to show her. First, that he meant what he said; he didn't care two pins about the opinion of society. And second, that their pointing fingers would not have the same effect on the Earl of Macklin.

But *how* to show her? What could he do? He was ready for anything. She'd made a tremendous sacrifice when she suggested being his mistress. He could do no less. He was ready to offer up his dignity, his social prominence, for her. Arthur walked faster and racked his brain.

The silly pranks of society's young bloods would not do. If he began boxing the watch or downing tumblers of blue ruin or racing his curricle through the London streets, society would merely think he was growing senile. And those sorts of antics were not enough. Most laughed at them. They certainly did not rise to the level of ruin as Teresa would see it. At the other end of the spectrum, the behavior of scum like Lord Simon Farange was out of the question, obviously. What lay between these two? And had he actually never tried to plan a bit of public mischief before?

After further contemplation, and more disappointment in his own inventiveness, a possibility occurred to him. That might do. If it was properly managed. Yes, he thought he could make it fit very nicely indeed.

Practically at his own front door, he turned his footsteps toward another address not far away and prepared to pay a social call.

The object of his visit would be quite surprised to receive him, since he had never called upon her before. All the more, as the accepted time for morning calls was well past. So here he was, already embarking on his life of social crime.

Fifteen

"Macklin," Miss Julia Grandison said as she sailed into her drawing room some minutes later. "How very unusual. Not to say unprecedented."

Arthur rose from the seat where he had been waiting and greeted her in turn. They sat down. He made a few opening remarks.

"Yes, yes, the weather has been most clement," Miss Grandison said after a few minutes. "And Lady Jelleby's rout party was quite amusing. To what do I owe the…curiosity of your visit, Macklin? Is it not the done thing, you know, for a lone gentlemen to call on a single lady in the afternoon. Not for any…acceptable purpose. But of course, you do know that."

He acknowledged this with a nod and started to speak.

"Unless they have clandestine dalliance in mind," added Miss Grandison with a thin smile. "Which I am confident you do *not*."

His reputation for solid, upright reliability would have to be demolished. Oddly, Arthur found he was looking forward to it.

"If you are seeking a donation to your curious new…charitable endeavor, Miss Finch has already approached me. I declined." The lady's tone was dry and disapproving.

Arthur jumped in before she could continue. "You had asked me, once, to aid you in your…endeavors with your brother."

His formidable hostess eyed him as if he had suddenly turned into a completely different creature. "More than once, if memory serves," she replied. "Which it always does. And you were slippery, but immovable, in your refusals."

"Well, I have changed my mind. I wish to help. I am here at your service."

Miss Grandison's eyes narrowed suspiciously, as if he'd offered to steal the ornaments from the mantel shelf rather than assist her. "Indeed?" she replied, drawing out the word. "Why?"

"You *did* ask."

"And you *did* say no. Repeatedly, as we have observed. What has changed?"

"Perhaps I have come to see that you deserve my aid."

"Perhaps. I suppose stranger things have happened. Although none immediately spring to mind."

"Do the reasons matter?"

She stared at him a moment longer and then shrugged. "I suppose not. It's very odd, though, and I'm not fond of the odd. I like knowing what's what. It has something to do with Señora Alvarez, I suppose."

Arthur was too surprised to reply.

"Most things you do lately seem to," Miss Grandison added.

He hadn't realized it was so obvious. He should have. All the better, he decided. He would declaim his love from the rooftops if that would make a difference. But words were not enough.

"And *many* of them are odd," his hostess added. "Your recent houseguests, for example!" Her gaze grew speculative. "Señora Alvarez is an…unorthodox connection for you. People are wondering just where she came from."

This was the sort of insinuation Teresa dreaded. "Spain," said Arthur.

"Well, yes, but that is hopelessly vague, you must admit."

"No," said Arthur.

"I beg your pardon?"

"I don't have to admit anything at all." He discovered that there was an almost joyous freedom in throwing society's rule book overboard. But Teresa would want him to do it kindly. So best to change the subject. "I believe your retaliation should be very public," he said. "As was the original incident."

This diverted Miss Grandison. "Indeed. I agree. But I have not been able to think of a scheme that satisfies me. I had thought to expose John's opera dancer. But it seems that most gentlemen see her as an… accomplishment of some sort rather than a failing." She scowled at him.

"Not I," Arthur said. And then remembered he was supposed to be demolishing his sterling reputation.

"Now that Ada is married and gone, no one cares

much about the hussy," continued Miss Grandison. "Except Gertrude, I suppose. And I don't really wish to humiliate her."

Gertrude was her brother's wife, Arthur remembered, relieved that the dancer was to be left out of this. Teresa would not have liked involving her. "What if you were to subject your brother to the same fate that befell you? And dowse him with a bowl of punch?"

Miss Grandison blinked, startled.

"Before a large crowd, of course," added Arthur. "At a great society squeeze. I had thought the Overton ball? Next week. That is one of the last big events of the season."

His hostess appeared dazed by this flow of detail.

"Your...contretemps took place at a ball, after all," Arthur added.

"Well, I..."

"It seems a kind of...poetic justice. To close the books on the whole matter."

Miss Grandison gazed at him with puzzled wonder. "Yes, I see. I agree with your assessment. But I'm afraid... That is, I'm not certain I could bring myself to overturn a punch bowl before all those people. I would be all too likely to botch it." She shook her head. "A lowering reflection. I am quite disappointed in myself. But I don't think I have the temerity to do it."

"I'll do it for you," declared Arthur.

"You?"

Under her astonished gaze Arthur felt a pulse of excitement. This would work. She couldn't believe he would to do such a thing. All society would be agog.

As a young man, Arthur had never indulged any of

his wild impulses. He'd watched some of his fellows develop unfortunate habits or make fools of themselves, but he'd always been restrained. Not prudish or judgmental, he fervently hoped, but correct. That had simply been his inclination. But now it seemed that he'd had enough of strict propriety. He'd met Teresa and ended up bundling a half-conscious villain onto a ship for the Indies. Which must certainly rise from unorthodox to outrageous. Or worse. Something had ignited his madcap streak at this point in his life, and he gloried in it.

"What in heaven's name are you up to, Macklin?" asked Miss Grandison.

Fleetingly, he was drawn back into old habits. He started to rationalize. And then realized that he had no idea how to do so. Love was not reasonable. But that was none of Miss Grandison's affair. He owed no explanations. She could take or leave his aid. If she didn't want it, he'd think of something else. "Offering to help you? Do you really care what else?"

She took a moment to consider this. "I suppose not," she said slowly.

"And why should you? If your goal is accomplished."

"Well, I am very curious," she answered. "Intensely so."

"They do say not to look a gift horse in the mouth."

"Indeed," said Miss Grandison. "Why is that? I have often wondered."

"One judges the age of a horse by its teeth," Arthur replied. "To look in its mouth would be to question the value of the *gift*." He emphasized the last word.

Their eyes met for a long moment. Arthur wondered

how many people would stare at him with such wild surmise after this. The question made him want to laugh.

"The punch could do," Miss Grandison said then.

And so his fish was hooked. "There are people who recall what happened to you," said Arthur. "They will understand the message."

"You think so?" Her tone was very dry.

"Turnabout is fair play," he suggested.

"You believe in fairness, do you, Macklin?"

This was not the time for a philosophical discussion. "You could repeat what he said to you years ago, when he is sitting there covered in punch. What was it?"

"He said, 'You are always so clumsy, Julia.'"

"Yes. You should say something like that to him. In your best public voice."

"My public voice?"

"It is marvelously penetrating," Arthur pointed out.

"What in the world has come over you, Macklin?"

"Ingenuity?"

"In…" She frowned at him. "You are behaving quite unlike yourself."

"Perhaps you don't know me very well. Perhaps no one does. Oh! I've thought of something else. We should include the others. The fellows who plotted against you to overturn the punch. You told me who it was, but I've forgotten."

"Trask and Quigley." Miss Grandison had begun to look morbidly fascinated.

"That was it," said Arthur.

"Quentin Quigley is a high-court judge now," his

hostess pointed out. "And Ralph Trask is a solemn paterfamilias. Bald as an egg, of course, as I knew he would be."

"He'd look like an Easter egg covered in punch."

Miss Grandison was surprised into a laugh. And once she'd begun she couldn't immediately stop. "To think of them," she gasped finally. "All soaked, dazed, and dripping on the carpet."

"Sticky as well, I suppose," said Arthur.

"Oh yes. It was terribly sticky. But I do not see how it can be done, Macklin. How would we get them all together at the right moment?"

"Leave that to me." He had no idea how, but he would think of something. "You might start retelling the old story, as if it was just amusing now. Remind people who was responsible. You could call it a lark, or some such thing. Set the stage as it were." He had learned from Tom's experience.

"Lord Macklin, I am beginning to feel that I should refuse your extremely…surprising offer."

"Really? Why?"

"Because I very much fear you've gone mad."

"I haven't."

"Are you sure?" Her tone was desert dry. "How would you know?"

"I am very well aware of what I'm doing."

They engaged in another lengthy staring contest. Arthur settled in. He would have to become accustomed to astonished gazes. And mouths agape and dumbfounded gasps, he supposed.

"And you do not intend to tell me what that is," Miss Grandison said finally.

"Do you want your revenge, or not?" Arthur asked.

She considered this for some time, finally letting out a sigh. "I do. Though perhaps I should not. My mother used to say that one should strive to be the larger person. But she never actually had to occupy that position." Miss Grandison gestured at her massive figure.

"So we go forward with the plan then?"

"I feel as if I've harnessed a tiger to my carriage."

"Thank you." Arthur smiled. She looked taken aback by his expression. "So we are agreed it is to be at the Overton ball?" he asked.

"Yes."

"I will set things in train." He could get Tom and some of the actors to help. That was a good notion. Tom was always a wellspring of ideas.

"Things," repeated Miss Grandison, voice and expression wary. "I believe I won't ask what things."

"Probably best." Particularly as he had no details to give her as yet.

"Do you think it could be rack punch?" she added wistfully. "Not scalding, of course. But rather hot?"

"I will see what I can do." He was pretty well acquainted with Mrs. Overton. He had done her a favor or two over the years. But he was not sure he could dictate the menu at her ball. Still, the request would be another eccentricity, and he was ready to pile up as many of those as possible in the time allotted.

❧

"I never heard of such a thing as that," said Tom. "It's like a play, but at a ball?"

"You might say so," Arthur replied. They were drinking mugs of beer at Rigby's pub. The dim establishment had seemed to Arthur a fit place to plot new mischief. Not that he intended anyone else to know the whole of his plan. The retired boxer was throwing doubtful glances their way from behind the bar as if he suspected the worst.

"But why?" asked Tom. "And how will we work it so everyone can see?"

Arthur ignored the first question. "We'll have a sufficient audience. The young ladies who investigate mysteries have agreed to urge people along at the right moment."

"Huh." Tom nodded. "So what do you want me to do?"

There was no argument or talk of madness. Arthur was touched by the lad's implicit trust in him. "You will be instructing the actresses and shepherding one of the most important bystanders through the…action," he answered. "Here are cards of invitation." Arthur handed Tom three white squares. His reputation for correctness had stood him in good stead with Mrs. Overton. It had never occurred to the society hostess that the august Earl of Macklin might be planning a prank. "I've written out the…script for the ladies." He passed over the handwritten pages.

Tom scanned them. "Seems like Moll and Kate are the professionals, like, making certain your friends are in the right place at the right time?"

"A fine way of putting it."

"They can calm their nerves as well."

Arthur bit down on an antic smile. "I'm sure their

presence will be…soothing. But they must seem simply to be enjoying the ball. With no mention of any other purpose."

"They ain't to let on," said Tom with a nod. "They stay with their characters."

"Exactly. The…outcome of the scene is a surprise, you see."

"For the players too?"

"For everyone."

"Right." Tom put the papers in his pocket. "Moll and Kate will do just as you ask. They're first-rate onstage. And they're over the moon about going to a real ball. Not to mention the dresses you're buying for them."

"Splendid."

"Is it a surprise for the señora as well?" Tom asked.

"Most particularly for her."

This did earn Arthur a speculative glance. But Tom said only, "We'll keep mum at the theater then."

❧

Teresa examined the ornate invitation that had been delivered to her door by a liveried footman. It had come in an envelope with a note from Lord Macklin. She picked that up and reread the brief message.

> *You have been kind enough to say that you owe me thanks for recent efforts. I would consider it an equal favor if you would accept this invitation.*

The true meaning was no clearer this time than when she'd first opened it. He seemed to imply that her appearance at this Mrs. Overton's ball was a... payment for his help. But he had rejected the very idea of gratitude, had seemed revolted by the concept, in fact. He might have changed his mind, of course. But that didn't explain why her attendance at a ball should satisfy him. Were they to dance? Did he mean to repeat his proposal? A ball was a poor place for that. She felt the queasy combination of righteousness and regret that had afflicted her since he'd asked. She shouldn't go.

"That's a fine-looking bit of writing," said Eliza, shifting over the pasteboard as she set down the tea tray. "What's in it?"

"It is an invitation to a ball."

"A real ball? Like Cinderella?"

Was she the girl in the ashes? And Lord Macklin the handsome prince? But Teresa had no magical helpers. This was reality, not a fairy tale. Yet she'd missed him dreadfully since she'd sent him away.

A knock on the door heralded Tom's arrival. He had invited himself today for some of Eliza's lemon tea cakes and an unspecified discussion.

He devoured three of the former before tapping a finger on the invitation. "I came to see if I could escort you to this Overton ball."

"*You* are going?"

He grinned at her surprise. "Not very likely, eh? His lordship arranged it. I reckon seeing a proper society ball will help me play a toff onstage."

This might be so, but it didn't really explain.

"I've spoke to Vining and hired his hack for that night. Be almost like having a private carriage."

"What in the world is going on, Tom?"

"A ball?" He ate another cake. "No need to worry. I've had dancing lessons at the theater."

As if *that* was her concern. "This makes no sense. Why am I invited to this ball? Why are you? Who are these Overtons? Surely they cannot have heard of either of us?" They had better not have heard of *her*.

Tom was nodding as if he agreed. "Like I said, it's his lordship's scheme."

"Scheme?"

"Plan," corrected Tom quickly. "I got an idea about it."

"I would be delighted to hear this."

"Well, what they call the season is just about over, eh? I reckon Lord Macklin will be leaving town soon. So I'm thinking he's seeing this ball as a way of saying goodbye."

"Goodbye." Of course he would be going. Society streamed out of London when the season ended. It would be months before he returned, and by then perhaps he would have forgotten her. He ought to. But she couldn't bear the thought. Surely she could see him once more. She could have that. They might even waltz. "I will go," she said. She simply couldn't resist.

"Good," said Tom.

Teresa began reviewing her gowns to decide which would dazzle one particular, discriminating member of the *haut ton*.

Sixteen

HE HAD PERHAPS WORKED HARDER AT OTHER THINGS IN his life, Arthur decided several days later, but never in such a concentrated burst. He was accustomed to having a large staff making arrangements for him. He hadn't wanted to involve them in his plan for Miss Grandison's brother, however, and he didn't really mind the effort. He told himself he was like an ancient knight on a quest to win his lady. An odd sort of quest, to be sure, but the intent was there. A massive effort was the point, wasn't it? He didn't feel in the least as if he'd lost his senses. Had he not rather found them?

By the day of the ball, he had checked off all the tasks on his list. He'd made certain that Quigley, Trask, and John Grandison all planned to attend. He had used all his powers of persuasion on Mrs. Overton and convinced her that serving rack punch at her ball might set a new fashion, though Arthur suspected that she was moving over into the category of those who thought he'd gone a bit mad. The idea filled him with an unfamiliar glee. It had been a very long time since he'd confounded anyone. Had he ever? Really? He couldn't recall an instance, but he did have a great deal on his mind.

Tom and the two actresses from the Drury Lane Theater had been provided with the right sort of clothing and fully primed for the "scene" they were to perform. The ladies seemed to find the whole idea good fun. Miss Grandison had done her part as well, reminding the *ton* of her youthful embarrassment despite rising doubts about Arthur's mental stability.

On the night, Arthur dressed to be more conspicuous than usual. Actually, he never was the least bit conspicuous. So this ensemble would be a first attempt. "I beg your pardon, my lord," said his valet, Clayton, when he discovered a certain garment that Arthur had dug out of the back of the wardrobe. "There has been some mistake. I will just…"

"No, I'm wearing that one," Arthur interrupted.

Clayton turned, holding the waistcoat that they'd rejected as unacceptable, its cherry-red and silver stripes too garish for public view. "*This* one?"

Clayton had been with him for more than twenty years, and Arthur valued his canny insights as much as his personal services. But in this case the valet wasn't aware of the plan. "*That* one," Arthur confirmed.

"But, my lord."

Arthur saw that he'd gained another recruit into the ranks of those who feared for his sanity. So all was going well. "I am determined to wear it. A bit of a change, eh, Clayton?"

Though Clayton was an unassuming figure in middle age, with a round face that was pleasant rather than handsome and quiet brown eyes, he had the ability to exude disapproval. He exercised it to the fullest as Arthur finished dressing.

The waistcoat had the desired effect. It drew astonished stares when he entered the Overton house, and Miss Grandison couldn't seem to tear her eyes away from the garment when he went up to speak to her at the beginning of the ball. "The event will take place at the interval, when the refreshment room is most crowded," he told her.

"Event?" She stared at his midsection.

"Delayed justice? Act of redemption? What do you wish to call it?"

"At this moment, Lord Macklin, I cannot find a phrase that satisfactorily expresses my feelings."

"Well, you needn't worry. The plans are all in place."

"Worry. Am I worried? I don't seem to be able to discern what I am."

Arthur offered her a polite nod, as if they had been discussing commonplace matters and stepped away.

"How do you intend…" she began.

"It would be best if you were not aware of the details, don't you think?"

"Best," repeated Miss Grandison as if the word was untranslatable. He left her before she could figure it out.

His waistcoat attracted more attention, with smiles or frowns depending on the source. Certainly he was being noticed much more than usual. It was an interesting experience.

And then Teresa arrived with Tom, and he forgot everything else. In a gown of deep-blue silk with sprays of tiny sapphires sparkling in her earrings, she was gorgeous. Arthur's heart began to pound like that of a gambler who was risking all on one desperate throw.

Just as she'd imagined, Lord Macklin came up to Teresa and asked her to dance. She accepted and took his arm to join the set. It was more than a pleasure to walk across the floor beside him. Although he didn't look *quite* like himself. It was the stripes, she decided. "Your waistcoat is certainly…festive."

"Worthy of a celebration," he replied. Incomprehensibly. His blue eyes had an almost feverish sparkle.

"Why have you invited me here tonight?" Teresa asked him.

"I? Mrs. Overton invited you."

"That would be the lady who greeted me at the entrance? The one who clearly had no idea who I was?"

"There are so many guests," the earl replied. "This will be the last great squeeze of the season."

The music began. They moved through the first steps of a country dance.

At the next opportunity for conversation Teresa said, "Tom thinks that we—he and I—are here because you will be leaving London soon and wished to say a…ceremonial goodbye."

"Does he?" Lord Macklin looked pleased. "He is a clever lad."

"So it is that? You wished to make some…grand gesture of farewell?"

"Grand but not goodbye, I hope," Arthur muttered.

"What? I didn't quite hear you."

"You look ravishing tonight," he said. "You throw all the other ladies into the shade."

Teresa felt her cheeks flush. She was glad he found her beautiful. She thought him...everything a man should be. When he swung her around in a turn of the dance, her senses swam. She saw herself throwing her arms around him and begging him to carry her off, right here, in front of everyone. If he proposed marriage now... She shoved the idea away. It was no more possible than it had been before. Music and movement and a glittering crowd made no difference. And men didn't ask again when they'd been refused. Of course, they didn't invite one to balls and call one ravishing either. In eye-popping striped waistcoats. "It isn't like you to make dramatic gestures," she said.

"No? Are you sure you know me so well?"

She met his gaze and couldn't look away. Love was there. As well as...anticipation? Something was happening tonight. She didn't know what, but she had the sudden sense of a turning point looming. "What..." she began. And the set ended.

People stepped apart, dispersed. Lord Macklin turned and was inundated by a bevy of young ladies in pastel ball gowns and a babble of greetings.

"My brother Cecil is full of admiration for your waistcoat," said Miss Deeping to the earl.

"You do understand that this is ominous?" asked Miss Finch. "To be admired by Cecil Deeping is to destroy any aspirations you might have to good taste."

"Oh, Harriet, he's not so bad," said Miss Moran. "Have you seen *his* waistcoat?"

"I was too dazzled by the coach-wheel buttons and

the many fobs," said Miss Deeping. "Henry said he looks like a mountebank."

"I have never regretted having no brothers," said Miss Finch.

"Yes, you have," replied Miss Moran. "When you were wishing you could learn swordplay back at school."

"Ha! I'd forgotten." Miss Finch laughed. "A brother like Cecil would be no use for *that*. And one doesn't get to choose."

"I'll bring Cecil to compliment you *later*," said Miss Deeping to the earl, giving the final words an odd emphasis.

Before Teresa could do more than wonder about undercurrents, Miss Moran burst out with "Your earrings are lovely. Did you design them?"

Teresa nodded. Tom joined them. There was a general milling about. Couples moved in for the next set. And somehow Lord Macklin was gone. Teresa looked for him, but he seemed to have disappeared.

He wished he could dance every dance with Teresa, Arthur thought as he edged his way into the card room. But he couldn't. He wanted to attract attention to himself, not to her. And if he talked to her anymore, he might give things away. His…cast clearly couldn't resist dropping hints. So that great pleasure was denied to him. He had to stay away from her. He would lurk here until nearer the time. He found a place at one of the card tables and joined the hand, receiving gibes about his waistcoat with a witless smile.

Arthur emerged as the set before supper was forming. He didn't seek a partner. Rather, he located

Miss Grandison's brother, who also was not dancing, and went to stand near him. Just as the music ended, Arthur stepped forward and said, "Good evening, Grandison, how are you?"

The man looked surprised to be addressed. They were not well acquainted. But he responded civilly.

"I've heard there is to be rack punch with supper," Arthur added. "Shall we go and see?"

"At a ball? That is most unusual."

"Mrs. Overton assured me." He edged the other man toward the doorway to the refreshment room. Grandison let himself be herded. Arthur saw the three young ladies leading groups of their friends in the same direction. Miss Julia Grandison was approaching as well. She grimaced at him. He ignored her.

The young actresses had been put in charge of Quigley and Trask, to maneuver them into position at the proper moment. They'd been given free rein as to how this was to be accomplished. When Arthur brought his charge into the room he saw the two gentlemen who had tipped a punch bowl over Miss Julia Grandison many years ago looking a bit dazed by the unexpected female attention. They were also precisely in place near the rack punch. Arthur brought John Grandison to join them, nodded a dismissal to the actresses, and then moved behind the refreshment table. "Look, it is rack punch," he said.

When they turned, Arthur picked up the large bowl—heavy, but he'd been braced for that. He raised it high and, with a great heave, tossed the warm liquid over the unsuspecting trio.

A gasp swept through the room.

Arthur experienced a barrage of appalled stares from the cream of society. Mouths hung open; some pointed at him. He spotted Tom, looking poleaxed. He noticed Miss Finch, her brows raised in startled surmise.

Trask, Grandison, and Quigley wiped sticky punch from their faces. It dripped from the tails of their coats. They gazed at Arthur, stunned.

"How very clumsy of you, John," someone declared. It was Julia Grandison, in her best public voice. It was indeed marvelously penetrating.

The room erupted in a storm of talk. Arthur felt a tremor of anxious gratification as he continued to search for the one person he most wanted to find. And then he saw her. Teresa stood near Tom. She'd been hidden by another lady's headdress, but she'd obviously seen the whole. Her amazed expression said so.

Arthur stared at her with his heart in his eyes. He couldn't speak to her now. He mustn't involve her in his notoriety. But he hoped for some sign that she'd understood his message. He didn't care one snap of his fingers for social ruin. Let them bring it on! After an endless moment, she started to smile. He held her gaze until the smile seemed likely to turn to a laugh, then turned on his heel. His work here was done. He walked out of the room and the house.

❦

"He threw it right over them," Tom told an awed audience at the theater workshop the next day. He shook his head. "The look on his lordship's face when he heaved that punch bowl. I'll never forget it."

"But *why* did he do it?" asked Miss Moran.

The three young ladies had shown up first thing, and Teresa's suspicions that they had been in on the prank had been partly confirmed. They'd settled with a group of artisans in the courtyard to hear and rehash the tale.

"It was so unlike him," declared Miss Deeping. "I've always found Lord Macklin stuffy."

"But we know you are a poor judge of people, Charlotte," said Miss Finch.

"I may miss some things, but I'm not usually that far off!"

"Yes, you are," said Miss Moran. "Haven't you noticed the twinkle in his eyes?"

He had done it for her, Teresa thought. She still couldn't quite comprehend the enormity of it. The scene kept playing in her mind—the heft of the bowl, the slosh of the punch, the utter stupefaction of the three victims. And most vividly, the earl's look at her afterward. His expression, his gaze, said that this was a message for her. A weird sort of gift. When she'd smiled at him, he'd looked…satisfied?

"His lordship didn't say nothing to me about tossing punch," replied Tom. "I reckon he decided to help Miss Grandison get back at her brother in the end." Tom grinned. "She tried ever so hard not to look pleased, but she didn't quite manage it."

"Ada will be furious to have missed this," said Miss Deeping.

"*I'm* right furious," said Poppy, who'd joined the workshop staff only a few days ago and was settling in admirably. "What a sight to see. Why didn't you take me along?" she asked Tom.

"I told you, I didn't know what his lordship was

going to do. And I couldn't just march you into a grand society ball without an invitation, could I?"

"You think I couldn't have done as well as Molly and Kate?" Poppy glared at him.

"You ain't an actress."

"Yet," muttered Poppy.

"Ada wouldn't have liked seeing her father embarrassed," said Miss Moran.

"After the hints about an opera dancer?" said Miss Finch. "I disagree."

"He looked so bewildered," said Miss Deeping. "Even after Miss Grandison spoke up. He didn't seem to have the least notion that his sister might resent the way he treated her years ago."

"And so perhaps he deserved a shock," replied Miss Finch. "How could anyone fail to realize that?"

Teresa wondered if kindness had been part of Lord Macklin's motive. No. He was kind, but this wasn't the sort of benevolence he practiced. He'd done it to show her that he meant what he said—he didn't care a whit about society's opinion of him. She also wondered how he was feeling this morning in the… aftermath of his outburst? Was he full of regret? She would hate to learn that he was sorry now. She half rose, full of a need to see him.

"The bald fellow, Trask, took it the best," Tom went on. "After the first shock, he started laughing. With punch running down his bald head and onto his shoulders. The other one, Quigley, looked like he was going to explode. Lord Macklin might want to watch out for him."

"He has already sent me a fiery protest," said a deep

voice from the courtyard doorway. Teresa turned with all the others to find the earl approaching. She sank back into her chair. "We are exchanging... correspondence, trying to avoid a duel," he added. "I think we shall succeed if I offer up enough abject apologies. He *is* a high-court judge. He can hardly put a bullet in me."

The earl joined them on a chorus of exclamations.

"I wouldn't be too concerned," he responded. "It is not exactly a matter of honor to be dowsed with rack punch. Quigley was not...impugned. Though we have not quite settled what it *is*." He smiled.

Teresa could see no signs of regret in his face. He sounded much as usual. He looked as urbanely handsome and assured as ever.

"We are all wondering *that*," said Miss Deeping. "Have you heard the wild theories racing around the ton?"

"I have not." Lord Macklin looked merely amused.

Miss Deeping counted them off on her fingers. "One, the most convoluted—that Miss Julia Grandison knows some dark secret about you and threatened to reveal it unless you did as she asked. Two, the strangest—that opera dancers have sent you out to pay off past humiliations. In a demented kind of chivalry. Several men have looked *quite* concerned about that one. And three, the simplest—that you've just gone mad. Of course."

"Charlotte is making a chart," said Miss Moran. "With subcolumns for what your dark secret might be and which gentlemen had best watch out for retribution."

The earl burst out laughing. Teresa listened as if the sound might give her clues. It seemed a carefree laugh.

"Why *did* you do it?" asked Miss Finch.

"To make a point."

"What point?" wondered Miss Moran.

Lord Macklin met Teresa's eyes and held them as he said, "That I am quite willing to be notorious."

There was no mistaking the message in his gaze. He had done this thing for her, to prove he meant what he'd said. And he had not changed his mind about marriage. Teresa's pulse sped.

"Why would you want to be that?" asked Poppy. "Won't it be a great trouble?"

"No. Not the least in the world."

"But people might snub you," said Miss Moran.

He turned and looked at her with slightly raised brows. His expression seemed politely inquiring, but Teresa could see the unshakable aplomb behind it. "If they like," he said, his voice laden with indifference.

"They won't," said Tom. "Not his lordship. The gossips will yammer and sniggle, the dog-hearted foot lickers. And then I expect everybody'll end up admiring him in the end."

There were murmurs of general agreement. Teresa looked around the group. These individuals of different outlook and degree all thought Tom was right. She hadn't taken the earl's quality and history into account. *He* would not be scorned. He made that impossible.

He was watching her. *Not* like a cat waiting for a mouse to scurry past. More like a supplicant daring to hope. She felt her face heat with a dizzying mixture of anticipation and amazement and desire. Could it be happiness, trembling in the balance? She saw him recognize…something in her face.

Arthur's spirits soared. His stubborn love had been swayed by his…heroic deed. He was sure of it. Nearly sure. He had to ask her. He was wild to do so. She was sitting so close to him, and yet an inconvenient crowd away. He must be rid of all these people!

He hadn't counted on the young ladies being present. He couldn't command them as he might Tom and his comrades. Well, nothing to do but make a start. "Is there no work to be done here today?" he asked the air. The outer circle of artisans reacted to the voice of authority and began to disperse. But Tom and the young ladies, including Poppy, made no move. He was left within their circle of interested gazes. Arthur searched for words.

But he'd forgotten. He'd thrown off the shackles of propriety. He wasn't hemmed in by them any longer. Noting that it was deuced difficult to establish new habits, he said, "Will you all please go away and let me talk to Señora Alvarez?"

"Are you finally going to speak?" asked Miss Deeping. "We have been wondering *why* you were waiting."

"Charlotte," said Miss Finch.

"Well, but we…"

"Charlotte," said Miss Moran.

Miss Deeping held up a hand to forestall them. And then all three young ladies spoke in a practiced chorus. "It's more complicated than that."

"What is?" asked Poppy. "Do you practice speaking all together? It's funny."

"Let's get back to it, Poppy," Tom said to her. He rose and offered his arm. With a giggle, she stood and took it. As they walked out, Tom looked back over his shoulder, grinned at Arthur, and gave him a quick salute with his free hand. Arthur could only smile back.

The three young ladies gathered their things, of which they seemed to have an inordinate number. Then they too departed. At last he and Teresa were alone in the courtyard.

They were not overlooked. There were no windows into the workshop. Arthur found himself thinking that a few windows would be pleasant, for the light, and realized he was putting off hearing his fate. "Well," he said.

"Do you intend to explain yourself?" Teresa asked.

He was momentarily concerned. Then he saw the gleam in her dark eyes. She wasn't quite laughing, but she wasn't cool either. Strong emotion stirred there. "You worried that you would ruin me," he said. "I did not agree, but you weren't open to my arguments. So I decided to do it myself, to remove your...anxieties."

"Remove?" She shook her head. "When I saw you lift that punch bowl, I thought *I'd* gone mad."

"It was quite heavy."

Her lips twitched. "And the looks on those men's faces!"

"I do wish I might have seen that," he said. "But their backs were turned to me, you know."

Teresa gazed at him. It seemed that doubt still plagued her. "Perhaps you have lost your mind."

"Some people think so. Let them." He leaned closer to her. "I am simply in love."

"Do you say I have driven you mad?"

"No. I say you have let me find myself once again."
He dared to take her hand. She didn't pull it away. "I
have been…muted for some years. By circumstances.
And rules. Now I'm ready to come to life."

"Which means behaving outrageously?"

"That was only to convince you. Have I? Because I
can indulge in more and more outrageous pranks until
you are."

"You are being ridiculous."

"Am I? It is a new and interesting behavior for me.
Quite stimulating."

"Lord Macklin…"

"I wish you would call me Arthur. I really long to
hear my name on your lips."

The word led Teresa to focus on *his*. Those lips that
had sent fire through her veins.

"I hope it's clear that I am offering for you again,"
he said. "Is it? If I went down on one knee this time,
would it help?"

"Will you be serious?"

His expression shifted. "I've never been more so,
Teresa. I don't think I can be happy without you."
He frowned. "That did not sound well. If you really
do not wish to be my wife, then of course I won't
continue to plague you." He looked into her eyes. "I
dearly hope that is not the case."

"Must I marry you to keep you from making a fool
of yourself? Again."

A smile curved those seductive lips. "Absolutely. It
is your duty to redeem my reputation, to save me."

"I? To save you!"

"I believe you have. At least I hope you will agree to do so. Continue to do so. For the rest of my life."

The clumsiness of his words, so unlike the ever-confident earl, enchanted her. "How can I refuse?"

He sprang to his feet and reached for her, then hesitated. "Would you mind very much saying 'yes'?"

"Yes," Teresa said. "Yes, I will marry you, and we will save each other for the rest of our lives."

He pulled her up into his arms and kissed her as she had been longing to be kissed—tenderly, ruthlessly, softly, passionately. The world disappeared into a languorous flurry of kisses.

Some indeterminate time later, they sat side by side with his arm around her waist. "Will you wear your striped waistcoat to the wedding?" Teresa asked him.

"I will wear it every day from now on, if you like. Unless…" He looked concerned.

"Unless?"

"Clayton, my valet, has been rather furtive since the Overton ball. I fear he might have burnt that waistcoat. But I will buy another exactly like it."

Teresa held up a hand. "No. I would not like to begin our marriage by offending Clayton. He was very kind, and most imposing, when I stayed at your house."

"You will be there always now," he replied with complacent delight. "So we will do without the stripes, if necessary?"

"We will."

"But nothing else. Anything you want, you need only name it."

"I have always been fascinated by elephants," said Teresa.

"By…" He looked down at her, caught the joke, and smiled. "It would serve you right if I purchased an elephant and put it in your care."

"With one of those seats they wear on their backs," she retorted. "Like the pictures from India. We could ride it about your estate. That would certainly confirm your…transformation."

"Do you dare me? Or tempt me?"

"I retract everything," said Teresa, and kissed him again.

They were both laughing when Tom's head appeared in the doorway. "Are you finished?" he asked. "It's just that everyone keeps asking me."

"Señora Alvarez and I are going to be married," answered Arthur.

"Oh, good!" Tom looked back and perhaps made some gesture. In the next moment, he and the three young ladies had surged back into the courtyard. It seemed that no one had gone farther than the workshop.

"I told you so," said Miss Deeping as they surrounded Arthur and Teresa.

"You promised you would stop saying that, Charlotte," said Miss Moran. "We wish you every happiness."

"Indeed," said Miss Finch. "When is the wedding to be? Ada will be furious if she cannot attend."

"We haven't planned—" began Teresa.

"It will be quite soon, by special license, and pay no heed at all to other people's convenience," said Arthur.

"Are you going to let him dictate to you?" asked Miss Deeping, censure in her face.

"A lady gets to decide everything about her wedding," said Miss Moran.

"Her last, and often only, efficacy," added Miss Finch dryly.

Teresa looked up at her earl. His gaze was warm and caressing. Love brimmed up and filled her. "Well, you see, he has promised me an elephant."

"What?" asked the three young ladies in unison.

"Did he really?" Tom looked delighted. "Can I come and see it? We had one in a play once, and I wondered if…"

"Go away," Arthur said. "All of you. You ladies, go home. Tom, return to your work or wherever you please. As long as it is not here."

There were protests. Arthur summoned up his new habit of impertinence and pointed a finger at the door. Slowly, reluctantly, they went. He then returned to the much more pleasant matter of kisses.

DIANA GRESHAM HUGGED THE THIN COTTON OF
her nightdress to her chest and snuggled deeper into
the pillows of the posting-house bed. She had never
been so happy in her life, she told herself, and today
was just the beginning of a glorious future. This afternoon, she and Gerald would reach Gretna Green and
be married, and then no one could part them or spoil
their wonderful plans—not even her father.

Of course, Papa was unlikely to protest *now*. Diana's
lovely face clouded as she considered the terrible step
she had been forced to by her father's harshness. If
he had only *listened* this once, it wouldn't have been
necessary to defy him. But almost eighteen years as
Mr. Gresham's sole companion had repeatedly—and
painfully—defeated any such hopes. Papa was impla-
cable; he had never shown the least interest in her
ideas or opinions, except to condemn them. Diana felt
only a small admixture of guilt in her relief at having
escaped her rigid, penurious home.

A tap on the door made her expression lighten.
Sitting up and smiling expectantly, she called, "Come

in." The panels swung back to reveal first a loaded tray, then an extremely handsome young man.

"*Voilà*," he said, returning her smile possessively. "Tea. And hot toast." He swept a napkin from the tray to display it. "I play servant to you."

Diana clapped her hands. "Thank you! I am so hungry."

"The unaccustomed exertions of the night, no doubt," he replied, placing the tray across her knees and resting a hand on her half-bare shoulder.

Diana flushed fiery red and gazed fixedly at the white teapot. She would get used to such frankness concerning the somewhat discomfiting intimacies of marriage, she thought. Her first experience last night had not been at all like the stolen kisses she and Gerald had exchanged in the weeks since they met. Yet Gerald had obviously seen nothing wrong so Diana dismissed her reaction as naiveté. She knew she was less sophisticated than other girls, even those not yet eighteen. Because her father had never allowed her to attend any party or assembly, nor meet any of the young men who visited her friends' families, Diana was deeply humble about her ignorance, while passionately eager to be rid of it. Until Gerald's miraculous appearance during one of her solitary country walks—an event she still could not help but compare to the illustration of the Archangel Michael in her Bible—she had never spoken to a man of her own age. That her sole opportunity should bring a veritable pink of the ton (a term Gerald had taught her) had been overwhelming. From the first, she had joyfully referred every question to him, and taken his answers as gospel.

Diana raised her eyes, found her promised husband gazing appreciatively at her scantily clad form, and promptly lowered them again.

For his part, Gerald Carshin was congratulating himself on his astuteness. He had been hanging out for a rich wife for nearly ten years, and his golden youth was beginning, however slightly, to tarnish. Even he saw that. His sunny hair remained thick— automatically he touched its fashionable perfection— and his blue eyes had lost none of their dancing charm, but he had started to notice alarming signs of thickness in his slim waist and a hint of sag in his smooth cheeks. At thirty, it was high time he wed, and he had cleverly unearthed an absolute peach of an heiress in the nick of time.

Carshin's eyes passed admiringly over Diana's slender rounded form, which was more revealed than hidden by the thin nightdress and coverlet. Her curves were his now; he breathed a little faster thinking of last night. And her face was equally exquisite. Like him, she was blond, but her hair was a deep rich gold, almost bronze, and her eyes were the color of aged sherry, with glints of the same gold in their depths. She wasn't the least fashionable, of course. Her tartar of a father had never allowed her to crop her hair or buy modish gowns. Yet the waves of shining curls that fell nearly to Diana's waist convinced Gerald that there was some substance in the old man's strictures. It had taken his breath away last night when Diana had unpinned her fusty knot and shaken her hair loose.

"Your tea is getting cold," Carshin said indulgently. "I thought you were hungry."

Self-consciously Diana began to eat. She had never breakfasted with a man sitting on her bed—or, indeed, in bed at all until today. But of course, having Gerald there was wonderful, she told herself quickly. Everything about her life would be different and splendid now. "Are they getting the carriage ready?" she asked, needing to break the charged silence. "I can dress in a minute."

"There's no hurry." His hand smoothed her fall of hair, then moved to cup a breast and fondle it. "We needn't leave at once." But as he bent to kiss Diana's bare neck, he felt her stiffen. She won't really relax till the knot's tied, he thought, drawing back. A pity she's so young. "Still, when you've finished your tea, you should get up," he added.

Diana nodded, relieved, yet puzzled by her hesitant reaction to Gerald's touch. This was the happiest day of her life, she repeated to herself.

Gerald moved to an armchair by the window. "Once we're married, we'll go straight to London. The season will be starting soon, and I...*we* must find a suitable house and furnish it." Gerald pictured himself set up in his own house, giving card parties and taking a box at the opera. How the ton would stare! He would finally have his revenge on the damned high sticklers who cut him.

"Oh, yes," agreed Diana, her breakfast forgotten. "I can hardly wait to see all the fashionable people and go to balls."

Gerald scrutinized her, the visions he had conjured up altering slightly. Diana would of necessity accompany him. "We must get you some clothes first, and do something about your hair." She put a stricken hand to it. "It's lovely, but not quite the thing, you know."

"No." Diana looked worried. "You will tell me how I should go on, and what I am to wear, won't you?"

"Naturally." Gerald seemed to expand in the chair. "We shall be all the crack, you and I. Everyone will invite us."

Diana sighed with pleasure at the thought. All her life she had longed for gaiety and crowds of chattering friends rather than the bleak, dingy walls of her father's house. Now, because of Gerald, she would have them.

"You must write at once to your trustees and tell them you are married," he added, still lost in a happy dream. "We shall have to draw quite a large sum to get settled in town."

"My trustees?" Diana's brown eyes grew puzzled.

"Yes. You told me their names, but I've forgotten. The banker and the solicitor in charge of your mother's fortune—yours, I should say, now. You come into it when you marry, remember."

"Not unless I am of age," she corrected him.

Gerald went very still. "What?"

"Papa made her put that in. Mr. Merton at the bank told me so. Mama would have left me her money outright, but Papa insisted upon conditions. It is just like him. The money was to be mine when I married, unless I should do so before I came of age. Otherwise, I must wait until I am five-and-twenty. Isn't that infamous?"

Carshin's pale face had gone ashen. "But you are not eighteen for…"

"Four months," she finished. Sensing his consternation, she added, "Is something wrong?"

His expression was intent, but he was not looking at her. "We must simply wait to be married," he murmured. "We cannot go to London, of course. We shall have to live very quietly in the country, and—"

"Wait!" Diana was aghast. "Gerald, you promised me we should be married at once. Indeed, I never could have"—she choked on the word "eloped"—"left home otherwise."

Meeting her eyes, Gerald saw unshakable determination, and the collapse of all his careful plans. One thing his rather unconventional life had taught him was to read others' intentions. Diana would not be swayed by argument, however logical.

Why had she withheld this crucial piece of information? he wondered. This was all her fault. In fact, she had neatly trapped him into compromising her. But if she thought that the proprieties weighed with him, she was mistaken. The chit deserved whatever she got.

He looked up, and met her worried gaze. The naked appeal in her dark eyes stopped the flood of recrimination on his tongue, but it did not change his mind. Hunching a shoulder defensively, he rose. "I should see about the horses. You had better get dressed."

"Yes, I will," replied Diana eagerly, relief making her weak. "I won't be a minute."

Gerald nodded curtly, and went out.

But when Diana descended the narrow stair a half hour later, her small valise in her hand, there was no sign of Gerald Carshin. There were only a truculent innkeeper proffering a bill, two sniggering postboys, and a round-eyed chambermaid wiping her hands in her apron.

Diana refused to believe Gerald was gone. Even when it was pointed out that a horse was missing from the stable, along with the gentleman's valise from the hired chaise, Diana shook her head stubbornly. She sat down in the private parlor to await Gerald's return, concentrating all her faculties on appearing unconcerned. But as the minutes ticked past, her certainty slowly ebbed, and after a while she was trembling under the realization that she had been abandoned far from her home.

Papa had been right. He had said that Gerald wanted nothing but her money. She had thought that his willingness to marry her at seventeen proved otherwise, but she saw now that this wasn't so. Gerald had simply not understood. Hadn't she *told* him all the terms of her mother's will? She thought she had, but her memory of their early meetings was blurred by a romantically golden haze.

It hardly mattered now, in any case. Gerald was gone, and she must think what to do. With shaking fingers Diana opened her reticule and counted the money she had managed to scrape together. Four pounds and seven shillings. It would never be enough to pay the postboys and the inn. She could give them what she had, but where would she go afterward, penniless?

Tears started then, for her present plight and for the ruin of all her hopes and plans. Diana put her face in her hands and sobbed.

It was thus that the innkeeper found her sometime

later. He strode into the parlor with an impatient frown, but it faded when he saw Diana's misery. "Here, now," he said, "don't take on so." His words had no discernible effect, and he began to look uneasy. "Wait here a moment until I fetch my wife," he added, backing quickly to the door. Diana paid no heed. She scarcely heard.

A short time later a small plump woman bustled into the room and stood before Diana with her hands on her hips. Her husband peered around the door, but the older woman motioned brusquely for him to shut it, leaving them alone. "Now, miss," she said then, "crying will do you no good, though I can't say as I blame you for it. An elopement, was it?"

Diana cried harder.

The woman nodded. "And your young man has changed his mind seemingly. Well, you've made a bad mistake, no denying that."

Still, the only response was sobs.

"Have you any money at all?"

Diana struggled to control herself. She must make an effort to honor her obligations, however she felt. "F-four pounds," she managed finally, holding out the reticule.

The innkeeper's wife took it and examined the contents. "Tch. The blackguard! He might have left you something more."

"He only cared about getting *my* money," murmured Diana brokenly.

The other's eyes sharpened. "Indeed? Well, miss, my advice is to put him right out of your mind. He's no good."

Diana gazed at the carpet.

"You should go back to your family," added the woman. "They'll stand by you and help scotch the scandal. You haven't been away so very long, I wager."

Diana shuddered at the thought of her father. She couldn't go back to face his contempt. Yet where else could she go?

"Tom and me could advance you some money. Not for a private chaise, mind, but for the stage. You could send it back when you're home again."

"W-would you?" She was amazed.

Something in the girl's tear-drenched brown eyes made the landlady reach out and pat her shoulder. "You'll be all right once you're among your own people again," she said. "But you'd best get ready. The stage comes at ten."

In an unthinking daze, Diana paid the postboys and dismissed them, gathered her meager luggage, and mounted the stage when it arrived. A young man sitting opposite tried to get up a conversation, but Diana didn't even hear him. Her mind was spinning with the events of the past few days. As the miles went by, she recounted them again and again. Why had she not seen Gerald's true colors sooner? Why had she allowed him to cajole her into an elopement? What was to become of her now? She was surely ruined forever through her own foolishness. How could she look anyone in the eye again after what she had done?

Wrapped in these gloomy reflections, Diana was oblivious until the stage set her down at an inn near her home in Yorkshire. And once there, she stood outside the inn's door, her small valise beside her, afraid to reveal her presence.

"Yes, miss, may I help you?" asked a voice, and the innkeeper appeared in the doorway.

Diana tried to speak, and failed.

"Did you want dinner?" he added impatiently. She could hear sounds from the taproom beyond. "Are you waiting for someone to fetch you? Will you come in?"

"No," she answered, her voice very low. "I...I am all right. Thank you." She would walk home, she decided. The house was four miles away, but all other alternatives seemed worse.

"Wait a moment. Aren't you the Gresham girl?" The man came out to survey her, and Diana flinched. "I've seen you with your father. They managed to get word to you, then, did they? There was some talk that Mrs. Samuels didn't know where you'd gone."

Diana frowned. Mrs. Samuels was their house-keeper. What did she have to do with anything?

"You'll just be in time for the funeral. It's tomor-row morning. Was you wanting a gig to take you home?"

"Funeral?" she echoed, her lips stiff.

"Well, yes, miss. Your father..." Suddenly the innkeeper clapped a hand to his mouth. "You ain't been told! My tongue's run away with me, as usual. Beg your pardon, miss, I'm sure."

"But what has happened? Is my father...?"

The man shook his head. "Passed away late yester-day, miss. And I'm that sorry to tell you. I reckon Mrs. Samuels meant to do it face to face."

"But how?" Diana was dazed by this new disaster.

"Carried off by an apoplexy, they say. A rare temper, Mr. Gresham had...er, that is, I've heard folk say so."

He had died of rage at her flight, thought Diana. Not only had she ruined herself, she had killed her father. With a small moan, she sank to the earth in a heap.

The furor that followed did not reach her. Diana was bundled into a gig like a parcel and escorted home by a chambermaid and an ostler. Delivered to Mrs. Samuels and somewhat revived with hot tea, Diana merely stared.

Finally Mrs. Samuels said, "I told them you had gone to visit friends."

Diana choked, then replied, "But you knew... I left the note."

"I burned it."

"Why?"

"It was none of their affair, prying busybodies."

The girl gazed at the spare, austere figure of the only mother she had ever known. Her own mother had died when Diana was two, but she had never felt that Mrs. Samuels cared for her. She did not even know her first name. "You lied to protect me?"

The housekeeper's face did not soften, and she continued to stare straight ahead. "'Twas none of their affair," she repeated. "I don't hold with gossip."

"So no one knows where I went?"

Mrs. Samuels shook her head. "No one asked, save the doctor. The neighbors haven't taken the trouble to call."

And why should they? Diana's father had had

nothing but harsh words for them during his life. Part of the burden lifted from her soul. She still felt ashamed, but at least her shame was private.

"Are you home to stay?" asked Mrs. Samuels, her expression stony.

"I...yes."

"And will you be wanting me to remain?"

Diana stared at her, mystified. The woman had saved her, yet she seemed as devoid of warmth and emotion as ever. If she felt nothing, why had she bothered? What was she thinking? "Of course."

Mrs. Samuels nodded and turned away. "Mr. Gresham is in the front parlor. The funeral is at eleven tomorrow." She left the room with Diana's valise.

Diana hesitated, biting her lower lip. She walked slowly to the closed door of the front parlor, stepped back, then forward. She could not imagine her father dead; his presence had always pervaded this house. Her whole life had been turned upside down in a matter of days, and she was far from assimilating the change. She could not even imagine what it would be like now. Slowly her hand reached out and grasped the doorknob. She took a deep breath and opened the door.

Two

On the day after her twenty-fifth birthday, Diana Gresham followed a second coffin to the churchyard. Mrs. Samuels had been ill all that winter, and late in February she died, leaving Diana wholly alone. Diana had nursed the old housekeeper faithfully, and she tried to feel some sadness as she stood beside her grave and listened to the rector intone the ritual words, but she could not muster much emotion. She and Mrs. Samuels had never been true companions. The closeness that Diana had imagined might come from their shared adversity had never emerged. Indeed, the older woman had merely become more dour and reclusive as the years passed, and Diana had felt increasingly isolated.

When the rector and the few mourners were ready to depart after the brief service, Diana resisted their urgings to come away and wrapped her black cloak more closely around her shoulders as the sexton and his helpers began to fill in the grave. It was a dreary morning, with low gray clouds and a damp bitter chill. Warm weather earlier in the week had turned the winter earth to mud, but there was as yet no hint of green to reconcile one to the dirt. The moors rolling away beyond the stone church were bleak. Yet Diana did not move even when the wind made her cloak billow out around her, bringing the cold to her skin. She did not want to return to her family house, whose cramped rooms were unchanged since her father's death.

For some time, Diana had been feeling restless and dissatisfied. The shocked immobility that had followed her disastrous rebellion seven years before had modulated through remorse and self-loathing into withdrawal, contemplation, and finally, understanding. She had forgiven her younger self a long while ago. Her faults had been great, but they sprang from warmth of feeling and lack of family love rather than weakness. Her mistakes had been almost inevitable, given her naiveté and susceptibility.

But with greater wisdom had also come a loss of the eager openness that younger Diana had possessed. The habit of solitude had become strong; Diana seldom exchanged more than a few sentences with her scattered neighbors. I am like Mrs. Samuels myself now, she thought, gazing over the moors. I have no friends.

Her restlessness reached a kind of irritated crescendo, and she felt she must do something dramatic, or else she would scream. But she did not know what to do. Some change was inevitable. Even had she not been inexpressibly weary of living alone, she could not remain completely solitary. Yet she had no family to take her in. Mr. Merton, the banker, had called yesterday to congratulate her and solemnly explain that she was now in full possession of her fortune. She was a wealthy woman. But she felt resourceless. Money was useless, she realized, if one did not know what to do with it.

Shivering as the wind whipped her cloak again, Diana felt she must come to some conclusion before she returned to the house. If she did not, some part of her suggested, she would slip back into her routine of isolation and never break free. She would indeed become a Mrs. Samuels, reluctant to venture beyond her own front door.

I must leave here, she thought, looking from the small churchyard to the narrow village street with its facing rows of stone cottages. All was brown and gray and black; there was no color anywhere. She had never learned to love the harsh landscapes of Yorkshire, a failing, no doubt. But where could she go?

Diana felt a sudden sharp longing for laughter and the sounds of a room full of people. Wistfully she remembered her short time at school. Her father had kept her there less than a year, concluding that she was being corrupted by association with fifty empty-headed girls. Diana recalled their chatter and jokes as part of the happiest time in her life. If only she could return to that time! But her new financial independence would not give her this, however pleasant it might be.

Briefly she was filled with bitterness. It seemed a cruel joke that she should get her fortune now, when events had rendered her incapable of enjoying it. She could buy a different house, hire a companion, enliven her wardrobe, but she could not regain her

old lightheartedness or her girlhood friends. If only
her father had been kinder, or Gerald… But with this
thought, Diana shook her head. She could not honestly blame them for her present plight. Her father
had been harsh and distant; Gerald had treated her
shamefully. But she herself had repulsed the world in
her first remorseful reaction, for no reason that the
world could see. Naturally, those she rejected had
withdrawn, and it seemed to her now that she had
been foolish in this as well as in her rash elopement.

Gathering her cloak, Diana turned and walked
through the churchyard gate and along the street
toward home. Her father's house, hers now, was
beyond the edge of the village, surrounded by high
stone walls. As she approached it, Diana walked more
slowly, a horror of retreating behind those barriers
again growing in her. Was she fated to spoil her life?
Had some dark destiny hovered over her birth?

"Diana. Diana Gresham," called a high, light voice
behind her. "Wait, Diana!"

She turned. A small slender woman in a gray cloak
and a modish hat was waving from a carriage in the
center of the village. Her face was in shadow, and
Diana did not recognize her as she got out and hurried
forward.

"Oh, lud," the newcomer gasped as she came up.
"This wind takes my breath away. And I had forgotten the dreadful cold here. But how fortunate to
meet you, Diana! Cynthia Addison said you had left
Yorkshire, and so I might not even have called! Are
you back for a visit, as we are?"

When the woman spoke, Diana recognized

Amanda Trent, a friend she had not seen for eight years. Amanda, two years older, had married young and followed her soldier husband to Spain. They had exchanged one or two letters at the beginning, but Amanda was an unreliable correspondent, and Diana had ceased to write after her elopement, as she had ceased to see acquaintances like Cynthia Addison, who could not be blamed for thinking her gone. "Hello, Amanda," she answered, the commonplace words feeling odd on her tongue.

Amanda peered up into her face, sensing some strangeness. She looked just the same, Diana thought— tiny and brunette, with huge almost black eyes. Those eyes had been the downfall of a number of young men before Captain Trent won her hand. "Diana?" Amanda said, a question in her voice.

Making a great effort, Diana replied, "I am not visiting. I never left. After Papa died…" She didn't finish her sentence because the story seemed far too complicated to review; none of the important things could be told. And she didn't want pity.

Amanda held out both hands. "Yes, they told me about Mr. Gresham. I am sorry, of course, though…" She shrugged. Long ago, Diana had confided some of her trials.

Awkwardly Diana took her hands. Amanda squeezed her fingers and smiled. "Come back with me, and we shall have a cozy talk. I want to hear everything!"

Diana wondered what she would say if she did. Amanda seemed the same gay creature she had been at nineteen; she felt ancient beside her. Yet the chance to put off going home was irresistible, and shortly they were sitting side by side in Amanda's carriage riding toward her parents' house a few miles from the village.

"George is invalided out," Amanda told her. "He never recovered properly from the fever he took after Toulouse, so we decided to come here for a good long visit. I am so happy to be in England again! You cannot imagine how inconvenient it sometimes was in Spain, Diana."

Thinking that "inconvenient" was an odd characterization of the Peninsular Wars, Diana watched her old friend's face. Now that they were closer, she could see small signs of age and strain there. Amanda was no less pretty, but it was obvious now that she was nearly a decade past nineteen. Her friend's chatter seemed less carefree, more forced. Diana felt relieved; it had been daunting to think that only she was altered. "You have been in Spain all this time?"

"Oh, lud, no! That I *could* not have borne. I spent two seasons in London, and I was here for the summer a year ago. I am sorry I did not call, Diana, but I was… ill." She turned her head away. "Here we are. Mama will be so pleased to see you."

Wondering uneasily if this was true, Diana followed Amanda into the house. Mrs. Durham was one of the acquaintances she had ceased to see years ago.

As it happened, none of the family was at home. George Trent was riding with Amanda's father, and Mrs. Durham had gone to visit an ailing tenant rather than share Amanda's drive. The two women settled in the drawing room with a pot of tea and a plate of the spice cakes Diana remembered from childhood visits.

"Are you still in mourning?" asked Amanda then,

her expression adding what politeness made her suppress. Diana's clothes and hair were even more unfashionable than before her father's death.

Diana put a hand to the great knot of deep golden hair at the back of her neck as she explained about Mrs. Samuels. Amanda's dark cropped ringlets and elegant blue morning gown brought back concerns she hadn't felt for years. The black dress she wore was the last she had bought, for her father's mourning.

Amanda looked puzzled. "But, Diana, what have you been doing all this time? Did you have a London season? Or at least go to York for the winter assemblies?" When Diana shook her head, she opened her eyes very wide. "Do you mean you have just stayed here? But *why*?"

It must indeed seem eccentric, Diana thought, and she could not give her only plausible reason. Her neighbors had probably judged her mad.

Amanda was gazing at her with an unremembered shrewdness. "Is something wrong, Diana? You…you seem different. You were always the first to talk of getting away."

Miserably Diana prepared to rise. She could not explain, and Amanda would no doubt take that inability for coldness. Their long-ago friendship was dead.

But Amanda had lapsed into meditative silence. "I suppose we are all changed," she added. "It has been quite a time, after all. What else could we expect?"

Surprised, Diana said nothing, and in the next moment their tête-à-tête was interrupted by the entrance of Amanda's family.

The Durhams were familiar, though Diana had not

seen them recently, and their greetings were more cordial than she had expected. They did not mention her strange behavior or seem to see anything odd in her sudden visit to their house. But as they spoke, Diana gradually received the impression that they were too pre-occupied with more personal concerns to think of her.

One cause, at least, was obvious. Diana had never seen a greater alteration in a person than in George Trent, Amanda's husband. She remembered him as a smiling blond giant, looking fully able to toss his tiny bride high in the air and catch her again without the least strain. Now, after seven years in the Peninsula, he retained only his height. His once muscular frame was painfully thin; his bright hair and ruddy complexion were dulled, and he wore a black patch over one blue eye. Diana's presence appeared to startle and displease him, though he said nothing, merely retreating to the other side of the room and pretending interest in an album that lay on a table. His family watched him anxiously but covertly.

"George," said Amanda finally, when his conduct was becoming rude, "you remember Diana Gresham. She was at our wedding, and I have spoken to you of her."

George was very still for a moment. Then he turned, squaring his shoulders as if to face an ordeal. "Miss Gresham," he said, bowing his head slightly.

"Doesn't George look dashing and romantic?" Amanda continued, her tone rather high and brittle. "I tell him he is positively piratical and he must take care not to set too many hearts aflutter, or I shall be dreadfully jealous. Don't I, George?"

"Me and everyone else," he replied, and strode abruptly out of the room.

Amanda made a small sound, and when Diana turned she saw that her old friend's eyes were filled with tears. She felt sharp pity and fear that she intruded.

"It was only a tiny wound," said Amanda shakily. "But they could not save his eye. And then he took the fever as well. I had hoped that being home again would be good for George, but he doesn't seem to want to recover."

"You've been here only a week, Amanda," answered Mr. Durham. "Give him time."

"Yes, darling." Amanda's mother looked as if she might cry too. "I'm sure it is very hard for him, but he will come round."

Diana rose. "Perhaps I should take my leave."

The Durhams exchanged a glance.

"Please don't," cried Amanda. Then, realizing that she had spoken too fervently, added, "I beg your pardon. Why should you wish to stay, after all? It is just that I have been so…" She broke off and dropped her head in her hands.

Diana moved without thinking to sit beside her friend and put an arm around her shoulders. "Of course I will stay if you wish it. I feared I was prying into private matters."

"George does not allow it to be private." Amanda's voice was muffled. "I am selfish to keep you, Diana. It was just so splendid to see someone from the old days." She raised her head. "The things we remember of each other are so…simple."

It was true, Diana thought, and the idea appealed

to her as much as it did Amanda. Whatever worries each might have, between them there was nothing but pleasant recollections. Here was an opportunity to end her loneliness without explanations or the great effort of finding and cultivating new acquaintances. At long last, fate seemed to be coming to her aid. "I should like to stay," she said. "I should like it very much."

Amanda met her eyes, and for a moment they gazed at each another as two women, a little buffeted by the world and sadder and wiser than the girls they had been when they last met. A flash of wordless communication passed between them. Then Amanda smiled and clasped her hands. "I'm so glad. We will have another cup of tea and talk of all our old friends. Do you know what has become of Sophie Jenkins?"

Returning her smile, Diana shook her head.

"She married an earl!"

"But she wished to become a missionary!"

"So she always *said*," replied Amanda. "But when she got to London, she threw that idea to the winds and pursued a title until she snared one. They say her husband is a complete dunce."

Diana couldn't help but laugh, and Amanda's mischievous grin soon turned to trilling laughter as well. They both went on a bit longer than the joke warranted, savoring the sensation.

"I hope you will stay to dinner, Diana," said Mrs. Durham then. "I know you are alone now."

Diana had nearly forgotten the older couple. Turning quickly, she saw encouraging smiles on both their faces. "I should like that. Thank you." Did they really want her?

"That's right!" Amanda's dark eyes widened as she thought of something. "Diana! You must come and stay here. You cannot live alone, and I should adore having you. Wouldn't we, Mama?"

"Of course."

Mrs. Durham did not sound as enthusiastic as her daughter. But neither did she seem insincere. Suddenly the idea was very attractive. Diana would not have to go back to that dreary house for a while; she could put off the decision about what to do. Yet the habit of years was strong. "I don't know…" she began.

"You must come," urged Amanda. "We shall have such fun." Tension was in her voice, and Diana could not resist her plea. She nodded, and Amanda embraced her exuberantly.

"For a few days," murmured Diana, her eyes on the Durhams.

But the older couple was watching their daughter with pleased relief.

And so it was that Diana closed up her father's house on the day after Mrs. Samuels' funeral and settled into a pleasant rose-papered bedchamber at the Durhams'. The room was much more comfortable than her own, attended to by a large staff of servants. Diana had dismissed all the servants but Mrs. Samuels after her father's death, taking on household chores herself as a kind of penance. She had never learned to enjoy the work, however, and she decided now that there was no further need to punish herself.

As the days passed it became more and more obvious that Diana's presence was good for Amanda, and Diana took this as reason enough for the Durhams' kindness. That the opposite was also true, she did not consider for some time. Yet at the end of the first week, Diana realized that she was happier than she had been for months, perhaps years. Amanda's companionship filled a great void in her life, and a more luxurious style of living suited her completely.

At the beginning of the second week, as she and Amanda walked together on a balmy March afternoon, Amanda said, "We are the only two of our friends who have stayed the same, or nearly the same, anyway. I have seen Sophie and Jane and Caroline in town, and they are all vastly changed. They talk of people I don't know, and they seem wrapped up in town life. I suppose it is because you and I were cut off from society."

"Did you see no one in Spain?" Diana was curious about her friend's experiences abroad, though she did not wish to call up any painful memories.

"Some other officers' wives, but they were often posted away just as we became friendly. And I never got on with the Spanish and Portuguese ladies." She sighed. "George was most often with the army, of course. I spent a great deal of time alone."

"You came back for visits." Diana wondered why she had not stayed in England, as most army wives did.

"Yes. But then I missed George so dreadfully." Amanda's smile was wry. "We were...*are* so fond of one another. It is very unfashionable."

"I remember when you met him. One day you were perfectly normal, then you went to an assembly in York and came back transformed. We could hardly force a sentence from you. It took days to discover what was the matter."

Amanda laughed. "We were both bowled over. We married six weeks later."

"And the rest of us nearly died of jealousy."

They laughed. But Amanda's expression soon sobered again. "And now we are all scattered—Sophie in Kent, Jane in Dorset, and Caroline flitting from London to Brighton to house parties. It all seems so long ago." She paused. "Of course, they all have children, too. It makes them seem older."

Diana sensed constraint. "When you and George are settled…" she began.

Amanda shook her head as if goaded. "I have lost three. I…I don't hope…that is…" She bit her lower lip and struggled for composure. "But what am I about, discussing such things with you? An unmarried girl! Mama would be scandalized." She paused again, taking a deep breath. "You know what we must do, Diana? We must find you a husband. You are…what? Five-and-twenty now? Nearly on the shelf. How careless of you!" Abruptly her eyes widened. "I did not mean… Oh, I haven't offended you, have I? My tongue runs away with me sometimes."

"Of course you have not." But Diana did feel uneasy. "I have never had the opportunity to marry. I don't suppose I shall." Even if she did have the chance, it was impossible. No man would wish to marry her once he learned of her past. Diana knew she could never keep such a secret from a husband.

"Nonsense." Amanda examined her friend with a more critical eye than she had used so far. Diana had been very pretty at seventeen. Now, her color was not so good, admittedly, but her deep golden hair had lost none of its vibrancy, and the unfashionable way she dressed it was somehow very attractive. Her face was thinner, but her brown eyes with those striking gold flecks remained entrancing. Her form was slender and pleasing, even in the poorly cut black gown. Amanda's own dark eyes began to sparkle. It was unthinkable that Diana should not marry, and this was just the sort of problem that appealed to her. A keen interest that Amanda had not felt for some time rose in her, temporarily banishing worry. How could her plan be best accomplished? Slowly an idea started to form, which, she reasoned, might work for George as well.

About the Author

Jane Ashford discovered Georgette Heyer in junior high school and was captivated by the glittering world and witty language of Regency England. That delight was part of what led her to study English literature and travel widely. Her books have been published all over Europe as well as in the United States. Jane was nominated for a Career Achievement Award by *RT Book Reviews*. Born in Ohio, she is now somewhat nomadic. Find her on the web at janeashford.com and on Facebook at facebook.com/JaneAshfordWriter, where you can sign up for her monthly newsletter.

A DUKE
TOO FAR

Secrets to reveal, legends to unravel,
and a love to fight for...

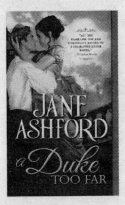

Peter Rathbone, Duke of Compton, is struggling to handle the
responsibilities of his family home and his grief over his sister
Delia's death when he's astonished by the arrival of Miss Ada
Grandison, who bears a mysterious letter that she claims holds
the secret to saving his ancestral home. Peter's life is about to get
even more complicated...

**"All the sparkling wit and flirtatious
banter of a Georgette Heyer novel."**

—*Publishers Weekly*

AN INCONVENIENT DUKE

When the duke starts searching for
answers, no one's secrets are safe

Marcus Braddock, former general and newly appointed Duke of
Hampton, is back from war. Now, not only is he surrounded by
the utterly unbearable *ton*, but he's mourning the death of his
beloved sister, Elise. Marcus believes his sister's death was no
accident, and he's determined to learn the truth—starting with
Danielle, his sister's beautiful best friend. But Danielle might be
keeping secrets of her own…

**"As steamy as it is sweet as it is luscious.
My favorite kind of historical!"**

—Grace Burrowes, *New York Times* bestselling author,
for *Dukes Are Forever*

ONLY A DUCHESS
WOULD DARE

Dazzling Regency romance from *New York Times* and *USA Today* bestselling author Amelia Grey

Alexander Mitchell, the fourth Marquis of Raceworth, is shocked when the alluring young Duchess of Brookfield accuses him of being in possession of pearls belonging to her family. The pearls in question have been in Race's family since the sixteenth century. And while Susannah Brookfield is the most beautiful, enchanting, and intelligent woman he has ever met, he's not about to hand over a family heirloom. But if he didn't steal her pearls, how exactly did he get them, and what are he and Susannah to do when they go missing once more?

"Exemplifies the very essence of what a romance novel should be...superbly written."

—*Love Romance Passion*

For more info about Sourcebooks's books and authors, visit:
sourcebooks.com

Also by Jane Ashford

The Duke's Sons

Heir to the Duke
What the Duke Doesn't Know
Lord Sebastian's Secret
Nothing Like a Duke
The Duke Knows Best
A Favor for the Prince (prequel)

The Way to a Lord's Heart

Brave New Earl
A Lord Apart
How to Cross a Marquess
A Duke Too Far

Once Again a Bride
Man of Honour
The Three Graces
The Marriage Wager
The Bride Insists
The Bargain
The Marchington Scandal
The Headstrong Ward
Married to a Perfect Stranger
Charmed and Dangerous
A Radical Arrangement
First Season / Bride to Be
Rivals of Fortune / The Impetuous Heiress
Last Gentleman Standing
Earl to the Rescue
The Reluctant Rake